CAFFA

By the same author:

BARBAROSSA

CODENAME APHRODITE

BEYOND REPAIR

WILLFUL NEGLECT

OPERATION HOTEL CALIFORNIA

CAFFA

Charles S. Faddis

Orion Strategic Services | Edgewater, Maryland

All statements of fact, opinion or analysis expressed are those of the author and do not reflect the official positions or views of the CIA or any other U.S. government agency. Nothing in the contents should be construed as asserting or implying U.S. government authentication of information or Agency endorsement of the author's views. This material has been reviewed by the CIA to prevent the disclosure of classified information.

Production Editor: Hannah V. Faddis
Design: Charles S. Faddis
ISBN: 978-0615568492

DEDICATION

To the men and women of the Clandestine Service,
out there now as they have been for sixty years, on
the ridge tops, in the back alleys, hunting the
monsters the world prefers to pretend do not exist.

Caffa

"In October 1347, at about the beginning of the month, twelve Genoese galleys, fleeing from the divine vengeance, which Our Lord had sent upon them for their sins, put into the port of Messina. The Genoese carried such a disease in their bodies that if anyone so much as spoke with one of them he was infected with the deadly illness and could not avoid death. The signs of death among the Genoese, and among the Messinese when they came to share the illness with them, were as follows. Breath spread the infection among those speaking together, with one infecting the other, and it seemed as if the victim was struck all at once by the affliction and was, so to speak, shattered by it. This shattering impact, together with the inhaled infection, caused the eruption of a sort of boil, the size of lentil, on the thigh or arm, which so infected and invaded the body that the victims violently coughed up blood, and after three days' incessant vomiting, for which there was no remedy, they died – and with them died not only anyone who had talked with them, but also anyone who had acquired or touched or laid hands on their belongings."

The Chronicles of the Franciscan Monk
Michele da Piazza, 1347

CHAPTER ONE

2150 HOURS. 16 JULY 2002.
NATIONAL INSTITUTE OF HEALTH. ISLAMABAD, PAKISTAN.

"Good evening," said Dr. Bashir Mahmud to the night watchman. He smiled his broad, doubt free smile and strode past the small desk at the entrance to the building.

"Good evening, Professor Doctor," said the watchman as he stumbled to his feet. It was late, and the building was long deserted, but one did not ask questions of the director nor inquire as to his business. It was his Institute. If he wanted to come in that was his right.

Bashir scuffed his way down the hallway to his office, leather sandals slapping the floor as he went. He was dressed in salwar kameese, the loose traditional Pakistani garb, with a wool sleeveless vest over his top. It was a costume more suited to a shopkeeper on the street than a man with a PhD in microbiology from Oxford, but completely in keeping with his status as a devout Muslim of the Ahl-e-Hadith school.

On Bashir's left, he passed glass windows giving a view into the interior of the mammoth Biological Security Level 3 (BSL3) laboratory that was adjacent to his office. Visible through the windows were banks of refrigerators, incubators and ventilated hoods for use in working with dangerous microbes. Stacks of petri dishes and racks of test tubes and pipettes cluttered the countertops.

A short distance past the lab, Bashir unlocked a door and entered his office. The furniture inside was heavy and ornate, and the walls were covered in awards and commemorative photos from a long and distinguished career. Bashir saw none of it. He crossed the office, unlocked another door in the back wall and stepped into the room behind it.

This was Bashir's private lab. It was intended to be a space for the director to putter with his own pet projects as he waited out the days until his retirement. It had a different purpose now.

To the left was a refrigerator filled with petri dishes and bacterial samples. On the right were several boxlike incubators. Straight ahead on a black laminate countertop was a tall glass cylindrical container filled with liters of what appeared to be thick, yellow custard.

Sprouting from the top of the cylinder were wires and metal tubes leading to a stack of white plastic boxes covered with controls and digital displays. Together the cylinder and the attached stack of instruments constituted a fermenter. It was designed for the precise, controlled cultivation of microorganisms. It monitored temperature, fed nutrients and measured growth. It made sure that all conditions were optimal.

Bashir checked the displays on the white boxes and glanced quickly at tables of numbers he had jotted down in a notebook sitting next to the fermenter. He was simply confirming what he already knew. It was time.

Putting the notebook back on the counter, Bashir disconnected the tubes and wires connected to the glass cylinder and moved it to one side. Then, moving smoothly and efficiently, he used a large pipette, a long glass tube with a narrow tip at one end and a large rubber ball at the other, to suck up quantities of the custard-like substance and squirt it into long glass tubes with tight plastic tops. Once he had filled two dozen of these he slipped each one into a protective, airtight plastic sleeve. Lastly, he opened a special freezer next to the refrigerator and took out a foam cooler with five kilograms of dry ice in the bottom of it and slipped each of the plastic sleeves into a compartment inside the cooler.

Once finished, Bashir stood up from the wooden stool on which he had been sitting, took off the reading glasses he had been using while he worked and rubbed his tired eyes. He checked his watch. It was close to midnight. He needed to hurry.

Bashir walked out of the Institute with the cooler in a small rolling Pelican case — a hard, black, plastic shell designed for the transport of breakable items. The night watchman staggered to his feet to say goodnight and then settled back into watching an old Bollywood flick on a small black and white TV at his desk.

Outside the front doors to the Institute, Bashir handed the case to his driver, Hussain, who put it in the trunk of the official vehicle he was driving and then rushed to open the car door for Bashir. Bashir settled into the back seat of the black sedan.

"Where would you like to go, Director?" asked Hussain as he climbed in the car and started the engine.

"Let's go see the Colonel, please," said Bashir.

"Yes, Director," said Hussain crisply. No matter how long the hours, driving for the Director of the Institute was a great honor.

"How is your family, Hussain?" asked the Director. He was staring out the window of the sedan at the open countryside rolling by.

"Thanks to God, they are well, Director," said Hussain. "The youngest turns five tomorrow."

"Seven children. You are blessed, Hussain," said Bashir. He closed his eyes for a moment and let a feeling of contentment wash over him. It was good to be able to be of use in such a great cause.

Traffic was light and the trip down Muree Road and then Kashmir Highway to Islamabad from the Institute's site on the fringes of the city was uneventful. In fifteen minutes, Hussain was turning into the neat residential streets of the I-8 sector of town. On both sides the empty streets were lined with walled residential compounds.

Islamabad was one of those planned cities that were the vogue in developing nations after the Second World War. The rest of Pakistan was chaos, filth and noise. Islamabad, by contrast, was sterile, cold and artificial. It was a joke among diplomats posted to the city to say that it was only "minutes from Pakistan", a reference to Islamabad's sister city of Rawalpindi, which teemed with crowds and traffic.

Hussain pulled the car up to the heavy metal gate at the entrance to their destination. Two uniformed guards with submachine guns scrutinized the car for a moment and then, satisfied that they recognized the occupants, opened the gates and waved the car inside. As Hussain shut off the engine and opened the door for Bashir, the gates closed behind them.

"I will not be long, Hussain," said Bashir. He smiled and his long, bushy beard bristled.

"Shall I carry this for you, Director?" asked Hussain. He motioned to the Pelican case, which he had removed from the trunk.

"I am old, my friend," said Bashir. "I am not yet dead."

"Of course, not, Director," said Hussain as Bashir took the case from him.

"Get some tea in the guard house," said Bashir. The temperature was still close to ninety degrees and the air was steamy from the rain earlier in the evening, but there was always time for tea in Pakistan.

"Yes, Director," said Bashir. He walked toward the small cinderblock building set just inside the gate and in front of the main house. The door to the building was open and a light on inside. Two off-duty, uniformed guards were sitting around a small electric hot plate with a tin kettle on it. Scratchy, thumping Punjabi pop music was coming from a radio somewhere inside.

Bashir went up the short flight of stairs to the front door of the home pulling the wheeled Pelican case behind him. The plastic case bumped on each stair as he went. He was met at the entrance by the Colonel's assistant, Ahmed.

"Let me help you with this, Director," said Ahmed. He was a tall, thick man with no neck and black pitiless eyes. He took the case from Bashir and carried it by the handle on one end as he motioned for Bashir to enter. "The Colonel is in his office."

"Thank you," said Bashir. He stepped inside as Ahmed pushed the front door closed with his free hand. Then he followed Ahmed across the sterile front room with its cold furniture and bare walls and down a short hallway.

"The Director is here, Colonel," called Ahmed. He pushed open a door off the hallway into a small office with dark wooden furniture and heavy curtains on the windows. "I will take your case to the back room."

"Good evening, my brother," said Colonel Javed Khan. He was a short man with a long, wispy beard, a belly and a cylindrical white skullcap on his bald head. He stood from behind his ponderous desk and came around to embrace Bashir and usher him into an armchair in front of the desk.

"Peace be unto you," said Bashir.

"And unto you, brother," said the Colonel as he settled back into his desk chair. Behind him on the wall was a large framed photograph of the Great Mosque in Mecca. On one of the other walls was a poster showing the silhouette of India with an Islamic crescent superimposed on it. In the corner of the poster was the emblem, a Koran resting on crossed swords, of the Jamaat-ud-Dawa, the political arm of the Pakistani terrorist group Lashkar-e-Taiba.

"I have brought everything," said Bashir.

"You left nothing behind?" asked Javed.

"Nothing," said Bashir. "The work is complete."

"Thanks to God," said the Colonel. He held his hands up with the palms open to heaven to emphasize his piety. "I had no doubt that you would succeed, brother."

"What they have done in Afghanistan is an abomination," said Bashir.

"You are a soldier of God," said the Colonel. "You recognize evil when you see it."

"How will you move it?" asked Bashir.

"Best to leave that to the professionals, Professor Doctor," said the Colonel. "We have great experience in this kind of thing. More than our brothers in Al Qaeda I think." He wagged his finger gently to remind the Director that his role in the operation was almost at an end.

"Of course," said Bashir hurriedly. "I forget myself."

"You are only interested in the success of our cause, my brother. I understand," said the Colonel. "You have donated much money to us in the past, and now you have given us the greatest gift of all."

"Inshallah, you will win a great victory," said Bashir.

"Inshallah," said the Colonel. "Now, show me what you have brought us." He stood and motioned Bashir to his feet. The two exited the office and walked toward the back of the building.

Ahead of the pair was a door that led to a storage room that had been added on to the back of the home. The Colonel pushed the door open and stepped down and inside. There was a rustling sound as he did so.

"Watch your step," said the Colonel. He moved away from the doorway into the center of the room.

"Why the plastic?" asked Bashir. As he entered the room he saw that black plastic sheeting had been put down on the floor from wall to wall.

"Just in case something in the case breaks," said the Colonel. Behind him on a wooden table was the Pelican case.

"If anything breaks, my brother, plastic will not help you," laughed Bashir. He did not notice that the door swung shut silently behind him.

"Of course, you are right, brother," said the Colonel softly. He looked past Bashir and nodded his head.

Bashir started to turn. It was too late. Ahmed shoved the heavy, black barrel of the Russian TT-33 pistol tight against the base of Bashir's skull and pulled the trigger twice. The Director crumpled to the ground, rolled over on his side and then lay motionless. Thick, dark blood began to pool around him. The hair on his neck where the bullets had entered was smoking. His eyes were wide open but already hard like glass.

"The driver?" asked the Colonel.

"I will handle him next, Colonel," said Ahmed. "As loud as the music is in the guard shack he will have heard nothing."

"Place the bodies back in the vehicle and run it off the road out in the country near the Institute. When they're found in the morning, the press will think it's another case of bandits at work on the edge of the city."

"And then, Colonel?" asked Ahmed.

"Bring me the American. It is time."

CHAPTER TWO

2132 HOURS. 5 AUGUST 2002.
FELL'S POINT, BALTIMORE, MARYLAND.

"Hey, man, you got a dollar?" said the kid with his ball cap on sideways and his pants belted below his ass.

"No," said Bill. He kept walking. Aphrodite was next to him on the sidewalk. There was graffiti on the brick wall beside them and a boarded up second hand store across the narrow street.

"Yo, fuck you, man," said the kid. He spat on the grimy sidewalk to one side for emphasis.

"What did you say?" responded Bill. He stopped and turned to look at the kid. He was maybe nineteen, with a weak moustache and pale, acne-pocked skin. Bill had probably fifty pounds on him.

"You got money, man," said the kid. He looked away for a moment as if reconsidering the conversation. The fat, black chick next to him in the torn jeans took a couple of steps back, and the thin white girl with the stringy, pink hair behind him stared at her feet. Bill's dark brown hair was graying around the temples, but there was something about the way he filled out his tight black t-shirt and brown, leather jacket that suggested danger.

"That's not the issue, dickhead," said Bill. "The issue is why the fuck I should give it to you."

"Bill," said Aphrodite. She was standing a pace behind him and to one side.

"I'm just saying," said the kid. "Trying to get my life together. A little dough would help."

"Yeah, you're on the fast track to stardom, buddy," said Bill. The kid looked away again and wiped his nose on the sleeve of his dirty flannel shirt. There were three empty bottles of malt liquor in a paper bag on the sidewalk behind him.

"Bill," said Aphrodite again.

"Yeah?" said Bill. He turned his head toward Aphrodite. She smiled back. She was wearing tight black jeans, high-heeled boots and a black tank top under a black leather jacket. Her long blond hair was bouncing slightly in the light breeze. She looked like a million bucks.

"You gonna throw down with this guy or what?" She cocked her head quizzically to one side.

Bill paused and looked down for a moment. He was conscious suddenly that he had squared his stance, put his feet shoulder width apart and brought his arms to a tense ready position at his sides.

"Let it go," said Aphrodite. "We don't have time for this. We need to go find Irene, not fuck around with these kids."

"Yeah, you're right," said Bill. Feeling suddenly ridiculous, he turned away from the punk in the ball cap and followed Aphrodite down the sidewalk.

"That's right, walk on," said the kid behind them. Aphrodite reached out instinctively and grasped Bill's hand to make sure he kept moving.

"You need to relax, Captain America," said Aphrodite. "This is Baltimore, not Beirut."

The pair rounded the corner onto Aliceanna Street. Ahead on the right was their destination, The Full Moon Saloon. The gilt-lettered front glass window vibrated. Inside somebody was hammering out the final chords of "Tail Dragger' by Howlin' Wolf. There were two young white men in jean jackets sitting on the curb in front of the bar smoking cigarettes and talking about kicking ass. Parked on the sidewalk were three heavily customized Harley-Davidson motorcycles.

"Must be the place," said Bill. He opened the front door and followed Aphrodite into the dim, smoky interior.

The bar was long, narrow and crowded. Immediately in front of Bill and Aphrodite were wooden tables and chairs jammed with patrons. Toward the rear of the bar, just in front of the small stage, were what looked to be church pews. Along the left wall was a wooden bar with a brass foot rail. Every available foot of space was filled with people.

"How will we know her when we find her?" yelled Bill over the sound of the music and the crowd.

"She'll be in charge," said Aphrodite. Then she led the way, pushing her way through the sea of denim, leather and tattoos toward the stage.

"Thank you," yelled the lead singer of the band as they finished the song they were playing. "We're going to take a little break, and then we'll be back to play some John Lee Hooker!" The crowed bellowed its approval, as the band members put down their instruments and filed out the side door onto the street for a smoke and some air.

"I don't see anybody who looks like they are running this place," said Bill. He and Aphrodite stopped just in front of the stage and scanned the bar as best they could. Somebody had kicked on the stereo system and "Honky Tonk Woman" by the Stones started playing.

"Let's ask the bartender," said Aphrodite. She pointed at a bony white girl with spiked black hair and metal studs in her eyebrows behind the bar.

"You talk to the chick with the metal in her face," said Bill. "I'm gonna hit the head real quick."

"Ok, Tarzan," said Aphrodite. She pushed her way up to the bar as Bill disappeared in the direction of the men's room down a hallway behind the stage. The bartender had her back to the bar and was pouring a glass of whiskey. Aphrodite waited for her to finish.

"Fuck you!" said a loud, angry male voice behind Aphrodite. She turned.

"No, fuck you, asshole!" yelled someone else. Aphrodite could see three guys in motorcycle jackets with the name "Huns" on them in front of her. The crowd had parted slightly around them.

"I'm gonna fuck you up, dickhead!" yelled the biggest of the three guys in motorcycle jackets. He swung a huge, meaty fist and then began to kick at something on the floor. From somewhere came the sound of a woman screaming. A man in front of Aphrodite moved hurriedly to one side, and suddenly she could see. There was a thin man in his fifties with a long, gray ponytail lying on the floor doubled up in a fetal position. He was bleeding heavily from his mouth.

"Beat his ass, Weasel!" yelled one of the three guys Huns. He swigged his beer in satisfaction as his buddy, a tall, balding man with a large gut, kept kicking.

"Ain't nobody tells us what tits we can and cannot touch!" yelled the third member of the trio. He had a long, hooked nose and small, black eyes. He was staring at a woman in a black skirt and white top with long blond hair streaked with gray. She was standing behind the man on the floor, screaming for the big man to stop and clutching the front of her blouse where the buttons had been torn away.

14

Aphrodite turned around and looked at the bar. The bartender was standing petrified. On the counter behind her were a gallon jug of vodka and a net bag of lemons.

"Empty the bag and put the bottle in it," said Aphrodite to the bartender.

"What?" said the girl.

"Do it now," said Aphrodite. She turned back to look at the men. The big man was still kicking the man on the ground.

A short woman with red hair and the build of a fire plug shoved her way out of the crowd and stepped in front of the big man. She was wearing an apron over khaki slacks and a white polo shirt.

"Cut the crap, Weasel!" yelled the woman. She pushed the big man with both hands to add emphasis. "I'll call the fuckin' cops if I have to!"

"Call 'em, Irene," said Weasel. He backhanded her across the face with one meaty hand and sent her tumbling into a table covered in beer bottles and shot glasses.

"Stop it!" barked Aphrodite. Her voice was surprisingly strong and clear. The crowd noise dropped. The woman in the white blouse stopped shrieking and looked startled. All three of the Huns turned around to look at Aphrodite.

"Shut up, bitch," said the big man with the gut. He grinned to show a row of gold teeth. "Or I'll teach you a lesson next." He turned back to the man on the ground. "Now where were we?"

"Please," said Aphrodite. "Educate me". The bar went dead quiet. Even the music in the background seemed to dim.

"Ok, whore!" yelled the big man. He spun around with a fist raised and a grimace on his fat, red face.

Aphrodite was standing facing the bar when the big man turned, her head cocked to one side so she could see over her shoulder and her hands clutching the net bag with the bottle of vodka inside. As the big man spun to face her she unwound like a discus thrower going for the world record, pivoting on her feet, swinging the bag in a wide, fast arc and connecting with the man's skull at full extension.

The bottle exploded. The bag disintegrated. A spray of blood, glass and vodka shot across the room.

The big man went down like he had been shot with a cannon, out cold with blood dripping from his nose and eyes and his fingers twitching spasmodically.

"Holy shit!" yelled the Hun with the long, hooked nose. "You fuckin' killed Weasel."

"Bad move, bitch," said the other Hun. A long Italian style stiletto had appeared in his right hand. He had a ragged scar on one cheek that made the sick smile on his face that much more twisted.

"Put it away," said Bill. Aphrodite turned at the sound of his voice. He was standing beside her in a firing stance, holding a Glock 19 9mm pistol in front of him with both hands. His sights were positioned directly on the bridge of the nose of the guy with the knife.

"Here to save your girlfriend?" asked the Hun with the knife.

"She's my wife," said Bill. "And from the looks of things, I'm here to save your sorry ass." He looked pointedly at Weasel who was still unconscious on the floor in a puddle of blood, glass and booze.

"I'm going to cut your throat, prick" said the Hun with the knife. But, he didn't move. His buddy, with one with the hooked nose, said nothing.

"Put the knife away," said Bill "Walk out now. Take your buddy to a hospital."

"Or?"

"Or I am going to put two rounds between your eyes and three more in your chest."

"Let's go," said the guy with the hooked nose.

"He's bluffin," said the guy with the knife. He didn't sound sure.

"He ain't fuckin' bluffin'," said the other Hun. He was edging backward toward the door. The room had gone deathly silent.

"No, he's not," said Aphrodite calmly. She saw that Irene had gotten to her feet and was standing silently to one side. Bill's hands were rock steady. It was maybe five feet from the muzzle of the pistol to the Hun's face.

"Fuck!" said the Hun with the knife. He closed the blade and shoved the knife back in his pocket. "Fuck," he said again. Then he turned back toward Weasel. "Help me get his ass up," he barked to his buddy. The two of them began to struggle with lifting the considerable dead weight.

"What took you so long?" asked Aphrodite. She looked at Bill and smiled. He had lowered the pistol to his side but not put it away.

"Line at the urinal," said Bill. He was still watching the Huns, making sure they didn't reconsider their decision to retreat. "What did you hit him with?"

"A gallon jug of vodka," said Aphrodite.

"Ouch," said Bill.

"I guess I owe you guys," said Irene. She had walked over and was standing next to Aphrodite. Behind her the Huns were dragging Weasel out the side door.

"I'm Eleni," said Aphrodite. She used her true name rather than the codename, Aphrodite, by which she had been known to Bill all these years.

"Nice to meet you," said Irene. She reached out and shook Aphrodite's hand.

"And, I'm Bill," said Bill. He put the pistol back in his shoulder holster and shook hands as well.

"I don't recognize you guys," said Irene. "Any special reason you dropped in to my place tonight? We don't get a lot of tourists."

"Well," said Aphrodite. She glanced briefly at Bill before continuing. "Actually, we were looking for you."

CHAPTER THREE

Below it was pitch black. Above, there were countless stars, more stars than Anwar Al-Amriki had seen anywhere other than the mountains in Pakistan. They reminded him of days in training, of the camaraderie of the mujahiddin and of the joy he felt in being part of a just and righteous cause. Reclined in the rear seat of the ultra-light aircraft, listening to the whir of the pusher propeller behind his head, he felt almost peaceful. He might be here on a mission of death, but right now he was enjoying the splendor of the universe that Allah had made.

"Welcome to gringo land, bro," said Rico, the pilot. "We just flew over the border." His voice crackled in the bulky, duct-taped headphones on Anwar's head. Anwar leaned over and looked down. Somewhere below them was the twelve-foot fence the Americans believed protected them. It was invisible in the darkness.

It had been a long trip already, more than two weeks since he left Pakistan and began his multi-leg journey to his final destination. There would be plenty of challenges ahead before his mission was complete. Still, it felt good to have made it this far and to be beginning his real work.

"About two minutes 'til we land, bro," added Rico. The nose of the ultra-light dipped slightly, and Anwar could feel it drop in the pit of his stomach.

"Ok," said Anwar via the small microphone attached to his headset. They hadn't been above one hundred feet since their takeoff from a dry lakebed in Mexico twenty minutes before. He could see they were lower than that now. As he watched, the lightweight aluminum and fabric aircraft passed over a small stream lined with short, gnarled trees and tall grass. Reflexively, in anticipation of the coming landing, he reached up and confirmed that the wallet containing his identification documents was still in the inside pocket of his jacket

"Be ready," said Rico. He was dimly illuminated by the green light of the instrument dials in the small open cockpit in the front of the aircraft. Anwar could see him craning his neck around searching for landmarks. "I am staying on the ground thirty seconds, man, that's it."

"Got it," replied Anwar. They continued to descend. Somewhere off to their left a mile or so was a dim yellow light from a ranch house.

"Stop fucking with your cell phone," said Rodrigo. He was sitting behind the wheel of a green and white Border patrol pickup truck parked a few miles north of the Mexican-American border.

"What the hell else is there to do?" said Mac. He was sitting next to Rodrigo in the front seat of the pickup. "We're just sitting on our asses, as usual."

"This is the job, gringo," said Rodrigo. "Been doing it for twenty years. Rain or shine."

"Right, right," said Mac. "And you walked five miles to school in the snow, uphill both ways." He looked up, smiled and then went back to trying to get a signal.

"Hear that?" asked Rodrigo. He leaned over toward the open window of the green and white Border Patrol pickup truck in which he was sitting.

"What?" asked Mac. He swatted at some non-existent insect and scratched his short, blond crew cut

"That," said Rodrigo.

"What?" repeated Mac. He didn't look up from the screen of his cell phone as he spoke.

"That," snapped Rodrigo. He smacked the steering wheel with the palm of his hand. "Put the fucking phone away and listen." He stuck his head out the window into the night air and closed his eyes in concentration. There was a distant whirring sound, almost like that of a window fan.

"I don't hear anything," said Mac sulkily. He shoved the phone into the pocket of his jacket and did his best to look disgusted.

"Fuck you, college boy," said Rodrigo. "You can't hear shit." He reached down, turned the ignition key and started the car. The headlights came on and illuminated the landscape of scrub brush, cactus and sand in front of them.

"Where are we going?" asked Mac. He sat up reflexively in his seat and put his hand on the handgun on his hip.

"To catch a goddamn ultra-light, gringo, that's where," said Rodrigo. He dropped the truck in gear and began to move.

◆ ◆ ◆

"Thirty seconds," said Rico. He had dimmed the dials in front of him even more so that now they gave off only the faintest glow. They were down to less than thirty feet, with the throttle pulled way back and their airspeed down to less than fifty miles an hour. Anwar leaned over and looked down. They were directly over a wide, level dirt road.

"I'm ready," said Anwar. He put his hands on the buckles to the safety harness that held him in his seat, so that he was ready to exit the aircraft as soon as it touched down.

"You better be, bro," said Rico. "I ain't going to sit around and wait for those migra assholes to show up." To their left, the broken shell of an old cattle truck skidded by, and Anwar realized they were now only a few feet off the ground.

Rico ran flights over the border two or three times a week, carrying weed for a cartel in the south. Those flights were a totally different animal, though, because he did not land. He loaded the packages of marijuana in a cage under his seat, and when he was over the drop zone he pulled a lever and dumped his cargo. He spent less than a half hour in the air. He cleared close to a thousand dollars a run, and the risk was minimal.

This time it was different. This time he was taking live cargo, not merchandise. More than that, he was freelancing, carrying a passenger about whom he knew almost nothing and whom the cartel did not know at all. Had it not been for the ten thousand bucks he had been paid in advance, he would never have even considered taking the gig.

There was a brief pause and almost total silence. The engine was throttled all the way back now and the prop turning only lazily as the aircraft glided forward on its black nylon wings. Then, there was a bump, a skid and a momentary sideways hop. The ultra-light rolled to a stop surprisingly suddenly, and a small cloud of dust and sand drifted down in its wake.

"This is it, hombre," said Rico. "From here on you're on your fucking own." He strained to turn around in the front seat to see whether Anwar was out yet.

Anwar pulled off his headset, unsnapped the buckles on his harness and pushed himself up and out of the deep bucket seat. Underneath the aircraft in a metal cage was his backpack with his clothes and other possessions. He squatted momentarily, retrieved the bag and then turned away from the ultra-light and began to walk quickly toward the brush at the edge of the road.

Behind him, the propeller began to spin, and Anwar could hear the crunch of small stones as the aircraft began to roll forward. He stopped momentarily at the side of the road and turned to look back. The aircraft was already speeding away and, less than a hundred feet down the road, it jumped suddenly into the air. Rico banked it hard left as it climbed, and, within moments, it was swallowed by the night.

◆ ◆ ◆

"We're too late. He's headed home," said Rodrigo. He had stopped the truck on a slight rise above a wide dirt road that lead to an abandoned ranch below. He was standing next to the truck with a pair of night vision binoculars to his eyes.

"Why would he land?" asked Mac. He was still sitting in the cab of the vehicle.

"I don't fucking know, Mac," said Rodrigo. "All I know is that he landed and that he is already taking off again."

"He could dump his cargo without landing," said Mac. "They always dump their cargo without landing."

"Thanks for that information," said Rodrigo. He climbed back in the truck and cranked the engine. "Now, let's go do our jobs and find out what the hell is going on."

◆ ◆ ◆

Backpack on his back, Anwar pushed his way through the grass and brush along the side of the road. Twenty meters in, he came to a gulley and crouched down momentarily to get his bearings. From one of the side pockets of the backpack he pulled a GPS unit and turned it on. After a brief pause, the screen came to life, and within moments, it began to acquire a location.

Anwar put the GPS down on the ground in front of him and sat down cross-legged in front of it. It would take a few moments for the device to be ready to navigate. Above him in the still warm night sky was the last thin sliver of a moon, making a beautiful golden crescent. He considered it an omen of great significance and yet another sign that he would be successful in carrying out his role in the coming operation.

Somewhere above and behind Anwar there was abruptly the sound of a truck engine starting. He froze and then turned slowly to look in the direction of the noise. A pair of headlights was bouncing along toward him down a rutted dirt road. They were perhaps four hundred meters away.

Anwar turned back to the GPS, scooped it up and shoved it back in his backpack. Then, slowly and cautiously he crawled into the tall, dry grass at the edge of the gulley and stretched himself out flat with his face down toward the earth.

From his time in the training camps Anwar knew that the first instinct in a situation like this was to run. He also knew that it would be a fatal mistake. He would make himself small, invisible and silent. He would disappear.

◆ ◆ ◆

"You can see the wheel marks right here," said Rodrigo. He had stopped the truck on the dirt road where the ultra-light had landed and was shining a big, black flashlight on the ground.

"Yep," said Mac. He was standing next to Rodrigo, and he had his pistol in his hand.

"But, there's nothing here," continued Rodrigo. "No merchandise."

"Maybe he didn't bring drugs," said Mac. He had his own flashlight out now, and he was shining it on the ground as well. "Maybe he brought someone."

"Fuck," said Rodrigo. He walked a few feet to one side of the tire tracks and swung his flashlight back and forth. There were unmistakable boot prints in the dirt and gravel. Mac saw them too.

"Shall we track him?" said Mac. He sounded excited for the first time that night.

"In the dark, gringo?" asked Rodrigo. "Whoever it was is moving out pretty good by now, probably headed due north like everybody else that jumps. Toward the highway."

"Maybe," said Mac. He was scanning the edge of the grass with his flashlight and pistol.

"Come on, gringo," said Rodrigo. "Let's call this in and then drive around and see if we can't get in front of this guy."

"Ok," said Mac reluctantly. He holstered his weapon and turned back toward the truck.

"Relax, white boy," said Rodrigo as he climbed into the cab. "However he got here, this guy's still an illegal. He'll have to be meeting some coyote somewhere nearby to help him with the next part of this trip.

Rodrigo started the truck and drove off down the dirt road in the same direction in which the ultra-light had taken off. Then, about three hundred meters away he made a hard right and headed due north in the direction of the closest two-lane state road.

◆◆◆

Anwar lay very still until he heard the sound of the engine fade and made sure the truck was not going to return. Then he sat up and pulled the GPS from his pocket. It had finished acquiring satellites now and had fixed his position. He toggled a switch, selected his first waypoint and pressed a button. The GPS displayed the distance to his next stop and the estimated time it would take to get there.

Anwar looked at the data, fixed it in his mind and then picked out a landmark ahead a few hundred meters by which to steer. It was a tall cactus on a low ridge in front of him. He would be walking due west, and according to the GPS it would take him two hours and nineteen minutes on foot to make it to the Nogales

Arizona bus station without stops. He figured that it would be easily double that with all the stops he expected to make, but that did not matter. He knew from the Internet that the first bus heading north left at 0630 the next morning, so he had plenty of time to burn.

After shoving the GPS into his right jacket pocket, Anwar stood and shouldered his pack. The desert air was beginning to cool now, and he felt a slight chill for the first time. From inside his left jacket pocket he pulled a black knit watch cap. Then he slipped it on over his long blond hair and took a moment to wipe some grit from his baby blue eyes. He had been away three years, but he was home now, and he had work to do. He took a last look up at the crescent in the sky, thanked Allah for his good fortune and began to move.

CHAPTER FOUR

2242 HOURS. 5 AUGUST 2002.
FELL'S POINT, BALTIMORE, MARYLAND.

"You were the last thing he talked about, before he died," said Bill. He was sitting on a wooden chair in Irene's small back office. Irene was in her black plastic desk chair a few feet away. Aphrodite was perched on Irene's desktop with her long legs dangling.

"That son of a bitch," said Irene. She shook her head slowly from side to side and looked at the scarred wooden floor. Aphrodite reached over and put her hand on Irene's shoulder for support.

"Maybe he could not find a way to show it," said Aphrodite. "But, he loved you."

"That son of a bitch," said Irene again. She dabbed at her damp eyes.

They had begun talking a few minutes after the Huns dragged themselves out of the bar and Irene ushered them into her office. Bill and Aphrodite had felt their way forward in the conversation, taking turns leading, searching for clues as to how to proceed. It was not easy, figuring out how to tell a woman you'd never met that her father, a man she hardly knew, was dead.

"He's the only reason I'm still here," said Bill. "If he hadn't taken point, I would have been the one to get it." His mind was filled with a searing vision, as he spoke. Jimmy, Irene's father, lying on the ground, bleeding from his eyes, killed by an improvised explosive device planted by Al Qaeda operatives intent on killing them all.

"I never really knew what he did," said Irene. "In my whole life, I only saw him a few times."

"He was a rolling stone. That's for sure," said Bill. It was still hard to accept. Jimmy Beard, living legend, bigger than life, dead.

"My Mom grew up in Columbus, Georgia," said Irene. She had given up trying to pretend that she wasn't crying. Tears streamed down her cheeks. "She met Jimmy when he was in jump school. Got pregnant. He moved on. She didn't."

"I'm sorry," said Aphrodite. She was a child of the street. She knew pain when she saw it.

"I hated him for it, for a long time," said Irene. "It wasn't until I was grown and Mom was gone that I finally figured out that it wasn't his idea that he stay away. It was hers."

"He had a good heart," said Aphrodite. She smiled at Irene and squeezed her shoulder.

"He gave me the money to buy this bar and get it going," said Irene. "Showed up at my Mom's funeral, waded through all the bullshit I threw at him and insisted on helping out."

"That was Jimmy," said Bill.

"Was he doing something important when he died?" asked Irene. It sounded like the answer was vital to her.

"Very," said Bill. He paused. It was impossible to know where to begin or where to end. He had already told Irene that he was ex-CIA and that Jimmy, Aphrodite and he had been on a job in the Middle East when Jimmy was killed. What more could he say?

"Tell her," said Aphrodite. There were things that were simple. This was one of them. Secrecy be damned. Jimmy was dead. His daughter needed to know why.

"I met Jimmy in the jungle in Central America when I was still in the Army," said Bill. "Another time. Another enemy. After I came on with the Agency, he and I worked together on several jobs. He was a legend. If you were going to a bad place, he was the man you wanted with you to make sure you came back alive."

"I believe that," said Irene.

"That's why they sent him with us into Kurdistan. We were looking for an atomic bomb. We were on our own. We needed the best."

"Did you find it?" asked Irene. She sniffled and dabbed at her eyes.

"We did," said Aphrodite.

"The world's safe for another day," said Bill. He smiled to lighten the mood.

"Thanks to your father," said Aphrodite. She slid down onto the floor next to Irene and squatted on her heels. "Because of his courage." She held both Irene's hands in hers as she spoke.

"God, I'm acting like a fool," said Irene. She had been looking down at the floor but now lifted her eyes to Aphrodite's and smiled weakly. "I don't have time for this. I've got a bar to run."

Bill's cell phone began to ring. He fumbled in his jacket for it, looked briefly at the number displayed on the phone and stood up. "Back in a minute," he said. Then he opened the door and stepped out of the office.

"You run this place all by yourself?" asked Aphrodite. She was still squatting in front of Irene and still holding her hands.

"Mostly," said Irene. "My husband and I split about a year ago. He vanished with a waitress from Hooter's. Since then it's been pretty much Eddie and me."

"Who's Eddie?" asked Aphrodite.

"My son," said Irene. She paused, looked away again, and then continued. "He's nineteen. Won't listen. Goes his own way a lot."

"Children are hard," said Aphrodite.

"Haven't seen him since yesterday," said Irene. She turned her head as searching the city through the walls for her son.

"Maybe we can help you straighten him out," said Aphrodite. She was on the street in Athens when she was sixteen, living by her wits. She knew about kids who went their own way. She knew how dangerous that way could be.

"Can't sleep worrying about him sometimes," said Irene.

The door to the office opened. Bill stepped inside. His brow was furrowed. He was troubled.

"What's up?" asked Aphrodite. She came to her feet smoothly.

"We need to go to Honduras," said Bill. "Now."

CHAPTER FIVE

2312 HOURS. 6 AUGUST 2002.
QISA KHAWANI BAZAAR, PESHAWAR, PAKISTAN.

"This is it," said Ali. He bent over and squinted through the hazy windows in the back of the sedan. The electricity in the bazaar was out again, and the only illumination came from the gas lanterns hung in the shopkeepers' stalls.

"You are sure?" said Sub-Inspector, Sardar Ghayur of the Khyber Pakhtunkhwa Police. He had not stayed alive this long by simply accepting the word of a source. He leaned over Ali and strained to see. Around them, the streets were filled with swarms of shoppers haggling for deals and lugging home their purchases in striped nylon sacks.

"This is the place," nodded Ali. His hair and beard, dyed bright orange with henna, bobbed and danced. He pointed out the window toward a narrow, filthy, cobblestone alley that disappeared into the darkness between two shops selling leather sandals and cheap plastic shower shoes.

"Stop," said Sardar to the driver in the front of car.

"Yes, sir," said the driver. He pulled the sedan abruptly to a one side, shoving aside a crowd of women clustered around a plastic bin full of underwear and two men haggling over cigarettes.

Behind them the Toyota pickup truck carrying the security element on bench seats in its bed pulled in as well.

"Wait here," said Sardar to the driver. He pushed open the rear door of the sedan on his side, grabbed Ali's hand and began to pull the man from the car behind him.

"I should not be going," said Ali. He waggled his head from side to side for emphasis as he spoke.

"You're going regardless," said Sardar. He was only a little over five feet six inches in height, but he was not yet thirty and still had the build of the wrestler he had been in university. He pulled on Ali again, and the man came tumbling into the street. *You lead us here*, thought Sardar. *You go first.*

"What are your orders Sub-Inspector?" asked Khan. He was the head of the Khyber Pakhtunkhwa Police security element that had dismounted from the pickup. The six men of his detachment had reflexively formed a ring around Sardar and Ali. They were dressed in identical clothing to Sardar: black boots, khaki trousers, black shirts and black berets. Each carried an AK-47 assault rifle.

"Up there," ordered Sardar. He pointed toward the narrow alley. Around them people stopped shopping and turned to stare. Sardar knew they needed to move fast or risk giving their targets time to escape.

Two of the men in the security element took the lead and trotted up the alley into the darkness. Sardar and Ali followed with the remainder of the security element. The gaslights of the bazaar stalls disappeared from view as they advanced. Underneath their feet, the cobblestone became broken and then gave way to bare earth. The ground was littered with trash. The air stunk of raw sewage.

The alley turned left and then abruptly right again. Ahead and above them on a slight rise appeared a ramshackle two-story wooden structure with a narrow wooden balcony running its width about twelve feet off the ground. Above the balcony six-pointed stars were cut into the building's white-washed masonry façade.

"They are on the second floor," said Ali. "In the back." He pressed himself against one wall of the narrow alley as if fearing some immediate and lethal reprisal for his treachery.

"Go," said Sardar simply. Khan nodded and made a series of hand gestures to his men. Two of them moved silently down the alley toward the rear of the building. The remainder followed him toward the front door of the building with weapons at the ready.

"If you are lying, Ali," said Sardar. "It will be the last lie you tell." He stepped into the shadows next to Ali and took a firm grip on his arm. The weight of the .45 Stoeger Cougar pistol on his hip was reassuring.

Seconds passed. The only sounds were the hubbub from the bazaar and a baby squealing somewhere above and behind them. Rats scurried in the dark.

"Don't move, don't move!" It was Khan yelling in Pashto somewhere inside the target building. A string of gunshots rang out, and someone started screaming in a high-pitched voice.

"Stay down!" commanded Khan. Something heavy crashed to the ground on the second floor of the building. Glass broke. There was more shouting. The wooden shutters that covered the doorway from the second story of the building to the narrow balcony burst open. A figure in dark salwar kameese flew out the doorway and into the air.

"Go," said Sardar. He pushed Ali away with one hand and drew his pistol with the other. There was no sense in letting the targets see the face of the source who had informed on them. Ali scuttled down the alley without making a response.

The man who had jumped crashed to the ground in front of Sardar, struggled to get to his feet and then fell to his side screaming, writhing in the dirt and grasping at his leg.

"Stand up and you will die," barked Sardar in Pashto. He advanced out of the shadows with his pistol trained on the man's head. The man clenched his teeth and stared back wide-eyed from behind his long wild beard. His hands were wrapped around his right leg just below the knee. A jagged piece of bone had torn through his trouser leg, and blood was seeping between his fingers.

"Are you alright, sir?" asked Ahmed. He was one of the two men who had gone around behind the dwelling when the raid began. He and his partner had come back to the front of the structure when they heard the screaming.

"I am," said Sardar. He looked up briefly. Ahmed had his AK-47 trained on the wounded man's head. Sardar holstered his pistol and knelt down.

"One dead up here. Two others in cuffs. All ours untouched, "called Khan. He was standing out on the balcony of the target home and looking down.

"Search the place," called Sardar without turning. There were cracks of light all around now where shutters had been opened and neighbors were peering out to see what transpired. He did not plan to stay long in this hole. Better that they completed their work and were on their way.

"I will check you now," said Sardar to the man in front of him. "If you move to resist, Ahmed here will blow your head off. Do you understand?"

The man nodded but said nothing. Sardar began to work his way over the man's body and through his clothes, checking first to make sure he was not wearing a suicide vest and not carrying any obvious weapons, and then shifting to a slower, more methodical approach looking even for small items that might have been sown into seams of his clothing.

"What is this?" asked Sardar. He felt something broad and flat stretched across the abdomen of the man. He ran his hands over the spot again. There was something there under the man's clothing.

"There are papers up here," yelled Khan.

Sardar pulled up the man's long tunic. Taped with medical tape to his stomach was a large flat manila envelope. He pulled it loose. He could feel that there were documents inside.

"Here, too," Sardar called. The envelope was sealed. He felt for his knife in his pocket. In front of him the man moaned and closed his eyes. He was losing consciousness.

"Someone coming, Sub-Inspector," said Ahmed.

Sardar turned and the looked down the alley toward the bazaar. There were at least a dozen men in casual civilian attire carrying AK-47's coming toward him. Behind them were two older, heavier men with heavy moustaches and dark suits.

"ISI," said Sardar. He stood and, without thinking, shoved the envelope inside his trousers in the small of his back. He had learned the hard way that it was often difficult to know whether the Directorate of Inter-Services Intelligence (ISI) was friend or foe.

"I can't read these," yelled Khan from inside the house. "Maybe you can."

"Come outside. Now," replied Sardar. He walked toward the men advancing in his direction. "We have company."

"Good evening, Sub-Inspector," called the older of the two men in suits. He was speaking Urdu with the distinctive accent of Lahore.

"Good evening, Colonel Shah," replied Sardar. "I did not expect to see you here this evening."

"This is Major Bhutto," said Shah gesturing to the man next to him. "This is his investigation. He will take custody of whatever prisoners you have and any evidence you have seized."

"What do you mean this is his investigation, Colonel?" asked Sardar. "This is a police operation. "

"Not anymore," said Major Bhutto. His white teeth gleamed under his bristling black moustache. He motioned to the armed men around him and they moved forward barking orders to Sardar's security detail.

"I demand an explanation," said Sardar.

"You will get none," said Bhutto. "Puissant tribal police officers don't demand anything from ISI." He showed a mouthful of teeth again to emphasize his contempt.

"Who told you we were here?" asked Sardar. *Was it Ali?* It wouldn't be the first time a source padded his pocket by passing the same information to more than one service.

"Take your Pashtun children and go home," said Bhutto with all the condescension he could muster. "Isn't there a camel that needs fucking somewhere?" He pushed past Sardar and headed in the direction of the house that had been raided.

"It's always the same isn't it, Colonel?" said Sardar. "You Punjabis. You think you own the whole damn country."

"This is an intelligence matter, Sub-Inspector Sardar," repeated the Colonel. He placed special emphasis on Sardar's rank to ensure he remembered where junior police officers stood in the pecking order relative to colonels of the Intelligence Service. "Stand down."

"What are you trying to hide, Colonel?" asked Sardar. "What is it that has you out from behind a desk so late at night?"

"You will lose this fight, Sub-Inspector," said Shah. Several more armed men in civilian clothes were coming up the alley behind him.

"Maybe," said Sardar. His blood was beginning to boil now.

"Let it go," said Khan. He had appeared at Sardar's side, and as he spoke he reached out and put his hand on the shoulder of the Sub-Inspector.

"Why?" said Sardar. "Because this arrogant Punjabi son-of-a-bitch says so? You know why he is here. We found something."

"It doesn't matter," said Khan. He squeezed Sardar's shoulder slightly as he did so. They had been together a long time, and he knew how close the Sub-Inspector was to doing something foolish.

"He's right," said Shah. "Listen to your boy." Then he clasped his hands behind his back and began to stroll up the alley.

"It doesn't matter," hissed Khan to Sardar as the Colonel moved away from them. "I still have the documents from upstairs." He patted his stomach as he did so to show that he had slipped them inside his uniform shirt.

"The documents," said Sardar. He had almost forgotten about them. He reached back and checked to see that the envelope was still safely tucked into his trousers. Shah's ISI personnel were clustered around the injured man on the ground while Sardar's men stood by and watched.

"Yes, boss, the documents," said Khan. "You need to look at them. I can't read them. They're in English."

CHAPTER SIX

1749 HOURS. 6 AUGUST 2002.
EAGLE RAY BAR, WEST END, ROATAN, HONDURAS.

Bill and Aphrodite parked their rental Jeep in front of the Lusty Lizard Bar and walked down the dirt main street of West End to the beach. Aphrodite was wearing a gold bikini with a silk sarong around her waist, and the wind of sea fluttered the fabric of her skirt as she moved. Bill was back in his habitual Caribbean attire, faded cargo shorts and a loose camp shirt. On either side the road was lined with rough wooden tiki bars and dive shops. An old Toyota pickup truck bumped by filled with mangoes, watermelon and vegetables, while the loudspeaker on the top of the cab blared scratchy reggae music.

"I hate that we left Irene without helping her more," said Aphrodite.

"Me too," said Bill. "But, I owe this man everything, and he sounded desperate." Bill looked over at Aphrodite briefly. "There'll be plenty of time for Baltimore later."

"I guess," said Aphrodite. She sounded unconvinced.

"This is the place," said Bill. He turned off the road, walked across an expanse of white sand and out onto a narrow, rickety pier.

The Eagle Ray Bar sat on pilings at the other end about a hundred feet from shore.

"Great," said Aphrodite. She reached over and held Bill's hand in hers as they walked. The sun was strong and low on the horizon, and the water below crystal clear, but her eyes scanned their surroundings relentlessly. What exactly had brought them here was still unclear, and that made her uneasy.

Stepping into the bar from the brilliant sunshine outside, Bill and Aphrodite were momentarily blind. The bar was open on all sides to the let the breeze through, but the broad roof created a pool of cool, dark shade. They paused to regain their vision and to survey the scene. The sound of "Hotel California" coming from speakers somewhere in the rafters engulfed them.

Across the bar through a sea of plastic tables and chairs, Bill could see a group of Australian backpackers with beaded hair and tie-dyed shirts arguing about a soccer game. The table in front of them was littered with bottles of Salva Vida beer, a local Honduran favorite. A chalkboard nailed to a wooden post behind them announced that tonight's special was conch fritters.

Directly in front of Bill was a table full of twenty something American scuba divers drawn to the island by its reef. The muscular white guy across from Bill was wearing a white t-shirt that said "Wanna See An Octopussy Squirt? Go Diving" in red letters. He had a hammerhead shark tattooed on one bulging bicep.

The woman next to him was still wearing her shorty wetsuit. The pink ball cap on her head said "Dive Chick".

Bill pushed forward through the crowd, and headed for a table on the far side of the bar. Aphrodite followed. A tiny black waitress in white shorts and a white tube top pushed past Bill, and a gaunt Jamaican man with long, dirty dreadlocks leaned out over from his table, grabbed her ass and yelled that he wanted more whiskey.

"Fuck you," said the waitress.

"Suck my deek," said the Jamaican in a slow, deliberate way that suggested he was more than a little high.

Seated on the other side of the bar with his back against one of the wooden posts that held up the thatch roof of the bar was a tall, thick man with skin so dark he looked like a great ebony tree. Bill slid in across the table from him. Aphrodite sat down next to him and instinctively turned her chair partially to one side, so she could see the room behind them and cover Bill's back.

"Solomon, my friend," said Bill. He reached out and grasped his hand as he spoke. "Are you well?"

"Praise the Lord," said Solomon. He grinned broadly, and the white of his teeth was dazzling against the darkness of his skin. "And who is this?" he asked. He was still holding Bill's hand but was staring at Aphrodite.

"My wife, Eleni," said Bill.

"Your wife," said Solomon. He sounded mildly disappointed. He let go of Bill's hand, took Aphrodite's, raised it to his lips and kissed it. "It is a great pleasure," he added.

"Thank you," said Aphrodite. She noted that the big man was speaking to her, but talking to her ample breasts. "I have heard a great deal about you."

"Have you?" said Solomon. He let go of Aphrodite's hand and turned back to Bill. "I hope all good things."

"How's business?" asked Bill.

"Thank you for coming, my friend," said Solomon. "It's been a long time. I didn't even know if the number I had for you would work." The smile was gone.

"You saved my life, Solomon," said Bill. "I don't forget things like that." He meant it.

"Treasure hunting can be a dangerous business," smiled Solomon.

"Treasure hunting?" said Aphrodite. She looked quizzically at Bill.

"Another time," said Bill. He looked embarrassed. "It did not end well."

"Well enough," said Solomon. "You are alive."

"Must be a good story," said Aphrodite.

"A very good story," said Solomon. He laughed. "And the treasure is still out there."

"Tell me how I can help," said Bill to Solomon.

"It's my nephew," said Solomon. He paused momentarily and looked around as if to assure himself that no one was eavesdropping. "Hotel California" had been replaced by "Red, Red Wine". The man with the long gray hair at the next table was swaying to the music and telling his companion, a rail thin woman with equally gray hair, about the weed he had back in his place on the beach. Solomon leaned in toward Bill and Aphrodite and spoke more softly. "I warned him. He didn't listen."

"Warned him about what?" asked Bill.

"The Muslims," said Solomon. His bright island shirt was partially unbuttoned to show the great expanse of his chest. A gold cross on a bright gold chain hung against it.

"In Roatan?" asked Aphrodite.

"On the mainland," said Solomon.

"What was your nephew doing?" asked Bill. He already knew the answer.

"The family business," said Solomon. Once again he paused and looked about. The Australians had started talking about Nicaraguan rum. No one was listening.

"Smuggling," said Bill.

The waitress in the white tube top appeared, and the conversation stopped momentarily. Solomon ordered a glass of rum and some limes. Bill and Aphrodite asked for two Salva Vidas.

"Yes, of course," said Solomon when the waitress had left. Behind him dive boats moored for the night bobbed at anchor in the tiny harbor.

"What did he smuggle?" asked Aphrodite.

"Where are you from, Eleni?" asked Solomon. "You do not have an accent like an American."

"Greece," said Eleni.

"You are very pretty, but somehow I think you know some things about how the world works."

"Life has not always been pretty for me," said Eleni. She had a hundred stories about drugs, violence and living on the edge of death, that she chose to leave untold.

"Do you know the history of our island, of the Garifuna?" asked Solomon.

"No," said Eleni.

"In the late 1700's there was a slave revolt on St. Vincent. It is an island in the Eastern Caribbean. There were big plantations there and many slaves then. The British controlled the island, and when they put down the revolt, they captured many thousands of people, including my ancestors."

"Here we go," said Bill. He rolled his eyes.

"This is the truth," said Solomon.

"Don't listen to him," said Aphrodite. She slapped Bill's hand and gave him a scowl. "Tell me your story."

"The British did not want these people on the island anymore. They knew these people would never stay slaves, and that they would fight for their freedom every chance they got. So, they put them on ships and brought them here. They marooned them on Roatan, which was uninhabited."

"They forgot you," said Eleni.

"They forgot us," agreed Solomon. "But, we did not die. We did not go away. We survived. We spread." He held his arms apart as if painting a picture in the air. "Throughout the Western Caribbean. On the mainland, on these islands. And, we did what we had to do to make money, to support our families and to live."

"What kind of trouble is your nephew in," asked Bill.

"I was in Belize City last week," continued Solomon. Once again, he leaned forward and lowered his voice. Once again, Bill met him in the middle of the table. "While I was there I got a phone call from Carlos. This is my nephew. He was there. He wanted to talk."

"So you met."

"We met. He talked. He was very worried. He wanted me to try to help him. He thought maybe I knew someone."

"Worried about what?" asked Bill.

"My nephew is a smart boy. But, not half so smart as he thinks he is. He has been working with a Muslim man, named Sultan. They have been moving things together and selling them."

"What kinds of things?"

"It started with weapons."

"To narcos," said Bill. Solomon just nodded gravely. "Fuck," added Bill. He looked down at the table momentarily and shook his head. This was getting deep quickly.

"Where do these weapons come from?" asked Aphrodite.

"From you," said Solomon. "I mean, from the USA."

"The USG sends weapons to governments all over Central America to use to fight the narcos," said Bill. "Then, enterprising fellows in the military sell them to smugglers who sell them to the narcos."

"Who use them to kill cops and the military," said Aphrodite.

"And then the USA sends more guns," said Solomon. "Sometimes I think maybe Americans are not so smart."

"How long's your nephew been in this?" asked Bill.

"A few years now," said Solomon. "I don't know exactly. He's my brother's son. Since my brother died I have been trying to watch over Carlos, like a godfather. But, he knows I don't approve of his business, so he doesn't tell me much."

"And, what has him so worried now that he's coming to you for help?" asked Aphrodite.

"People," said Solomon.

"I'm not tracking," said Bill.

"The Arab Carlos is working with lives just inside Mexico, across the border from Belize," said Solomon in a low, serious voice. Around them, the noise in the bar was increasing. Night was coming.

"Smugglers' heaven," said Bill.

"Like I said, at first he was moving mostly arms to the narcos in Mexico," said Solomon. "Then it was people. Africans. Chinese. All going north to the US. "

"Roger," said Bill.

"And, then an American," said Solomon. He pursed his lips and furrowed his brow. He assumed the gravity of what he had just said was clear.

"Whoa," said Bill.

"An American who wanted smuggled into his own country," said Aphrodite. She cocked her head and looked at Bill. He was staring at the table now with his eyes closed.

"A young man," said Solomon. "A white boy. Twenties. By himself."

"How long ago?" asked Bill.

"Recently," said Solomon. "I don't know exactly. But, it was a big deal. Just the one white boy. Had to be kept apart from anyone else. Like he was very special."

"That must have cost some money," said Aphrodite.

"Yes," said Solomon. "A lot."

"What else?" asked Bill.

"He did not tell me more," said Solomon.

"Where is your nephew now?" asked Bill. His mind was racing ahead now, planning moves, considering implications.

"He is in Belize," said Solomon. "He's scared. He feels that he has gotten into something very dangerous. He has a very bad feeling. He wants a way out."

"And you think we can help," said Bill.

"I can't take this to the police, my friend," said Solomon. "The honest ones would eat my nephew alive. The ones who are on the take would sell him to the narcos in a moment. I had nowhere else to turn."

"How soon can you get him here?" asked Bill.

"Maybe 48 hours," said Solomon.

"Good," said Bill. He looked at Aphrodite. He could tell by the expression on her face that she was already calculating the angles and measuring the risks.

"Thank you, brother," said Solomon.

"Thank me after we figure out what, if anything, we can do for you nephew," said Bill. "In the meantime, we are going to need some things from you to help us get ready."

The waitress reappeared with their drinks and began setting them on the table. The speakers in the rafters were blasting out "The Smuggler's Blues."

"Whatever you need," said Solomon.

CHAPTER SEVEN

2030 HOURS. 7 AUGUST 2002.
GREYHOUND BUS STATION, BALTIMORE, MARYLAND.

The bus rolled to a stop at the station, and the driver opened the door. Across the aisle, the fat man who snored got up from his seat and began to shove his bulk forward, dragging his duffel bag behind him. The two teenage girls, who had been sneaking swallows of tequila from a bottle in a brown paper bag for the last hour, got up and followed. Anwar decided to wait for the rest of the passengers to leave before he stood.

It had been two long days of riding. Still, he had found the time useful. It gave him time to reacquaint himself with the country. It gave him time to get his legs under him. It gave him time to study his enemy and prepare for what was ahead.

Anwar tried to avoid conversations. He was prepared to provide a cover story and to answer any questions a fellow passenger might have, but still he felt it best to keep his profile as low as possible. His trainers had ingrained in him the need to stay below the radar, to avoid attracting attention and to focus always on the objective. He was not here to chat. He was here to make sure the final arrangements were made and the operation was successful.

When the last other passenger had disembarked, Anwar got up, pulled his backpack from the overhead storage bin and walked toward the front of the bus. The driver was standing up and stretching. He showed no interest in anything other than his lower back, as Anwar walked past and trotted down the stairs to the pavement.

Anwar walked through the station and out onto the street without stopping. Stations were filled with cameras, cops and people who asked questions. He was done with the bus, and the faster he left the area the better.

Baltimore was a new experience for Anwar. He was a white kid from a middle class family in the Washington, D.C. suburbs. In school he played video games and smoked a little weed. Baltimore was the slightly scary place where affluent white people rarely went.

Still, based on the research he had done in an internet café in Karachi, he had a pretty good mental picture of the layout of the downtown area. He intended to use that knowledge now. He might be clear of the station but he needed to clean himself. His trainers had ingrained in him that discipline and tradecraft were everything. Before he did anything or met anyone he needed to make absolutely sure that he did not have a tail.

Anwar walked through the parking lot, past the Marine saying good bye to his girlfriend and the family of Salvadorans carrying their possessions in shopping bags, and out onto the main access road to the station. Ahead of him and to the right was an area filled with old brick warehouses and commercial businesses. It was deserted at this time of night, and most of the streetlights were out. He plunged in.

On Anwar's right was a rusty chain link fence overgrown with vines and weeds. He walked across the middle of a parking lot littered with debris. Shards of glass from shattered beer and whisky bottles crunched under his boots. He could smell stagnant, fetid water somewhere on the other side of a stand of scraggly, urban trees ahead of him.

Behind him somewhere he heard glass crunching under tennis shoes. Someone coughed into their hand in a failed attempt to remain undetected. Anwar knew there were at least two of them. He did not turn to look nor did he hurry his step. Ahead to the left Anwar could see a concrete sidewalk that led from the parking lot into a courtyard-like area between two one-story warehouses. One of the buildings had a sign on it saying something about salvage. There were a couple of beat-up vans parked inside a fenced-in area next to the warehouses. He headed that way.

Past the vans and around the corner, Anwar came to a spot where the warehouses closed in and a narrow brick alley ran ahead to the next block. A single light on a telephone pole cast a yellowish glow over the scene. In front of him were two black teenagers in heavy, oversized winter coats. The one on the left was holding a tire iron.

Glass crunched again behind Anwar, and he turned now to see who was behind him. There were two more young men there, one white and one Hispanic. As he watched, the white guy pulled a switchblade from his pocket and opened it.

"Give us your money, and we won't fuck you up," said the Hispanic guy.

Anwar didn't need this. On the other hand, he didn't have a lot of options. He couldn't call the cops. He couldn't stick around until somebody else called the cops. And he certainly could not afford to part with his wallet, his cash and his documents.

"Now," said the white guy.

Anwar turned back toward the two black kids. He began to walk forward.

"Don't be an asshole," said the black teenager on the left. He smacked the tire iron into his palm for emphasis.

"Allah protects," said Anwar in Arabic.

The kid with the tire iron came forward and swung it with both hands at Anwar's head. Anwar ducked and sidestepped, and the kid went past in a blur and almost fell on his face. The white guy came at him next swinging the knife from side to side at waist level. Anwar backpedaled as fast as he could.

"Cut the fucker," yelled the Hispanic guy.

Anwar came up hard against a wall behind him. He was out of room to run. His right foot slipped on something rotten and slick. The white guy slashed at him with his knife and the blade caught Anwar on the left forearm. Blood splattered across the pavement.

"Give it up," yelled the Hispanic guy.

"Allah protects," repeated Anwar in Arabic. He could feel blood running down his arm and onto his hand.

"I'm going to cut your fucking throat, prick," yelled the white guy. He was close enough that Anwar could smell the whisky on his breath. The knife came down from above this time, and Anwar barely blocked it with his right arm.

"Freeze!" The voice on the loudspeaker boomed across the filthy pavement. The white kid jumped and turned like he had been hit with an electric shock. His buddies turned as well.

A spotlight hit the group like an explosion and turned night literally to day. There was a police patrol car sitting at the end of the alley and a police officer standing next to it with his weapon drawn.

"Put your hands where I can see them and drop the weapons," yelled the cop. He was coming down the alley with his gun trained in front of him.

The Hispanic guy was already running, and the white guy was close behind him.

"Fuckin' pig!" yelled the black guy with the tire iron. He stepped forward shaking the tire iron in one hand.

"Don't be a dick, Ray," called the other black kid. He was backing his way in the direction that the other two punks had disappeared. "Let's get the hell out of here."

"Fuckin' pig," repeated the guy with the tire iron. He smashed the tire iron against the bricks in the alley and moved toward the cop again. The two were separated by less than ten feet now.

The officer fired twice. The black kid went down on his knees and then collapsed on his face. The officer started yelling for an ambulance and backup into the radio microphone clipped to his shirt. He continued coming forward with his weapon still trained on the black kid on the ground.

Anwar looked down at the blood dripping from his arm. He needed to take care of the wound. There was a bandanna in the side pocket of his jeans. He pulled it out and began to wrap it around the cut.

"You ok?" asked the cop. He was standing in front of Anwar now. He still had his gun in his hand, but he had lowered it to his side.

"Yeah, I'll be fine," said Anwar. He smiled to cover his discomfort. He needed to get moving. Fast.

"Ok, ok, take it easy," said the cop. He was a young, white guy with a Marine style haircut and bulging biceps. "An ambulance is on its way."

"Right," said Anwar. "I'll be fine." He smiled again.

The cop turned and walked back over to the body of the black kid on the pavement. He knelt down and put his fingers on the kid's neck. After a moment he took them away and shook his head. Blood was pooling at his feet. There was a siren wailing in the distance.

Anwar looked around. There was a piece of broken pipe with a jagged end on it a few feet to one side. The siren grew louder. He picked up the pipe.

The cop was still down on his knees a few feet in front of Anwar. It looked like he might even be praying. Anwar stepped forward, swung the pipe over his head and brought it crashing down on the top of the cop's head. He groaned and slumped to one side.

Anwar hit him again. And again. The cop stopped moving. The siren was louder still.

Anwar walked over to the line of low trees until he could see the fetid arm of the Inner Harbor behind them. Then he threw the pipe up and over the trees into the water. Tires screeched somewhere down the block, and the red and blue flash of police warning lights began to bounce of the pavement around him. He turned and ran.

CHAPTER EIGHT

2111 HOURS. 8 AUGUST 2002.
ROATAN, HONDURAS.

"Baby Boy's on his way to you," said Aphrodite softly into the encrypted Motorola radio cupped in her right hand. She was dressed all in black and stretched out flat on her belly next to a clump of palm trees at the top of a sharp ridge on Roatan's south coast. Her long blond hair was tucked up under an old Navy watch cap, and her face darkened with a mixture of lamp black and insect repellant that rendered her invisible and warded off the local bugs. In her left hand was the night vision scope she had been using to watch the vehicle carrying Solomon and his nephew as it made its way toward her. On the ground next to her was an FN FAL assault rifle with an Israeli Trilux scope mounted on it. All her gear, and Bill's, had been provided by Solomon.

"Roger," said Bill over the radio. His voice was low and husky, and the sound of the wind blowing across the ridgeline where he had set up a mile to the southeast was audible in the background. "Any sign of follow?"

"Negative," said Aphrodite. From her vantage point near the palm trees, she could scan all the way back up the dirt road below her to where it left the paved highway several miles away. Solomon's white pickup truck, with a red chem light taped to its antenna to ensure positive identification, had just passed her position. There were no other vehicles in sight and nothing moving other than the jungle life around her. "Your date is running free."

"Roger," responded Bill.

Bill was sitting at the crest of a rocky ridge overlooking a stretch of beach and a shallow bay. He put down the handheld radio and pulled a set of night vision goggles on over his eyes. The goggles gathered and amplified the ambient light and turned night into day. From his vantage point, Bill could now see the vehicle carrying Solomon and Carlos. There was nothing else moving, except for some land crabs in the brush behind him.

Bill watched for several minutes more, scanning continuously for any sign that anyone else was headed in his direction. He was dressed in blue jeans and a long, loose olive drab camp shirt. His Glock 19 9mm semi-automatic pistol was tucked into a concealed holster in the small of his back. Fifty yards away, well below the crest, so as to be concealed from view was an old Jeep with an M-4 carbine and several spare magazines filled with 5.56 rounds lying on the front passenger seat.

A mile from the ridgeline, the truck carrying Solomon and Carlos turned off the dirt road onto a narrow track through tall grass, as Bill had instructed Solomon to do the day before. The track went south toward the beach and the rusted metal skeleton of a shrimp boat grounded in a storm decades before. The track was littered with rocks and badly rutted, and as he watched Bill could see the vehicle's headlights bouncing up and down as it lurched its way forward.

After a·few minutes' drive, the pickup turned in a half-circle on the beach, came to a halt and shut off its lights. Bill waited. A few moments later, a cheap Nokia cell phone in his right breast pocket began to vibrate. He reached up, pulled the phone from his pocket and pressed the green telephone symbol to answer the call.

"Go," said Bill.

"Brother, we are here," said Solomon. He was whispering as if he were afraid of being overheard. Bill could almost smell the tension in his voice.

"I know," said Bill.

"Where are you?" asked Solomon. Part of the way you protected yourself in a high risk meeting like this with an unknown contact like Carlos was by not divulging your game plan in advance. Solomon knew he was to drive to this spot and make a call. He had no idea what was to happen next.

"Doesn't matter," said Bill.

"You are a very careful man," said Solomon.

"That's why I have all this gray hair," said Bill. "And, why I'm still standing." Solomon was an old, trusted friend. Carlos was an unknown. He would be treated as such.

"Yes," said Solomon.

"Tell your nephew to get out of the vehicle and walk west along the water until he is met," said Bill.

"And I will wait here?" asked Solomon.

"You will leave, my friend. After our meeting is done, I will get your nephew home," said Bill.

There was a pause of a few moments. Over the phone Bill could hear a muffled conversation taking place. Several times he heard the voice of Solomon's passenger saying he wasn't getting out of the vehicle.

"My nephew says he is afraid. He asks that you come to where we are now," said Solomon. Carlos was still jabbering away about something in the background.

"Negative," said Bill. "Give the cell phone to the boy. Tell him to get out of the car and walk until met. You drive home. I will contact you later." Bill pressed the red telephone symbol on the phone, terminated the call and stuffed the phone back in his pocket. Sometimes the most effective form of persuasion was silence.

Through the NVG's Bill watched the pickup. A full minute passed. Nothing happened. Another minute passed, then the passenger's side door opened. A figure in a shiny gray suit, a black silk shirt and pointy zippered boots got out, slammed the door and began hesitantly to move away from the vehicle. The lights came on in the truck, and Bill heard the faint sound of an engine against the silence of the night. Then the pickup turned away and began to bounce its way back toward the main road.

Bill watched and waited. The truck made its way to the dirt road, turned north and began to gather speed. A small herd of deer bounded across the road ahead of it and disappeared into the thick forest. Carlos, holding the hems of his suit trousers up like a woman in a long dress, picked his way slowly, hesitantly toward Bill.

Another five minutes passed. Carlos fell down, and Bill watched him pick thorns out of his hands, then get back up slowly and continue west. An owl called and then flapped away in the night. Nothing else moved.

Time to rock and roll, thought Bill. He inched back off the crest and then, still crouching, slid down the rocky slope of the ridge to his Jeep. Opening the door he climbed in and started the engine without turning on the headlights. He still had the NVG's on, and he intended to use them to drive. He picked up the M-4 and the magazines and stowed them between himself and the door, so that they would not be accessible to Carlos when he picked him up.

A narrow dirt and rock track ran down the backside of the ridge through dense forest and curled around toward the beach. Bill took it. The Jeep bumped its way forward over rocks and ruts. Outside there was nothing but jet black, jungle and the distant sound of the waves.

A few minutes later, the track came out of the forest and into an area of tall grass. Bill brought the Jeep to a halt just inside the trees. Less than a hundred meters ahead of him was the water. The track ran downhill to the water's edge and the rotting remains of an old pier and then turned hard right and ran west along the coast.

◆◆◆

Bill waited. Carlos came through some low brush about fifty meters away onto the dirt and rock road. That was it. He was on the "X". Bill stepped on the gas, sped forward, pulled the Jeep next to Carlos and stopped suddenly. The tires skidded slightly on loose stone.

"Get in," said Bill. He leaned across the front seat and opened the passenger door as he spoke.

Carlos hesitated briefly, no doubt startled by the sudden appearance of the vehicle, which seemed to have materialized from nowhere in the darkness, then got in and closed the door. Bill stepped on the gas again and shot down the dirt road into the black of night.

"Good to meet you," said Bill simply.

"I have thorns in my hands, man," responded Carlos.

"Sorry, kid," said Bill. *Why are all bad guys such pussies*, he thought.

"I didn't expect to go for a walk," said Carlos sulkily.   He stunk of cheap cologne and sweat. He had piled his long dreadlocks up on his head like a basket of snakes and tied them in place with ribbons.

"Again, sorry," lied Bill. He crested a rise, reentered the jungle and began a slow descent toward another small bay. On both sides of the vehicle, tall trees and tangled vines crowded in. The road was a little smoother and the potholes less numerous. Bill stomped on the accelerator.

"Did you have any trouble getting here?" asked Bill. His lights were still off, and he still had the NVG's on. He watched the rearview mirror and saw nothing following. Carlos was hanging onto the strap over the passenger's side front door with a look of terror on his face.

"No," murmured Carlos.

"Good," said Bill. He hit the brakes, turned hard right and flew down a side trail into a rough clearing surrounding two ruined wooden buildings with tin roofs. He brought the vehicle to a stop next to some rusted machinery and a sign that said Port Royal Timber, shut off the engine and turned around in his seat to take one last look behind him to make sure he hadn't missed anything. Nothing but dust hung in the air. Then he pulled off the NVG's, tossed them on the dashboard and turned to face Carlos.

"You drive well in the dark," said Carlos. He sounded terrified. He had a toothpick between his teeth, and he was working it back and forth in his mouth with his tongue.

"Practice, kid," said Bill. He reached forward and shook Carlos's hand. It was soft and smooth, the hand of a man who hadn't done a day's honest labor in his life. "Now please lean forward and put your arms on the dash in front of you," added Bill.

"Man, what's up? You don't trust me?" asked Carlos.

"I don't trust anyone," said Bill.

Carlos leaned forward and put both hands on the dash as instructed, and Bill began to methodically frisk him. He was looking for weapons and explosives, but he was also looking for recording devices, beacons and a host of other concealable devices that might tell him that Carlos was playing both sides in this game. He found only the cell phone that Solomon had given Carlos, a dirty wallet and a couple of cheap Honduran condoms.

"Thank you," said Bill. "You may sit back now."

"You must think I am a very dangerous man," said Carlos. He leaned back against the seat and turned slightly to his left to face Bill.

"I think you have dangerous friends," said Bill.

"No doubt."

"Tell me about these friends," said Bill. He turned sideways in his seat, so that he could face Carlos directly and readily reach the snub-nosed Model 360, 5 shot Smith and Wesson Airlight revolver in the holster, duct-taped to the back of Carlos's seat. It wasn't a very accurate weapon, but it did not matter. In this situation, it was what the old timers called a "belly gun," meaning that if it was ever fired it would be at such close range that you could literally shove it into the belly of the man you were shooting.

"Can you help?" said Carlos.

"Solomon says that you told him a story about being asked to move some white American kid into the United States," said Bill.

"That's not a story, man," said Carlos. He sounded almost insulted. "That's the truth."

"Of course," said Bill. That remains to be seen, he thought. "Tell me."

"I work with a guy in Mexico," said Carlos. "I get stuff for him. Guns, ammo, night vision devices, things like that."

"Where?"

"What?"

"Where do you get the stuff you move to the guy in Mexico?" asked Bill.

"Doesn't matter," said Carlos. "You don't need to know." The toothpick moved faster.

"Listen, kid," said Bill. "You're the one who's in deep shit. Not me. Talk to me or stop wasting my motherfucking time."

"I can tell you what you need to know without getting into all that," said Carlos. His voice was small and desperate.

"Roger," said Bill. He turned back to the front and started the Jeep. "Where am I dropping you?" He reached down and put the vehicle in gear.

"Whoa," said Carlos. 'What are you doing?"

"Leaving you to fend for yourself," said Bill. The Jeep began to move.

"Fuck," said Carlos. "Ok, ok, you win." The toothpick had come to rest in the corner of his mouth.

"What?" said Bill. He stopped the Jeep and turned toward Carlos. "What did you say?" The Jeep was still running.

"I said I get the shit from the mainland," said Carlos. "From the Honduran military. I buy it and then move it to my man."

"Cool," said Bill. He shut down the Jeep, pulled on the parking brake and turned to face Carlos again.

"I get it to my man. He sells it up in Mexico to the narcos," continued Carlos. "They're always in the market."

"Talk to me about people," said Bill.

"A year or so ago, we started moving people," said Carlos. "Africans, Arabs, even Chinese."

"From where to where?" asked Bill.

"From Honduras. From Belize," said Carlos. They get to Central America by air. Then we move them by boat or overland into Mexico and up to the border."

"Must be expensive," said Bill.

"Must be," said Carlos. "I've heard people say some of the illegals pay $60,000 for the whole trip. My split is usually around $5,000 a head."

"So, talk to me about this white kid," said Bill.

"That's some weird shit," said Carlos. There was sweat beaded on his coffee-colored forehead.

"Tell me how weird," said Bill.

"This guy I work with is a Pakistani," said Carlos. "He has contacts in the Middle East. He said we were moving the kid for them."

"For who?"

"I don't know," said Carlos. "No, really, no bull. I don't know. Man didn't tell me. Just said it was a big deal. Needed to be done right."

"And."

"So, usually I get help. If we're moving a bunch of "skinnies" from Africa or something, I don't need to waste all my time with feeding and watering, you know what I'm sayin'? But, with this kid, the deal was it had to be me, only me. Nobody else could touch him."

"I asked you about the kid," said Bill.

"White kid," said Carlos. "Like born and bred in the suburbs white, blond hair, blue eyes, whole deal. Early twenties, maybe. Quiet."

"What else?"

"Too weird," added Carlos. "Fuckin' skinny ass white kid like he fell out of California but Muslim."

"You're sure," said Bill. He wasn't feeling better.

"Fuck, I'm sure," said Carlos. "Had to pray five damn times a day, facing Mecca, the whole thing."

"Your uncle said the kid was carrying something," said Bill.

"A cooler," said Carlos.

"Describe it," said Bill.

"I worked with a guy who sold organs," said Carlos. "Kidneys, livers, that kind of shit. From China. No joke. For transplants in South America. People buy that shit bootleg."

"What's this have to do with the cooler?"

"That's what this kid was carrying," said Carlos. "In a backpack. A cooler like they use for moving transplant organs."

"Where's the kid now?" asked Bill. He needed to know exactly how many steps behind he was.

"Probably the States," said Carlos. "I left him with a guy in Chula Vista who takes shit over the border into Arizona in an ultralight. That was a week ago. "

"Why are you telling me all this?" asked Bill. He leaned forward so as to be able to look Carlos squarely in the eye. Even in the dark his gaze was piercing.

"I no saint," began Carlos. "I do some shit. But, I don't want to be part of this. I've got a bad feeling."

"You didn't think of this before you moved the kid?" asked Bill. He knew bullshit when he heard it.

"Sometimes you need to think for a while before you know what is right," said Carlos. He looked up and away to his right briefly as he spoke.

"What else, kid?" asked Bill.

"What do you mean?"

"I get you're in deeper than you want," said Bill. "But that ain't all that's going on here."

"I told you," said Carlos. He looked away and started working the toothpick again. "I don't know what the fuck is going to happen, but I don't need to part of that shit."

"How much?" said Bill.

"What?"

"Don't waste my fucking time, kid," said Bill. "How much do you owe him?"

"What…"

"How much?" said Bill. His voice was almost a whisper and all the more menacing because of it.

"Two hundred and fifty thousand dollars," said Carlos. He was staring at the floor. The toothpick was in his hand. "My man fronted me the money to buy rocket launchers from a colonel in Tegucigalpa. I was going to use it for a piece in a casino in Jamaica. I'd keep the winnings, then do the deal. Double my profit."

"How much did you lose?" asked Bill.

"All of it," said Carlos.

"You're done," said Bill. He grinned. Idealists made him nervous, but a scheming little weasel trying to keep his head on his shoulders was right up his alley.

"I'm dead," agreed Carlos.

"A few more questions," said Bill. "Then we'll move to a different place to continue talking." He was never comfortable spending too much time hunkered down in one spot. Better to be on the move. "Who is this man?"

"His name is Sultan Rashid," said Carlos.

"Where can I find him?"

"In Mexico. Near the Belize border."

"Where?" asked Bill. He knew the border well. It was not an easy place to find people.

"I don't know, man," said Carlos.

"Where do you meet him?"

"I meet him in different places," said Carlos. He shrugged his shoulders and turned his palms upward in front of him to emphasize his helplessness in these matters. "Where he tells me."

"How does he contact you?" asked Bill. It made sense to him that Sultan controlled the meeting places. A guy in his line of work who was not careful did not last long on the street.

"On the computer," said Carlos. "He calls me on Skype. He says that it is secure, that not even the Americans can break the encryption and tell where he is calling from."

Skype was a Swedish voice over IP application that allowed callers to place free telephone calls from computer to computer. It used a very advanced encryption program and also processed phone calls via random and continuously shifting transmission routes through dozens of servers around the globe. It was, unfortunately, pretty close to as impregnable, even to the National Security Administration, as Sultan believed it to be.

"What is his name on Skype?" asked Bill. Every user had to have a screen name to access the system.

"Sahaba," said Carlos.

"Of course," said Bill. It meant companions of the Prophet in Arabic, a reference to the inner circle surrounding the Prophet Muhammad in the early days of Islam.

"And my name is High Roller," said Carlos.

"Of course," said Bill.

"That's what I know," said Carlos. He shrugged his shoulders again for emphasis.

"And how do you send things to him?" asked Bill. It was the age-old challenge of any debriefing, figuring out exactly what question you had to ask to get the magic answer.

"There is a buoy," said Carlos. He pointed generally off in the direction of Belize. "Out there."

"You leave the items in the water?" asked Bill. He knew it wasn't actually as crazy as it sounded. Smugglers in the Gulf had been hiding caches of booze and other contraband in the shallows and on the sandbars of the area for centuries.

"There's a buoy southeast of Half Moon Caye," said Carlos. "It marks the location on the bottom where there is a box. I put whatever I'm moving in watertight bags or boxes, and I leave the things there for him. We arrange the time and the day on the computer." Half Moon Caye was one of several islands, which dotted Lighthouse Reef off the coast of Belize.

"And when is the next time you are to leave something in this box for your friend, kid?" asked Bill.

"I left them there yesterday," responded Carlos. "He asked me for some special things. Some sniper scopes. Some radios. An external drive. A scanner. Some of it's for his office, I think. I don't know when he'll pick it up. Maybe today. Maybe in a few days. Do you want to know how to find the buoy?"

"Yes," said Bill. "I would like that very much."

CHAPTER NINE

9 AUGUST 2002, 1243 HOURS.
BALTIMORE, MARYLAND.

Anwar came up out of the subway at the Charles Center station and walked west to the UPS store next to the Renaissance Hotel. He had spent the entire previous day moving around downtown Baltimore on foot, learning the area and confirming he was not under surveillance. Now it was time to go to work.

"May I help you?" asked a teenage girl behind the counter. She was busy painting rainbows on her nails. She looked up momentarily and then went back to work.

"No, thank you," said Anwar. "Just checking my mail." He smiled to emphasize his sincerity, then opened box 193 with a key he produced from his pocket. There was a single envelope in the box. He took it out, put it in his pocket, smiled again in the direction of the clerk and left the store.

Five minutes later Anwar walked into the McDonalds near the Market Place subway station, bought a Big Mac meal and took a seat by the window. He pulled the envelope from his pocket, opened it and unfolded the documents inside. Fastened to one of the sheets of paper inside were two credit cards in the name Michael P. Smyth.

It was strange to see the words spelled out, thought Anwar. Even though they were the same words on the identity documents he carried. Even though it was the name he had been given at birth. The words meant nothing to him anymore. He was Anwar Al-Amriki, and the person who had been called Michael P. Smyth was dead. He had been on his last legs when Anwar left the country two years before. He died forever in Pakistan, when Anwar pledged himself fully to jihad and accepted the instructions for this mission.

Still, Anwar thought, the cards were crucial to what would happen next. Cash was good for many things. For many others, like virtually everything you bought online, you needed a credit card.

Anwar put the cards back in the envelope and put the envelope in his backpack. Then he walked toward the Inner Harbor and up the steps into the giant Barnes and Noble bookstore. There was a slight breeze blowing across the water from Federal Hill, and the space in front of the nearby National Aquarium was packed with elementary school kids on a science field trip. Stretched across the entrance to the aquarium was a broad banner proclaiming it "Dolphin Week" and welcoming the Public Schools of Baltimore.

Inside, the bookstore was two stories with high ceilings, boilers and chimneys that soared above the surrounding stacks of books. The building had been a power plant for years before it was converted, first into a nightclub and then into a bookstore. Its cavernous spaces and multiple levels were perfect for what Anwar had in mind.

On the second floor, in a back row near the entrance to the video section, Anwar found some armchairs and cushioned stools and took a seat. Then he brought out his notebook computer from his backpack, turned it on and logged onto the store's complimentary Wi-Fi network.

Once on the web, Anwar logged into his Skype account and opened it to the main control screen. He glanced down at the time on the computer. It was precisely 1300 EST. That meant it was 2300 hours in Pakistan. Akbar should be contacting him any moment.

"May I help you?" asked a store employee who had stopped in front of Anwar. She was an older black woman with gray hair and bifocal lenses.

"No, thank you," said Anwar. He smiled to show how non-threatening he was. "Just working on my thesis."

"Good for you, dear," said the woman. "Education is important." She walked off in the direction of the science fiction section to continue re-shelving books.

Anwar's computer warbled to signal that one of his Skype contacts had become active. Anwar looked down at his screen. There were three contacts listed on his Skype homepage, Akbar,

Sahaba and Sumaya. The homepage also gave Anwar's contact name as Addas. Akbar had just come online.

A message appeared on the screen from Akbar. It said, "Confirm your status."

"Thanks be to God, I have arrived intact with the medicine," typed Anwar. "Am in position in the same city as Sumaya and the others. Have not yet made contact."

"Good," came the response. "Make contact immediately and initiate a test as quickly as possible."

"Understood," typed Anwar.

"That is all. God be with you. I will speak with you again tomorrow at this time per our plan." The message appeared and almost immediately Akbar went offline.

Anwar closed his computer, put it back in his backpack and walked downstairs and out of the store. Outside he headed west past the Harborplace pavilions and around the harbor to Federal Hill. Then he stair-stepped his way through the narrow back streets, watching to confirm that he was still clean and he had no tail.

Twenty minutes later, Anwar entered Spoons Café on Cross Street, purchased a cappuccino at the bar and settled into a seat at a table in the rear of the establishment. There were a handful of other patrons, engrossed in newspapers and small talk. He attracted no attention.

Anwar opened his computer and logged onto the café's wi-fi and then onto Skype again. Precisely at 1400, Sumaya came online.

"Blessings be to God, I am here and prepared to begin our great work," typed Anwar. As before his message appeared over the pseudonym Addas.

"Welcome," came the response. "All is prepared."

"Good," responded Anwar. "I will come to you tonight at the time and the location previously arranged. I will bring the medicine. We will conduct a test immediately."

"Tonight at the time and location arranged for this purpose," typed Sumaya.

"God is great," responded Anwar. Then he immediately logged off, shut down his computer and departed the café. He walked back the way he had come, toward the harbor, past the Science Center and north toward the cheap motel in the center of the city where he had taken a room.

School children were everywhere around the harbor now, all seemingly bound for the aquarium and all flanked by teachers and chaperones making valiant attempts to keep their charges orderly and quiet. He stopped and watched for a moment. He thought of similar field trips he had taken as a child. He thought of the moral bankruptcy of the culture around him. He thought of what was coming and the fate of the children and the teachers he was watching. He smiled.

Time to check on tickets and schedules Anwar thought, and he headed north toward another little coffee shop he knew that also had a Wi-Fi network and the privacy in which to work.

CHAPTER TEN

2117 HOURS, 10 AUGUST 2002.
PESHAWAR, PAKISTAN.

"Spange Baab," said Zakia Ghayur. She was two, and English was her third language, after Pashto and Urdu, so she could be excused the poor pronunciation.

"Sponge Bob," said her father, Sardar Ghayur slowly and distinctly. He was balancing the girl on his knee as he sat on the small sofa in his tiny, windowless living room. In front of him, on the flickering screen of a small television set with a bent wire antenna, "Sponge Bob Square Pants", was lecturing his best friend, Bob the starfish, on always telling the truth. In the narrow kitchen behind Sardar, his wife, Warda, was scraping plates and washing dinner dishes.

Someone knocked at the door. Sardar glanced instinctively at his pistol on the top shelf of a narrow, plastic bookshelf a few feet away. "Who is it?" he called.

"Khan," said a male voice from the hallway.

"Coming," said Sardar. He stood, walked to the kitchen and handed his daughter to Warda.

"Are you going out?" asked Warda. She had placed Zakia on one hip and gone back to scrubbing a large frying pan with her free hand.

"Yes," said Sardar. "But, I won't be gone long." He leaned over and kissed Warda on the cheek. Her long, black hair hung loose down her back, and the headscarf she wore when she went outside was draped over her shoulders.

"I will put this one to bed while you are out," said Warda. She looked up briefly and winked.

"And I will put you to bed when I come back," said Sardar. He grinned and walked toward the door.

"I will hold you to that promise, husband," said Warda behind him.

Sardar took his pistol down from the bookshelf and shoved it into the holster on his belt so that his long, loose shirt covered it. Then he opened the door and stepped out into the dim, narrow hallway with its single 15 watt bulb hanging on a bare wire from the ceiling.

"Tea?" asked Khan. He was standing a few feet down the hallway dressed in loose, traditional civilian attire.

"Sure," said Sardar. The two men descended the two flights of dusty, concrete steps to the ground floor and stepped out of the chipped wooden doors of the building onto the broken, uneven surface of the sidewalk.

Khan paused, lit a cigarette and turned toward Sardar and muttered in a low voice, "I counted four on my way in." Behind him, in a doorway about ten meters away, a man in the driver's seat of a tiny, white Suzuki van said something into a microphone in his sleeve.

"Usually six of them," said Sardar. He took a drag off of Khan's cigarette and then passed it back to him. "Counting the ones on the other side."

"Sounds right," said Khan.

"Started the day after we found the papers," said Sardar. The two men started off in the direction of a corner teahouse crowded with late night customers. Donkey carts and three-wheeled motorcycle taxis pushed their way down the narrow, pot-holed street beside them through crowds of men in skullcaps and Pakols, flat Pashtun hats. The air tasted of dust and diesel.

"ISI donkey fuckers," said Khan.

"How is it at the station?" asked Sardar. Across the street two young men in leather jackets kept pace.

"They've been in twice," said Khan. "Copied every piece of paperwork on the raid," said Khan.

"Good thing I've been on leave," said Sardar.

"Good for you, boss," said Khan. The two men crossed a narrow alley whose pavement had disintegrated into fragments of asphalt and rock. A hot breeze blew trash against their legs.

"I hid the documents where they can't find them," said Sardar.

"Don't tell me where, boss," said Khan.

"I wasn't going to," said Sardar. He stepped up out of the alley onto the high concrete sidewalk. Khan followed. Above them, in a riot of signs for local businesses, hung an advertisement for an astrologer. Behind them, skewers of lamb kebab were roasting on a bed of coals in front of a tiny, austere restaurant filled with angry, bearded men.

"What do they say?" asked Khan.

"They say our friends in the LeT are training people in explosives, firearms and killing," said Sardar.

"I thought we knew that," said Khan.

"Training people who need instruction manuals that are written in English," said Sardar. "American English."

"And the donkey fuckers know it," added Khan. He shook his head slowly from one side to the other.

"If they're not helping," said Sardar. The pair stopped at a teahouse. It was a sea of men squatting on low wooden stools in front of tables covered in glass teacups and metal kettles. The proprietor made a sign to indicate that he would have a table for Sardar and Khan in just a moment.

"Did they speak to you?" asked Sardar.

"Yes, twice," said Khan. "I told them their guys took everything at the site when they showed up. I didn't mention the papers, but they didn't say what they were looking for anyway."

"You didn't keep anything," said Sardar.

"No, thanks be to God," said Khan. "I gave it all to you that night." The television in the teahouse was showing a news program. The newscaster was bellowing about "American crusaders" and the latest "massacre" of civilians in Afghanistan.

"The papers also talk about other kinds of weapons, said Sardar. "Biological weapons."

"What are you going to do?" asked Khan.

"I don't know," said Sardar. He glanced across the street. The two men in leather jackets were gone.

"Best to destroy the papers, boss," said Khan. He finished his cigarette and stomped it out on the pavement.

"Are they watching your place?" asked Sardar. He turned to Khan and looked him hard in the face.

"No," said Khan.

"Then why are they watching mine?" asked Sardar. His face froze. "Why haven't they talked to me? What are they waiting for?"

"Mother fornicators," yelled Khan. He turned and began to run toward Sardar's apartment. Sardar was already ahead of him.

The two men covered the distance back to Sardar's apartment building in a quarter of the time it had taken them to walk it. Sardar lead the way up the stairs inside the building, breath coming in great gasps of spit and fear.

The first ISI agent met them at the top of the stairs in the hallway outside Sardar's apartment. He was a tall, big-bellied Punjabi with a wooden truncheon in his hand.

"Intelligence investigation in progress," sneered the Punjabi. Sardar went into him like a fullback without breaking stride. The truncheon came loose and skidded to one side. The Punjabi went down hard with a great explosion of air from his lungs and what sounded like the cracking of ribs.

"Keep going, boss," screamed Khan. Sardar, still scrambling to his feet, tumbled and lunged through the door of his apartment and into his living room. Khan scooped up the truncheon and began raining blows on the head of the Punjabi as he tried to stand.

Inside the apartment, Sardar staggered to his feet and pulled his pistol. The two men in leather jackets were standing in front of him cutting the cushions on his couch to shreds and working the stuffing through their fingers. Behind them on the floor were the smashed remnants of the television set.

Warda was screaming in the bedroom.

"Out," said Sardar. His voice was raw and edged with hate.

"You will regret being here," said the man in the leather jacket to Sardar's left.

"Not as much as you, shit eater," said Sardar. The sound of the pistol discharging in the small room was deafening. Sardar fired it directly into the man's foot, and the wounded man crumpled like a rag doll to the floor, shrieking hysterically. His partner dropped the cushion he was holding and stretched his arms high above his head to emphasize his compliance. His face had gone a ghastly shade of gray.

"You heard the man, dick sucker," said Khan. He had entered the room with the blood-stained truncheon in his hand. Behind him in the doorway lay the motionless body of the Punjabi. "Out, and drag your crippled monkey-fucking friend with you."

Sardar went into the bedroom with his pistol held tightly in both hands, arms stretched in front of him. Warda was on the bed. Her shirt was torn. There was blood on her face. She was clutching Zakia to her chest. Major Bhutto was standing next to the bed.

"Are you mad?" asked Bhutto? "Do you know the consequences for interfering with ISI?"

"Do you know the consequences for violating the family quarters of a Pashtun?" yelled Sardar. "Do you know that under tribal law I am not only allowed, but required to kill you for the insult to her honor and mine?" He advanced until the barrel of the pistol was pressed tightly into Bhutto's broad, fleshy face.

"Give me the papers, and I will go," wheezed Bhutto.

"I have no papers," said Sardar. "And you will go anyway." He reached up, grabbed Bhutto by the hair and then turned him around so that he was facing the door to the living room. With the pistol pressed tightly against the base of Bhutto's skull, Sardar led the man out of the apartment and down to the street.

Outside on the sidewalk, a crowd was gathering around the wounded ISI man with the hole in his foot. Sirens were sounding in the distance. Someone had dragged the Punjabi down the stairs, as well. He was lying to one side, bleeding but still breathing.

"Go," said Sardar to Bhutto. He pushed the man away and lowered his pistol to his side.

"We will end you," said Bhutto. He walked over toward the wounded ISI man, pulled a cell phone from his pocket and began to dial.

"Orders?" said Khan. He was standing next to Sardar expectantly.

"Get your car," said Sardar. "Meet me in the alley behind the apartment building in one minute."

"What's the plan?" asked Khan.

"Run," said Sardar. He turned and bounded up the stairs. Khan was already moving toward his vehicle.

CHAPTER ELEVEN

2205 HOURS, 10 AUGUST 2002.
CARIBBEAN SEA.

As soon as the boat passed the tiny, dark cay on the starboard side, Ganesh pulled the throttle back and began to shed speed. The depth finder showed the bottom was coming up fast underneath them. The twin 225 horsepower outboard motors whined, the bow dropped and the 25-foot fiberglass boat settled a little deeper in the water.

Bill was standing on the starboard side of the vessel holding onto a handrail with one hand and sipping a cup of coffee held in the other. He was wearing a fleece top and a pair of old khaki cargo pants. Behind him, with her arms wrapped around his waist stood Aphrodite, head pressed against Bill's back, eyes closed. On the horizon, the lights of cargo vessels and oil tankers bound for New Orleans and the Gulf Coast twinkled in the darkness.

"Won't be more than fifteen, twenty minutes until we are on site," yelled Ganesh. He was standing at the steering wheel of the vessel in a pair of loose khaki shorts and an olive-drab turtleneck sweater. He looked down briefly at the backlit navigation screen in front of him on the boat's instrument panel, then back at Bill again.

"Roger," yelled Bill. "It shouldn't take more than twenty minutes underwater. Then we can roll over to the reef, catch some fish and live our cover story for being out here." He grinned and then he went back to sipping his coffee. Against the bulkhead to his right several fishing poles rattled in brackets .

Ganesh was a tall, dark-skinned Indian. His family was from Goa, but he had grown up in Dhahran, Saudi Arabia as part of the vast expat community that worked the oilrigs in the eastern part of the Kingdom. Life after school had been a steady slide into ventures, legal and otherwise, that kept him in cash but also kept him moving one step ahead of the law.

Ganesh was a useful guy to know when it came to coming and going from an island without being detected. Over the years, Bill had done him a number of favors, and now was time for Ganesh to repay some of that kindness.

Their plan was simple. Ganesh would get them to the site of the underwater cache. Bill would dive down and add another waterproof bag to those already waiting to be picked up. This one would contain another type of scanner in addition to the one Carlos had already purchased. Carlos was confident that Sultan would assume that he was simply trying to make sure he satisfied a requirement and accounted for possible compatibility problems between different brands.

The scanner held an off the shelf tracking beacon, which would allow its location to be pinpointed within ten meters anywhere on the planet, based on satellite GPS signals. Assuming it was going to end up in Sultan's office, they would be one step closer to locating him. The beacon, like all their other gear, was courtesy of Solomon.

At least, that was the plan.

The boat followed a narrowing channel toward Half Moon Caye. On both sides, the water shallowed and coral reefs came almost to the surface. Plotted on the navigation system in front of Ganesh were the GPS coordinates they had been told marked the location of the underwater cache. Around them all was pitch black save for the distant lights of the ships and the stars above.

"So, how long you too lovebirds been married anyway?" yelled Ganesh. He flashed a broad, dazzlingly white smile.

"Not long," said Aphrodite.

"A few months," said Bill.

"And where'd this loser take you for your honeymoon?" asked Ganesh. He turned his head and looked at Aphrodite who had opened her eyes and stood up straight behind Bill.

"Nowhere," said Aphrodite. She punched Bill lightly in the ribs. "He never takes me anywhere."

"Wow," said Ganesh. He shook his head slowly from side to side to emphasize his sincerity. "You suck, Boyle."

"We will go on a honeymoon as soon as we get time," protested Bill. "Just need to take care of this business first."

"Right, always time later," said Ganesh.

"Exactly," said Bill.

"You are one dumb son of a bitch, I'll give you that, Boyle," said Ganesh.

The boat sped on. No one spoke. The time and distance melted away. There was nothing but the roar of the outboards and the night.

Then, abruptly, the engines went silent, the bow dropped completely and the boat wallowed to a slow drift forward.

"This is it," said Ganesh. "Do you see anything?"

"Not yet," said Bill. He had fished a pair of night vision goggles out of his backpack and was scanning the area in front of them.

"Has to be close," said Ganesh. "Hope we didn't pass it."

"No, there it is," said Bill. He extended his right arm and pointed. "Five degrees to starboard, twenty-five meters." He was looking at an orange round buoy like those that marked many fish traps in this area. This one, however, had the yellow diamond that Carlos had said marked the site.

"How close do you want me to get?" asked Ganesh, as they eased up toward the buoy. About fifteen feet out he could see it with his naked eyes.

"Right here is good," said Bill as he dropped the anchor. "Don't want to get snagged on the cage on the bottom."

"Right," said Ganesh.

Bill bent over and pulled his scuba bag out from under one of the seats in the boat. Moving quickly he pulled on his wetsuit, his BCD and tank, his fins and his mask. He also took the bag with the beaconed equipment in it and clipped it to one of the utility hooks on his BCD, just to make sure he did not drop it underwater. Only when he was sitting on the side of the vessel ready to roll over the side did he stop to make sure he hadn't forgotten anything.

"I'll be down twenty minutes tops," said Bill. He checked his air pressure gauge and confirmed he had a full tank. That should give him an hour underwater at least. "I'm going to open the box, stuff in this bag and then pop back up. Easy day."

"Ok," said Ganesh. "I'll be here."

"I just hope he hasn't already been here, picked up the stuff and left," said Bill.

"Yeah, and I hope he doesn't show up to get the stuff while I'm sitting here on my ass, anchored at his secret smuggling location," said Ganesh.

"The odds against him showing up here at exactly the same time we are on site are astronomical," said Bill. He winked.

"Thank you," said Ganesh.

"For what?" asked Bill.

"For jinxing us," said Ganesh. "You stupid American bastard. Just for that, while you're down there, I'm going to tell your wife all about your treasure hunting skills."

"Fuck you," said Bill.

"I'm all ears," said Aphrodite.

Bill seated his regulator in his mouth and then rolled over the side. He surfaced, gave a thumbs up to show he was okay and then began to kick his way over to the buoy. He would follow its anchor line to the bottom and the cage.

CHAPTER TWELVE

2230 HOURS, 10 AUGUST 2002.
HALF MOON CAY, BELIZE.

When Bill reached the cable that connected the buoy to the cage, he did a final check on his gear and began to descend slowly to the sea floor. Clipped to his BCD was a small electric light, which illuminated the area a few feet around him. In the weird, pale glow from the light he could see the wispy, greenish film on the anchor chain he was using to pull himself down and, occasionally, the brief silhouette of a fish sliding by on the edge of the surrounding darkness.

Twenty-five feet down, Bill came to the top of the cage. It was a rusty metal box about three feet high, five feet long and five feet wide. Inside, with the help of his light, he could see several black waterproof bags. He took a key from a pocket on his BCD and began to open the plastic-coated lock holding the cage closed. He had adjusted his buoyancy so that he was hovering just a few inches above the cage itself.

The water around Bill surged, and he slipped to the left and lost his grip on the lock. Below him on the bottom swirls of sand kicked up and drifted away. He turned.

Something big slid by from left to right just beyond the range of his light.

Then nothing.

Bill paused for a moment. Using his flippers to turn, he rotated 360 degrees, scanning the area around him. He was still hovering just above the cage. Nothing moved. There was no sound.

Bill turned back to the lock and opened it. Then he lifted the hinged top of the cage and opened it. Finally, he dropped down inside the cage, unclipped the bag holding the scanner from his BCD and placed it alongside the other items waiting to be picked up.

Somewhere to Bill's left and barely within range of his light a long, gray-white body shot by. It was there for an instant, and gone almost as if it had never existed. Bill pushed himself up out of the cage, swung shut the hatch and locked it. He put his right hand on the rope to the surface and put his left hand on the control on his BCD that would inflate it and send him to the surface.

Above, Bill heard the dull sound of metal on metal. It was Ganesh banging a hammer on a metal sheet as a signal. Bill listened carefully. Three strokes. Then a break. Then three strokes. The pattern continued to repeat. As they had agreed before Bill descended, it meant that another boat was approaching and Ganesh was temporarily vacating the area around the buoy.

The banging stopped. All was silence again. Bill heard the engines on Ganesh's boat start and then the whine of spinning propellers in the water. The sound peaked and then gradually dropped off to nothing as Ganesh left.

Bill hung on to the rope with one hand and listened intently. Against the silence that hung all around he began to hear another sound. It was propellers again, but these were different. They sounded bigger and heavier. A larger boat was coming.

At the edge of the range of Bill's light something appeared. It was round and smooth. It came closer. A snout appeared and then long, savage teeth.

The bull shark came steadily nearer. Its mouth was slightly open, and its dead eyes stared straight ahead. Above it was a dark, lifeless gray. Underneath it was a horrible, empty white.

Bill stayed frozen in place, one hand on the rope and one hand on the control that would send him up. Above him, the noise of the boat grew ever louder, until it stopped directly overhead. He could hear the muffled sound of someone grappling ahold of the buoy.

The shark was only feet away now and still edging closer. Above, the noise of men moving on the boat grew louder. The light on Bill's BCD continued to burn. He could not afford the chance that it could be seen from the surface. He reached up, put his hand on the switch on the side of the light and shut it off.

Only the dimmest light from the tiny crescent of a moon penetrated to the bottom where Bill clung to the cage. He could see nothing. Above him he heard more clanging, and he felt several hard tugs on the line to which he was clinging. The men above were fastening the rope to a winch and preparing to hoist the cage to the surface.

The water in front of Bill's face moved, and something rough dragged against the side of his body and pushed him aside. He remained motionless, willing himself to vanish into the black water around him. He could hear nothing but the pounding of blood in his ears and the sound of his own breath in the regulator.

The rough invisible body pushed against him on his other side and something grabbed at and pulled on his right flipper. Frantically, he pulled back and the flipper came loose. He saw nothing. In desperation, he reached down and pulled his dive knife from the scabbard on his ankle and then held the blade up in front of his face. Fighting off a ten-foot shark in the pitch black was pretty close to impossible, but he was out of options.

The shark's head appeared like an apparition out of the gloom directly in front of Bill. Its mouth was open and filled with long, ragged, pitiless teeth. Only inches separated the creature from Bill's facemask.

Bill swung the knife up into the bottom of the shark's jaw with both hands and drove it in up to the hilt. Dark blood exploded into the water around him. The shark twisted violently from side to side and then sped away with the knife still lodged in its jaw.

Bill clung to the rope. Huge clouds of bubbles were erupting in front of him as he panted to catch his breath. Under his feet the cage began to jerk upward. He had to move. Sooner or later, even in the dark, the men above were going to see the bubbles from his regulator on the surface and the game was going to be up.

Bill let go of the rope and dropped over the side of the cage. He released more air from his BCD and settled down onto the sand and gravel on the bottom. The cage moved upward and faded from his view.

Moments passed. Except for the sound of the squeaking winch above, it was once again silent. Bill began to slowly kick his way along the bottom, feeling his way forward with his hands. He needed to put distance between himself and the boat above.

Foot by foot, he pulled himself across the bottom, picking his way through utter, impenetrable darkness. Finally, when his gut told him he had moved at least a hundred feet, he stopped and lay still, allowing the weight belt around his waist to hold him motionless against the bottom.

The sound of the winch stopped. There was a period of distant banging and thumping, and Bill knew the cage was being emptied. Finally, there was a muted splash and the sound of the cage being lowered to the bottom.

Something smooth and rippling rolled against Bill's right hand, and reflexively he jerked it away. Whatever it was slapped the side of his neck and then his facemask. It the near total darkness, Bill saw for an instant the shape of a stingray. And then it was gone.

More minutes passed, the engines started on the boat, and it began to move away. The noise grew gradually fainter and finally disappeared altogether. Still Bill waited, breathing slowly and deeply, trying to conserve his air. He stole a look at the illuminated face of his dive watch. He had been under over an hour now. That meant his air was close to exhausted.

Finally, came the sound of another boat approaching. Minutes later, it stopped above and the metallic clanging began again. Ganesh was back. Bill pumped air into his BCD, turned on his light and began to ascend. It was only twenty-five feet. Decompression was not an issue. He ascended as quickly as he could. The knife was gone. He was defenseless if the shark returned.

Bill exploded onto the surface, pulled his mask down so it hung around his neck and looked around. Ganesh was standing at the side of the boat about fifty feet away waving a red-lensed flashlight as a signal. Bill swam to the side, clambered aboard as quickly as possible and collapsed onto the deck.

"You getting old?" asked Ganesh. He was standing over Bill with a half empty beer in his hand. "You seem out of breath."

"Shark," panted Bill. "Fuckin' shark."

"Right," said Ganesh. "You're old, and now you're seeing things." He stepped over to the wheel of the boat and started the engines. "I told you, Eleni, he's a loser."

"Yeah?" asked Bill. He pulled off his right flipper and tossed it toward Ganesh.

"Fuck," said Ganesh. He was looking down at the flipper. A huge, saw-toothed semicircle had been bitten out of one side.

CHAPTER THIRTEEN

1113 HOURS, 11 AUGUST 2002.
BALTIMORE, MARYLAND.

Charlene had never been pregnant, but she imagined that this was how it felt. Despite the headache and the fever and the congestion in her lungs, she felt beautiful. She felt powerful. She felt like she was creating something greater than herself and that she was one with God.

Growing up in Ohio, Charlene had never fit in. She hadn't been the pretty one. She hadn't been the smart one. She hadn't even been the easy girl that all the guys wanted to take to bed. She had just been forgotten, overlooked and adrift.

That was before Charlene discovered the world of Islamic radicalism on the Internet. That was before she realized that it was not she that was lacking, but the rotting corpse of the morally bankrupt society around her. That was before she made her way to the one true faith and discovered the great purpose for which God had given her life.

Charlene stepped out of the cab and handed the driver cash. She crossed the street and headed toward her destination. The sun was out overhead and a warm breeze was blowing. God was smiling on her, and she felt His favor.

◆◆◆

Mrs. Bonny was having a bad day. She had thirty kids from Booker T. Washington Primary School crowded in with half the other elementary school children into the Baltimore Aquarium at the Inner Harbor. Her teacher's aide, Dewanda, had called in sick. And, now, she couldn't find Billy.

"Stop that," said Mrs. Bonny. She reached out and pulled a little boy named Wayne down off the railing surrounding the shark tank.

"Why?" asked Wayne.

"Because I promised your Mom I would bring you home alive," said Mrs. Bonny. She scanned over the crowd of kids around her and did another quick headcount. Twenty-nine. No Billy.

"I think he went to the bathroom," said Tina, a small girl with her hair in neat cornrows standing next to Mrs. Bonny. Tina was the self-appointed teacher's pet.

"Which bathroom?" asked Mrs. Bonny. Tina usually annoyed her, but right now she was willing to take any help she could get.

◆◆◆

Charlene walked past the gift shop stuffed with fuzzy smiling sharks and cuddly squids and stepped onto the escalator to the upper levels of the aquarium. Her face felt like it had been welded on. It glowed with heat. She shook with a sudden chill and then coughed heavily into the handkerchief she was carrying in her hand.

Behind her, another group of young children stepped onto the escalator lead by a gray-haired black woman calling for everyone to stand still and keep their hands to themselves. Bringing up the rear of the group was a younger black woman pulling two struggling boys along with her. The air all around was filled with the sound of small running feet and excited voices discovering tropical fish, coral reefs and sea horses.

The escalator ended at a landing. A sign overhead indicated that a corridor to the left led to an exhibit on mountain streams, and a corridor to the right led to another escalator and the tropical rainforest arboretum. Charlene turned to the right.

◆ ◆ ◆

"Billy!" yelled Mrs. Bonny. She was getting desperate. Around her the rest of the class was getting restless.

"Can we go see the dolphins now?" asked Malcolm. He was always impatient.

"In a moment, we can," said Mrs. Bonny patiently.

"Lost someone?" asked Mr. Brown. His class was at the aquarium too, and he had spotted Mrs. Bonny from across the large exhibit hall and guessed she was looking for someone.

"Billy," said Mrs. Bonny with exasperation.

"Of course," said Mr. Brown. Billy had been in his class last year, and he was more than familiar with the challenges of keeping tabs on the child.

"I think he's in the bathroom," said Tina. She was still standing next to Mrs. Bonny.

"Let me look," said Mr. Brown smiling. He walked off in the direction of the men's room.

◆◆◆

Charlene stepped off the escalator and walked through the double doors that led to the huge glass arboretum at the top of the aquarium. In front of her, the space was filled with tropical flowers, palm trees, wooden walkways and crowds of small children. Parrots sat on branches overhead, and the air was warm and humid.

To the left, stairs led to an overhead catwalk. Wheezing and coughing, Charlene climbed the stairs and walked to a small platform above an artificial waterfall and a pool teaming with brightly colored fish. She leaned on the railing surrounding the platform, closed her eyes and let the heat of the air soak in. The chills were getting worse, and she was beginning to be conscious of feeling vaguely lethargic. Anwar had told her that all of this would happen. She knew it meant that her time was limited, and she smiled at the knowledge.

Charlene opened her eyes again and looked around. There was a small boy with thick black glasses standing next to her, tossing tiny stones he had picked up off the walkway into the pool of fish below. He seemed to be alone.

"Are you lost?" asked Charlene.

"No," said the boy. He stopped tossing stones for a moment and looked up at her. He could not have been more than eight. "I know where I am," he said unconvincingly.

"What's your name?" asked Charlene. Her head was pounding now, and she noticed that there was a slight bluish tinge to the skin on her hands gripping the railing in front of her.

"Billy," said the boy. His big glasses began to slide down his nose and he pushed them back in place with one small finger.

◆◆◆

"Not there," said Mr. Brown as he walked up to Mrs. Bonny. "I looked in all the stalls."

"I have no idea where he is," said Mrs. Bonny. "I think I'm going to find security and have them page him on the PA system."

"He'll be ok, Mrs. Bonny," said Tina. She really didn't care about Billy at all, but it struck her that comforting Mrs. Bonny right now would make her look good.

"Wait a minute," said Mr. Brown.

"What?" asked Mrs. Bonny.

"Isn't this your boy?" asked Mr. Brown. He pointed over Mrs. Bonny's shoulder.

Mrs. Bonny turned to look. There was a tall slender black woman wearing a long dress and a white head scarf coming toward them holding Billy by the hand. Billy was pointing excitedly toward Mrs. Bonny as the pair came closer.

"Thank you," said Mrs. Bonny. She reached out and took Billy by the hand as he approached. "You scared me to death," she said to the boy.

"You are welcome," said Charlene. She coughed heavily into her handkerchief and struggled to smile.

"Where was he?" asked Mr. Brown.

"Throwing stones at fish," said Charlene. She coughed again. Something heavy and wet came up her throat and into the handkerchief. It was thick, black blood. She coughed again. More blood came up. She doubled over and then collapsed on the floor.

"Are you alright?" asked Mrs. Bonny.

"I'll get help," said Mr. Brown.

"I love that I should be killed in the way of Allah; then I should be brought back to life and be killed again in His way," whispered Charlene to herself. Then she dissolved into uncontrollable spasms of coughing and spitting as a crowd of concerned teachers and students gathered around her.

CHAPTER FOURTEEN

0835 HOURS, 12 AUGUST 2002.
ROATAN, HONDURAS.

"What did she say?" asked Bill. He was standing in the Roatan airport. In front of him were two duffle bags. Solomon was standing to his left, looking concerned. They had tracked the beaconed scanner to the Mexican town of Felipe Carrillo Puerto, near the border with Belize. It was time to move.

"Irene said that Eddie was still gone, but that she knew where he was," said Aphrodite. She shoved the cell phone on which she had been talking for the last five minutes into her jacket pocket.

"Good news," said Bill. He glanced over at the single departure board in the airport. Their plane to Tegucigalpa was boarding in fifteen minutes.

"Definitely not," said Aphrodite. "She sounded terrified, like she was about to come apart. She said she was afraid Eddie was into something very bad."

"What's that mean?" asked Bill.

"She didn't want to say," said Aphrodite. "But, she kept saying people were going to get killed and she didn't know what to do."

"You think we need to go up there," said Bill.

"I think maybe one of us needs to go up there," said Aphrodite. She bit her lip and looked pained.

"Then who goes to Mexico?" asked Solomon. He sounded confused.

"You think it's that bad," said Bill.

"I think we never should have left her," said Aphrodite.

"We were going back," said Bill.

"Maybe too late," said Aphrodite.

Bill looked down and kicked the scuffed linoleum on the floor of the sweltering, one-room departure lounge. There was tinny reggae music playing over distant speakers in the background.

"You can't go to Mexico alone," said Solomon.

"Maybe we should both go to Baltimore," said Aphrodite. It was more a question than a statement.

"We can't," said Bill. "If we wait to go to Mexico we lose the window. Something will change. Or we'll be too late to make any difference."

"You can't go to Mexico alone," repeated Solomon. "You'll get yourself killed."

"He's right, Bill," said Aphrodite.

"You just said yourself someone needed to go to Baltimore, Eleni," said Bill. "We can't both be both places at once."

"I don't know what to do, Bill," said Aphrodite. "I don't have an answer. We need more time."

"We're out of time," said Bill. He looked back at the board and then out the dirty, cloudy windows of the terminal building at the parking lot filled with rusted pickup trucks and dented rental cars.

"You can't go to Mexico alone," said Solomon again. "If you have to go to Baltimore, then go."

"Goddamn it," said Bill. He turned his back on both Aphrodite and Solomon and paced slowly toward the corner of the room. There was a baby squealing in the corner and a crowd of backpackers sitting on the floor playing cards and quietly passing around a bottle of rum.

"This woman in Baltimore is important?" asked Solomon. He was talking to Aphrodite who was watching Bill walk slowly away.

"The promise he made to her father is important," said Aphrodite.

"Then he should go," said Solomon with finality.

"And his debt to you is just as important," said Aphrodite. She turned to look Solomon in the eye. "He believes he owes you his life."

"Then, I'll release him from that debt," said Solomon.

"He will not release himself," said Aphrodite. She looked back at Bill who had turned and was walking back toward them. "He is not built that way."

"You go to Baltimore, find Eddie and figure out what's going on," said Bill. He had stopped directly in front of both Sultan and Aphrodite.

"What about you?" asked Aphrodite.

"I'll go to Mexico, find this prick Sultan and figure out what he's up to," said Bill. "Then, I'll join you in Baltimore."

"No," said Solomon.

"Look, old friend," said Bill. "I promised you I would help. I am going to do that. I will sort out what is happening, and then we can figure out how to stop it and keep your nephew out of jail."

"No Captain America stuff," said Aphrodite.

"Promise," said Bill. "I'm just going to get the information we need to find a way to shut these guys down without getting Carlos killed or having him spend the rest of his punk ass life in prison."

"I mean it, Bill," said Aphrodite. She squinted her eyes for emphasis.

"You know me, Eleni," protested Bill.

"Maybe that's the problem," said Aphrodite.

CHAPTER FIFTEEN

**2045 HOURS, 12 AUGUST 2002.
ISLAMABAD, PAKISTAN.**

Andrew Peters paid the tailor for the repairs he had done on his favorite tweed jacket and walked out of the shop to his car. Andrew was short, balding and developing a modest paunch now that he was well into his forties. He was also an exceptional spy.

As he walked toward his vehicle parked against the curb in front of the tailor's shop, Andrew scanned the area around him out of reflex and training. Islamabad was, for Pakistan, a relatively safe area. It was not benign.

Nothing seemed out of the ordinary on the street. But something about his car caught Andrew's eye immediately. There was a folded sheet of notepaper tucked under one of his wiper blades. It had not been there when he entered the shop only minutes before.

Andrew approached the car, holding his jacket on a hanger in one hand, and pulled the paper out from under the wiper with the other. The paper felt thick and rough to the touch. It was definitely of local manufacture, not the slick, glossy paper used in the American embassy where he worked.

Andrew opened the paper and read the writing on it. It was in English but the letters were awkward and the spelling poor. This was not a message written by a native English speaker.

"DEER MR. ANDREW. I AM A FREND. I HAVE INFORMATION OF GRATE VALUE TO YOUR COUNTRY. PLEESE BE COMING TO MEET ME NOW AT THE FOUNTAIN IN THE LOBBY OF THE MARRIOTT HOTEL. I THINK THIS WILL BE A SAFE PLACE FOR TALKING FOR BOTH US. LOOKING FORWARD TO MEETING YOU."

Volunteers were not uncommon in the world of espionage. Sometimes they walked into the embassy. Sometimes these days they sent emails to a website. And, occasionally, they stuck notes on your windshield.

Andrew stuffed the note in his pocket and unlocked his car. Then he got in, hung up his jacket and sat behind the steering wheel for a moment. A guy offering to provide information of value to the United States was a good thing. Andrew had been a CIA case officer for a long time. He knew an opportunity when he saw it.

On the other hand, being told where and when to appear by a party unknown ran counter to every instinct Andrew had. Spies stayed alive by making sure no one could ever fix them in time and space. Stepping onto an "X" designated by someone else could get you killed in a hurry.

Andrew pulled the note out of his pocket and reread it. Then he read it again. Whoever wrote it had been careful to avoid giving any information about who he was or the nature of his information. That smelled right. That was how a guy would behave who was concerned about his security, afraid of getting caught and conscious that a note on a windshield could blow away or be snatched up by someone other than the intended recipient.

The choice of meeting site was also significant. The Marriott sat inside the diplomatic quarter. Access to the area was controlled, as was access to the hotel grounds. No jihadi terrorist would think of setting foot there. That suggested whoever wrote the note was someone who could pass through checkpoints without fear. It also suggested that they were aware that Andrew would not meet just anywhere and had deliberately picked a location where he would feel secure.

Andrew wasn't sure what all that meant. When he tallied up all those points, though, it tipped the scale. This was a lead he was going to run down. He started the car, pulled out into traffic and headed for the Marriott.

◆◆◆

Andrew walked into the Marriott twenty minutes later after leaving his car with an attendant in the parking lot out front. The lobby of the hotel was the same soulless blend of marble, overstuffed furniture and crystal chandeliers found in all five-star, third world hotels. After the heat, dust and confusion of the street, it felt chilly, sterile and out of place.

To one side, several fat Punjabi businessmen on a pair of gaudy, gold couches were haggling over the price of wheat. Beyond them, around a small, low table a group of Chinese officials in matching black suits were sipping tea and eying their surroundings suspiciously. From speakers in the ceiling came a syrupy sweet muzak.

At the back of the lobby was the entrance to the corridor that led to the hotel coffee shop. Standing against the wall next to the corridor was a short man with the build of a weight lifter. He was wearing an ill-fitting gray suit and no tie. He was alone.

That's my boy, thought Andrew, but he showed no outward sign that he had noticed the man at all. Instead he began to wander toward the large marble fountain in the center of the lobby. When he reached it he deliberately stood with his back to the man he had spotted and pulled out his cell phone as if to check his messages.

The actions were intentionally theatrical and transparent. I am here. I am not a threat. I am also not without other business to attend to. Make your move.

A moment passed. In a seating area nearby, two Azeri prostitutes in black spandex dresses with faux ostrich feather collars were laughing insipidly at the jokes of a couple of twenty-something Pakistani men in Savoy Row suits. The table in front of them was littered with ashtrays, glasses and cell phones.

"Mr. Andrew," said the man in the gray suit. He had appeared next to Andrew at the fountain. "Thank you for coming." He held out his hand, and Peters shook it.

"Your note was very interesting," said Peter. There was something about the man in the suit that seemed familiar, but he could not place it.

"You do not remember me, I think," said the man in the gray suit. He smiled slightly as if enjoying some private joke.

"Have we met?" asked Peter.

"Last year, Peshawar," said the man. "You were there working with ISI. I am with the tribal police. We were called in to assist. "

"I'm sorry," said Peter. "I should have recognized you." As he recalled, that operation went sideways in a hurry when someone in ISI leaked the information on the impending raid to the targets. Things had gotten ugly fast.

"You were I think focused on other things," said the man.

"I was," said Peter. He recalled coming very close to throttling the ISI colonel who was his counterpart. "I apologize if my temper got the best of me. Not my finest moment."

"On the contrary," smiled the man. "It is precisely because you are the only other person I know who has ever threatened to kill an ISI officer that I am here."

"How can I help you?" asked Andrew.

"My name is Sub-Inspector Sardar Ghayur. And, I think it is I that can help you. I think I can help you save a great many lives in fact."

CHAPTER SIXTEEN

1625 HOURS, 13 AUGUST 2002.
CANCUN, MEXICO.

The Cancun airport was sleek, modern and welcoming, designed to comfort the legions of American tourists flocking to the Mexican Riviera. Bill found it sterile and uncomfortable. He remembered the old terminal, the small, grimy structure that smelled and looked like Mexico not Disneyland. He shouldered his duffle bag, hustled out of the arrivals lounge and hailed a cab.

Twenty minutes later, he had the cabbie drop him downtown outside the Hotel Internacional, a seedy one-star joint several miles and a world away from the white sand and all-inclusive resorts of the hotel strip. When the cab had departed, he walked down the street to the Econo Car Rental near the bus station, picked up a dented Jeep Wrangler and headed south. He didn't really expect to be followed by anyone at this stage, but old habits died hard.

South of Cancun, the road was lined on both sides with the entrances to huge resorts catering to the Americans who came, not to see the real Mexico, but to spend time in the one they imagined. As the miles sped by, the resorts thinned out, the restaurants became fewer and further between and the real Yucatan began to

124

emerge. Bill passed Playa Del Carmen, where he was technically still partners with a Mexican named Paco in a dive shop, fought off the urge to stop in and find out if he was making any money, and kept moving. Akumal came and went. Then Xelha.

Two hours later, south of Tulum, the road was flat and straight and there was nothing but jungle in sight as far as the eye could see. Every few miles a dirt footpath disappeared into the trees, marking the route to another tiny Mayan village. The only gringos who came here were missionaries, adventure seekers and smugglers.

About thirty minutes north of Felipe Carrillo Puerto, Bill pulled the car over at paved pullout used by truckers driving between Belize and Mexico to rest. He got out of the Jeep, stretched and sniffed the air. The sun was setting fast in the west. A few howler monkeys called somewhere in the bush. Otherwise, it was silent. There were no other cars on the road and, other than the road itself, no sign that man had ever been here.

There were a lot of memories here, memories of years Bill had spent trying to find his soul after leaving the CIA. Some of those memories were sweet. Most were not. He had searched in vain for a way to forgive himself for the death of his wife on the streets of Athens. It the end, it had taken Aphrodite to show him there was nothing he had to forgive.

The Yucatan was a steamy, green, alien world to most outsiders. In many ways, for Bill, it was a home.

Bill opened his duffle, pulled out some clothes and changed. He put on an old olive drab t-shirt, tied a red bandana around his head and put on a pair of faded jeans with a rip in one knee. He stuffed a few key items in a backpack to carry, tossed it on the passenger's seat up front in the Jeep and headed south again. He could not make himself into a local. He could make himself look less threatening.

Thirty minutes later, Bill drove into the outskirts of Felipe Carrillo Puerto, a small, dusty town just north of Mexico-Belize border. Moments later he took a right turn, drove a few blocks further and parked the Jeep in the shadows behind the white-washed walls of a church compound.

Bill exited the vehicle, shouldered his backpack and began to walk. He had studied overhead imagery of his target location, and he knew Felipe Carrillo Puerto well enough to know exactly how to get there from his present location. He moved out quickly in the gathering darkness.

It took Bill ten minutes to cover the remaining ground to the target building. It was a standard white-washed, concrete structure, two stories tall and set along a narrow commercial boulevard in the heart of the old part of town. The ground floor was occupied with auto parts stores, cheap restaurants and a shop making corn tortillas. The second floor was all offices, which opened onto a breezeway that ran the length of the building.

On the ground floor of the building, between "El Patron" restaurant and "Los Hermanos" auto parts shop, was a doorway that led to the stairs for the second floor. Next to the doorway were several chipped plastic signs set one above the other. The second one from the top said "EMPRESA COMERCIAL YUCATAN, SULTAN RASHID DIRECTOR, SUITE 210". Just below that one was a sign for "SYLVIA RAMIREZ, ASTROLOGO, SUITE 200."

Bill glanced up at the signs as he walked by, but gave no indication of having any particular interest. Two short, dark Mayan men in broad, straw hats and blue jeans followed by several Mayan women in traditional trajes, white dresses with embroidered necklines, pushed past, and he stepped out of their way. Neither the men nor the women paid any attention to him.

In front of Bill, a crowd of young Mayan men were standing around the entrance to a small, open-fronted restaurant watching a soccer game on a small television mounted on the wall inside. Bill skirted around the crowd and no one even turned to look at him. He was another dusty, backpacking gringo in the Yucatan of no particular importance.

Twenty meters ahead, a narrow alley awash in garbage and stench ran behind the row of businesses Bill had just passed. He turned left into the alley and slowed his pace. He wasn't sure what he was looking for other than an opportunity, but it paid to get the best possible picture of the target.

Surreptitious entries were not something you just threw together on the fly. They were planned, thought out and executed by teams of individuals after careful study. You marked the target. You mastered the occupant's routines. You worked through every possible contingency. It might take months to actually get inside of a building. That was the right way to do it.

Bill had no time to do it right.

Whoever the white kid was who had gone north, he was well on his way already. Whatever plot he was part of might already be in motion. And, most importantly, Aphrodite was on her own in America digging into another totally unknown and likely dangerous situation. Bill wasn't just on thin ice. He was on ice that was melting under his feet. Whatever he was going to do, he had to do it now, and he had to do it fast.

As he moved down the alley, Bill studied the back of the target. The back of the building was essentially a blank wall except for small opaque windows that must have looked in on restrooms, and rectangular air conditioning units set in wire cages. Bill kept walking.

At the end of the alley, Bill found a space between a large metal trash container and a low wall and wedged his backpack in where it could not be seen. Then he took a left, and continued around to the doorway on the other side of the building, which led to the stairs. This time he went in.

At the top of stairs Bill came out onto the breezeway. It was lined with doors and small air vents set above the doors. He had no idea how the office numbers corresponded to the layout of the building. He took a guess and turned right. The first door was for the "ASTROLOGO". As Bill passed he could hear an animated conversation in Spanish going on inside. There were at least three voices, one of them female. She was saying something about the birth of a child.

There were light fixtures on the ceiling of the breezeway, but only about half of them were working. The floor was dirty concrete and looked that much more dingy in the dim, flickering light. Below in the street, pedestrian traffic was increasing as the temperature dropped and the crushing heat of the day dissipated.

The second door had no sign. There was no sound coming from inside.

The third was the charm. The sign on the wall next to it marked it as belonging to the "EMPRESA COMERCIAL YUCATAN". Bill paused briefly to listen. He could hear the sound of a Spanish news channel playing on a television and the voices of at least two individuals inside the office. They were speaking English. It was impossible to tell the layout of the office from the outside, but based on the dimensions of the building, he calculated that the space was one large room. He moved on.

At the end of the hallway, Bill came to a utility closet. He tried the doorknob, and the door opened. Inside were a utility sink, a broken mop and a push broom.

Behind Bill a door opened and an elderly Mayan man in a neat white button down shirt and crisp slacks stepped out in the hallway. The sign on the door to the office from which he had exited said something about insurance. The man glanced briefly in Bill's direction and then turned and walked down the hallway away from him. Bill waited until the man had begun to descend the stairs and then stepped into the utility room closing the door behind him.

Bill still had no plan.

This was a front office for a guy who, whatever else he did, smuggled drugs, weapons and people. That meant to maintain appearances, Rashid must do some measure of legitimate business out of this space. All around were small but ordinary businesses run by people who likely had nothing to do with terrorism or criminal activity. The men inside Rashid's office might be armed, but it wasn't likely that they would be expecting trouble. Bill's chances of getting shot were pretty slim. It did not, however, make getting in, stealing whatever was inside and getting out unseen any easier.

Bill looked around the small utility room. In one corner, he saw a metal panel set in a frame in the ceiling. The walls of the room were maybe three feet apart. Bill stood directly underneath the panel and braced himself with his arms against the walls. Then he brought his legs up quickly and did the same with his feet. Foot by foot, moving carefully so as not to slip on the smooth plaster, he worked his way up until he was only a few inches below the panel.

Bill pushed on the panel and it moved upward slightly then stopped. He repositioned himself against the walls to make sure he was stable and then shoved harder. The panel came loose suddenly and disappeared out of sight. There was a loud bang as it fell onto what sounded like concrete.

Bill froze. For several moments, while he silently cursed his carelessness, he listened for any indication that someone had heard the noise and been alerted. Nothing.

Reaching up with both hands, Bill got a grip on the rough concrete edge of the opening into the ceiling. He pulled himself up and shoved his shoulders through the narrow space until he had all but his legs out of sight. Finally, with one last heave he pulled his entire body up through the opening.

Bill was on the roof of the building. He rolled over on his back and looked at the night sky. There were a handful of stars visible, but the lights of the town around him drowned most of them out. Two blocks to one side, he could see the steeple of a church. In the street below men were yelling and clapping. Someone had scored in the soccer game.

The roof of the building was surrounded by an ornamental railing about two feet high. Being careful to stay below the level of the railing, to stay invisible to anyone down below, Bill worked his way forward through a crowd of television antennas and cheap metal satellite dishes. Cables and wires crisscrossed the roof, and the concrete was crusted with bird droppings

At the far end of the building, Bill stopped and turned around. There was no sign of any other access panels anywhere. He was virtually sitting on top of his target, separated by only a few inches of concrete, but he might as well be miles away.

Bill made his way to the back of the building and peered through the railing at the alley below. A couple of filthy dogs ran by yipping and fighting over some garbage that one of them had stolen. A gaggle of men walked underneath him, passing a bottle of tequila back and forth. All Bill could make out of their conversation was Spanish slang for "pussy".

Bill lifted himself up carefully and peered over the railing at the wall below him. He should have been directly over Rashid's office. The building wall was a straight drop to the ground twenty-five feet below. One of the small restroom windows was about three feet down. It appeared to have a cheap sliding panel in it that would be susceptible to forced entry. However, the window opening didn't measure more than ten inches by eighteen. There was no way Bill could fit through that.

A few feet to one side of the window was one of the air conditioning units. It appeared to have been fitted into a purpose-made rectangular opening in the wall. Surrounding it was a heavy metal cage, secured to the wall with massive iron bolts.

Bill slid down behind the railing and stretched out on the roof for a moment. He was coming up dry. He didn't just have to get into the office. He needed to get in and out again and leave no one the wiser. There was no point in acquiring intel on a threat and letting the enemy know you had it. They would simply change the plan and try again.

The geometry of the problem was simple. He needed to get into a room surrounded by solid concrete walls. A cube. There were by his count four openings into that cube, two of which he had just crossed off his list as not being feasible to exploit. A third, the air vent over the door, was far too small and, therefore, useless to him as well. That meant he needed to take another look at the front door.

Bill came up on his hands and knees and began the slow crawl back to the access panel through the filth and chaos of the roof. There was laughter in the street below now, and he suspected that the crowd watching the game had probably starting drinking mescal. A truck horn blared and someone yelled at the "illegitimate son of a whore" in Spanish.

When he reached the access panel, Bill stopped and listened carefully for a full minute. Then he cautiously peered down into the opening to make sure it was all clear below. It was close to 2030 hours now, and he was pretty sure the building would be all but empty, but he was taking no chances.

Once Bill was sure there was no one in the utility room, and that the door was still closed, he lowered himself down into the opening and braced himself again against the walls. Then, pulling on the crude handle welded to the inside of the panel, he pulled it firmly down into place. He worked slowly down the walls, landed lightly on the floor and brushed the bird droppings and whitewash from his clothes.

Bill opened the door a crack and peered down the hallway. There was no one in sight, and most of the offices were dark. It looked like he was right, that the place was closing up for the night. He stepped out of the utility room and began to pull the door closed behind him.

Two offices down, the door to the "EMPRESA COMERCIAL YUCATAN" opened. A young Mexican female in western clothing stepped out into the breezeway, called goodnight in Spanish over her shoulder and headed for the stairs without looking in Bill's direction. From the office, a deeper, male voice wished her good night, as well.

Bill stopped dead in his tracks. He had the door to the utility room almost closed behind him. Maybe he could still swing it back open and disappear inside.

A man came out onto the breezeway. He was tall and heavy, dressed in loose traditional Pakistani garb. He fumbled with his keys momentarily.

Bill stood perfectly still. The light above his head was out, and he was standing in shadow.

The man looked up, paused and then turned his head to stare directly at Bill.

"What are you doing there?" demanded the man in Spanish.

Bill made no response. He had a four-inch Emerson lock blade knife in his pocket. The man was perhaps twenty feet away. Bill could silence him in seconds and clear the area before anyone had any idea what had happened. That would get him out of this safely. It would also end the job.

"What the hell are you doing in there you lazy son of a pimp?" growled the man through a thick beard.

"Sir?" replied Bill in Spanish. He worked hard to make his pronunciation poor and stilted. Many Mayan people spoke Spanish as a second language.

"Do you know who I am?" asked the man. "I am Mr. Rashid. This is my office. You are supposed to clean it every Tuesday. This week you never came to work. My trashcan is full. My carpet is dirty."

"I am sorry, sir," replied Bill. He let his shoulders slump and avoided looking Rashid in the eye.

"I don't care if you're sorry, you donkey cock," snapped Rashid. "I'll bet you were drunk again. I'll bet that's what you're doing in there this late at night isn't it? Sucking on your bottle."

"No, sir," said Bill. He could feel the weight of the knife in his pocket and even as he was still trying to talk his way out of the situation he was measuring the exact number of steps it would take him to be on Rashid and done with it.

"Let me take a look then, you dog dick," said Rashid. He started to move toward Bill, but, mercifully, his cell phone rang. He looked like he might ignore it, but turned back the other way as he pulled the phone from inside his loose pants.

"Yes," said Rashid in Urdu. He listened momentarily, grunted short responses a few times and then hung up after saying he was on his way. Putting the phone back into his pocket, he turned back to Bill briefly.

"I want this floor clean on Monday," said Rashid. He pointed to the dirty concrete at his feet. "I want my office clean, as well. If not, I'm going to call Martinez and demand he fire you. Then you can pick through the trash for food for all I care, you worthless, lazy, Mexican dog."

"Yes, sir," said Bill simply.

Rashid turned back to his office door and locked the deadbolt. Then he folded over a heavy metal hasp set above the deadbolt and secured it with a combination lock. He gave the combination lock a yank to make sure it was secure, cast one more hard look in Bill's direction and went for the stairs.

Bill did not move until he heard Rashid step off the stairs at the bottom and start down the sidewalk. Bill moved to a spot on the breezeway from which, still covered in shadow, he could watch for several seconds more as Rashid walked away. There were no sounds coming from any of the other offices and no lights visible. The place appeared deserted.

In front of Rashid's door, Bill paused, bent over briefly and examined the locks closely. The deadbolt was a standard pin and tumbler lock manufactured in China. That meant it was cheap and had a lot of play in it. That was good for him. The combination lock looked to be some kind of Master Lock knockoff, probably also made in China. That should take seconds to defeat.

All he needed were tools.

Bill descended the stairs to the sidewalk below and then wandered around the block to the alley again. About midway down he stopped behind the auto parts store and peered into the jumble of trash cans and loose garbage on the ground. Within a minute or two he found what he needed: two used wiper blades and an empty Coke can.

Now, all I need is a place to sit down and work for a moment, thought Bill. Fifty meters away in the direction of a church was the concrete frame for a new office building. It looked deserted. Bill began walking in that direction.

CHAPTER SEVENTEEN

2030 HOURS, 13 AUGUST 2002.
MUSLIM COMMUNITY CENTER, BALTIMORE, MARYLAND.

Aphrodite parked the rental car against the curb on the dark street and got out. The neighborhood was completely alien and absolutely familiar at the same time. She was the only white woman in sight. The music coming from the windows of the surrounding homes meant nothing to her. Yet, the stench of alienation and despair was the same as it had been on the streets of the anarchist quarter in Athens where she grew up.

Across the street from where Aphrodite had parked the car was a small park strewn with trash and broken glass. A group of young black men in white t-shirts and baggy pants belted low were standing around a portable stereo of some sort, drinking beer and yelling about fucking somebody up.

Aphrodite checked the information on the creased business card Irene had given her a few hours before. It gave an address for the Baltimore Muslim Community Center. That was where Irene believed Eddie had gone.

An old black woman in a plain, cotton dress came out on the front porch of a row house next to the park and began to yell at the young men to turn down their music. They responded with a chorus of curses. Someone threw a beer bottle across the street in the direction of the woman and it broke in the street.

Aphrodite walked down the sidewalk toward the Community Center. The building sat at the end of a small drive, surrounded by ragged lawn. Behind it were several other smaller dilapidated, brick buildings that looked like they must have originally been a garage and servants quarters. This was probably once the home of a prominent white merchant family. That would have been a hundred years ago, before the migration of millions of African-Americans north to find work, before "white flight", before crack cocaine and drive-by shootings.

"Get your white Koran-kissing ass out of here!" yelled one of the men in the park.

"I understand your anger, brother," said a surprisingly calm female voice.

Aphrodite stopped and turned to look. There was someone else in the park. It was a woman. She was standing with her back to Aphrodite so that all that was visible was a long loose dress and a white scarf wrapped around her head.

"I don't give a fuck what you understand, bitch," said another male voice.

"Allah asks that you show respect for yourself and for your community," said the woman.

The response was another chorus of curses. Someone threw a glass bottle against a tree in the park and it shattered. The volume of the music increased. The old woman on the porch yelled something about the cops.

Aphrodite looked down at her feet for a moment and took a deep breath. This was none of her concern. She was here to find Eddie. It had been only a matter of days since she had told Bill to keep his focus and avoid pointless confrontations.

"How about we just fuck you up the ass?" yelled one of the young men in the park. There was a round of support from the others. Another bottle smashed against a tree. The woman in the headscarf was still standing still by herself in the dark.

This is different, thought Aphrodite. *This isn't just kids making noise.* She crossed the street, walked into the park and came up beside the woman who was being threatened.

"Who the fuck are you?" said one of the young men. He was maybe sixteen, short, skinny and already unsteady on his feet from alcohol. He was wearing a Baltimore Orioles hat sideways on his head.

"Go home," said Aphrodite. She looked briefly at the woman in the headscarf and was surprised to see she was a young white woman with pale blue eyes and wisps of blond hair visible around her head scarf.

"Or what?" said the young man. Behind him his buddies were laughing and clowning.

"Go home," repeated Aphrodite. "And don't ever talk to a woman like that again." She squared her stance and rolled her head around on her neck once to loosen up. Her eyes were on the hands of the young men in front of her.

"You going to fuck us all up?" said the young man with the Orioles hat. He reached in his pocket, pulled out a folding knife and opened it.

"No," said Aphrodite. "Just you."

The guy with the knife came forward suddenly swinging the blade in an awkward, looping manner at Aphrodite's face. She stepped back, let the blade go by, grabbed the punk's wrist with her right hand and then drove her left hand hard against his elbow. The kid's arm twisted, his elbow popped, and he landed on his face with his arm pinned behind him and Aphrodite's knee in the small of his back.

"Next?" said Aphrodite. She looked up and scanned the faces of the other young men. The knife was now somehow in her right hand. The guy she had pinned to the ground was yowling about his elbow.

No one spoke. Aphrodite came to her feet. There were people out on the porches of all the houses around the park now.

"Go home," said Aphrodite. "And put some ice on your friend's arm." She walked over to the boom box, turned it off and then handed it to the young man closest to her. He took it without comment, looked briefly at his buddies and then started walking away. His friends followed suit.

"Thank you," said the woman in the headscarf. "I was coming from the bus stop, and I heard the commotion in the park."

Aphrodite turned. The woman in the headscarf was still standing motionless. She had a calm, almost serene look on her face. She appeared to be in her mid-thirties.

"I'm Eleni," said Aphrodite. She held out her hand.

"I'm Afiyah," said the woman as she shook Aphrodite's hand. "Are you lost?" She smiled.

"I was looking for the Muslim Community Center," said Aphrodite. She cocked her head slightly to one side. "Is that it over there?" She gestured toward the red brick building across the street.

"Yes," said Afiyah. She smiled again. "May I ask what business you have there?"

"I'm looking for a kid named Eddie," said Aphrodite. "His mother seems to think he may be at the Center."

"Ah," said Afiyah. "I work at the Center, and I know Eddie."

"Any idea where he is?" asked Aphrodite.

"Let's go talk to the imam," said Afiyah. "He knows everything there is to know about young Eddie."

CHAPTER EIGHTEEN

2045 HOURS, 13 AUGUST 2002.
FELIPE CARILLO PUERTO, MEXICO

Bill squatted on his haunches in the darkness in the shell of the unfinished building. A few laborers and servants shuffled by on their way home from work, but no one paid any attention to him. Laid out on the concrete foundation of the house at his feet he had the wiper blades, the soda can and his knife.

There are some things that you could carry on your person or stuff into a bag without attracting any attention. There are other things you cannot disguise or explain away. Lock picks were in the latter category. So, Bill needed to make his own.

There were thin metal strips that ran the length of the wiper blades to give them some degree of rigidity. Bill pulled these loose and tossed the rubber blades themselves away. Then he bent the metal strips back and forth until they snapped and gave him two matching pieces about three inches in length.

The end of one metal strip Bill bent into a sharp "L". The end of the other strip he filed to a point on the concrete. Now he had a torque wrench and a pick with which to open the tumbler lock on the door.

With his knife, Bill cut both ends off of the soda can so that he had an open cylinder of aluminum. Then, he cut the cylinder lengthwise so that he could fold it out flat into a sheet. From this sheet, he cut a smaller rectangle, which he notched in two places on one side.

Finally, he folded the small rectangle over two times and then bent it into a tight "U" shape. At the point in the "U" where it bent, the notches had formed a tooth that stuck out. Now, Bill had a shim with which to open the padlock.

Bill picked up his new tools and his knife and slid them into his pocket. He got up and headed back in the direction of Sultan's office. It was time to go to work.

Across the street from the block of offices where Sultan's office was located, there were several Mayan men squatting in the dark on the curb, drinking rum and smoking to kill the time. Bill walked over within a few feet of a couple of the men and squatted down as if he was part of the group. Bill hadn't had eyes on the target for ten minutes now. He had no idea what had transpired during that time. He needed to watch for a while and make sure no one had gone back inside. Sitting by himself he would be conspicuous. Sitting with what looked to be a group of loafers helped him disappear.

"Have any cigarettes?" asked the man closest to Bill in horrible, guttural Spanish.

"No," said Bill in the same language.

"Fuck your mother," said the man next to the guy who had asked for cigarettes. He spit into the street as a taxi blew past in a cloud of exhaust. "You've got cigarettes." He was a small dark man with the face of a ferret.

"Eat shit, you sister fucker," said Bill. He figured the best approach was to go on the offensive. He looked directly at the man with the ferret face as he spoke and shifted on his feet like he was thinking about getting up. "If I had any cigarettes, I wouldn't give them to you."

There was a brief pause as the other men squatting on the curb looked at the ferret and waited to see if he would respond. Then the man grunted and chuckled under his breath and went back to picking at the black grime under his toenails.

Bill reached into his pocket and pulled out a pack of Marlboro cigarettes he picked up from a stand on the street earlier. He motioned to the guy next to him to pass the pack to the guy with the ferret face. The guy laughed, and the other men, including the ferret, joined in. Everyone enjoyed the joke. Then they all took cigarettes for themselves. The pack was half empty, and stank of sweat and rum by the time it made its way back to Bill.

Bill took a cigarette himself before he put the rest back in his pocket. He lit up and put the cigarette in the corner of his mouth and let it dangle, with a thin wisp of smoke bleeding off into the night air. He didn't smoke, but everyone around him did, and he needed to fit in. Conversation picked back up again.

Bill sat in silence for another twenty minutes as the men around him chattered away in Maya and Spanish. Traffic rumbled by in the road. No one took any notice of Bill.

Finally, satisfied that the lights were still out in the offices on the second floor of the target building, Bill got to his feet. He walked first down the street and away from where he was sitting, then crossed and walked back up the other side of the road until he was at the base of the stairs that lead up to Sultan's office. People pushed by on either side of him, and across the street the men with whom he had been sitting were still lost in conversation.

Bill leaned up against the wall next to the doorway for a moment and made a show of fiddling with one of his shoes. A bus roared by spewing exhaust and stuffed with passengers and bags. Bill rolled around the corner, into the doorway and up the stairs. By the time the exhaust and noise had passed, he had vanished.

At the top of the stairs, Bill went down on all fours so as to keep his head below the level of the railing that ran along the outside of the breezeway. Slowly and cautiously, he crawled to the door to Sultan's office. Once there, he pressed his ear up against the door and listened. There was no sound from inside. There was no light coming from under door. The office was empty.

Bill came up on his knees. His head was now slightly above the level of the top of the railing, but he was in shadow and from down below on the street anyone looking up would still have his view obscured. He was betting that no one would be paying close enough attention to notice him.

From his pocket, Bill produced the shim. He slid the "U" around the shackle of the lock, pushed the metal tooth into the space between the shackle and the body of the lock and pushed it in. The lock fell open. Not for the first time in his life, Bill wondered why anyone even bothered taking the time to close a padlock.

Bill slipped the lock off and put it in his pocket, so that he could keep track of it. He pulled out the torque wrench and pick that he had made from the metal strips off the wiper blades. He put the "L" portion of the torque wrench into the bottom of the key slot in the lock set in the door and applied a slight amount of pressure. The lock cylinder turned slightly and stopped with the torque wrench wedged into it.

Next Bill took the pick and began to feel along inside the top of the key slot. He closed his eyes and measured his breathing. Lock picking was all touch, and he needed to tune out everything to feel of the pins inside the lock that prevented the cylinder from turning.

All standard locks were pin and tumbler locks, and they were all the same. The design consisted basically of a rotating cylindrical tube inside of a larger locking mechanism. Around the circumference of the tube was the shell, which was fixed to the door. When locked, the tube was prevented from turning by spring-loaded pins, which protruded through the shell and into the tube.

Each pin was actually cut in one or more places perpendicular to its length. With no key in the lock, the pins protruded all the way in and held the lock from turning. When the right key was inserted the pins were raised to the shear line, the point where the cut in each pin aligned with the shell. Then the tube could turn, and the lock could open.

Picking a lock was simply a matter of raising each pin to the correct level while applying just the right amount of turning motion with the torque wrench. Ideally, the pinholes were supposed to be in perfect alignment. They never were, and in a cheap door lock like the one Bill was picking they were not even close. Raised in the right order, the pins would actually stick up and the tube would turn just the very slightest amount to hold them there. When all of them were up, the lock would open.

It was simple in theory. For Bill now, squatting in the dark, trying desperately to tune out the sound of the street and the beat of his own heart, it was anything but. For almost a full minute, he played with the pins, pushing them up one by one, feeling them slip back down when he got the order wrong, feeling the lock begin to turn and then jam on him. Finally, after what seemed in his exposed state an eternity, the lock turned, and the door opened.

Bill glanced around quickly and slid inside, closing the door behind him. He crouched down just inside the door and waited.

His eyes were already partially adapted to the dark from sitting in the shadows, but before he moved he wanted to allow his night vision to reach its maximum potential.

Around Bill shadows and shapes began to take form. On the floor in front of him was a woven Afghan war rug with images of the Twin Towers burning on it. Against the front wall of the office was a small desk with a chair in front of it. There were papers strewn across the desk, but no computer. He guessed this was where the younger man he saw earlier worked.

To Bill's left there were several large filing cabinets against the wall. On top of them were stacks of dusty books. Against the back wall was a large desk with a wheeled armchair behind it. There was a brand new MacPro desktop on it. Next to the desk was a shelving unit with printers and scanners on it. Bill recognized one of the scanners as being the unit he had placed in the cage off Belize.

More minutes passed, until Bill was confident that he could see as well as possible in the dim light. Gingerly, he stood up and began to walk across the floor toward the large desk. A surreptitious entry was no good unless it stayed surreptitious. That meant he needed to leave no trace that he had ever been here.

Slowly and deliberately, Bill came around behind the desk. As he did so he noted that it had a nameplate in a stand on it. The nameplate said Sultan Rashid. This was the big guy's desk for sure.

Bill had no idea how much time he had, but he was assuming it was not much. There might be a night watchman who was paid to check the doors, and the absence of a padlock on the outside of the office would be a giveaway that something was wrong. Rashid might just have gone to dinner and might return later. His assistant might work in the evenings. There were a million ways this could turn south in a hurry.

The file cabinets Bill decided to ignore. He was making some educated guesses he knew, but it was hard to fathom that a guy running illegal operations out of a front company office would keep hard copy records around for the cops to find if they every searched the place. No, if there was any trail here, it was going to be on the computer, and it was going to be encrypted.

Bill rolled the chair out from the desk and then sat down in it gently. It was a little high for him, but he did not adjust it. If he did so, it would be impossible for him to every get it back to exactly the same setting as when Sultan last sat in it.

Bill pushed the chair into the desk and touched a key on the keyboard. He noted as he did so that the keyboard was in English. Whatever else Sultan was, he was an educated man. The screen came to life and displayed a standard log in screen. To get any further he needed both a username and a password.

From inside his pocket, Bill brought out one of the things he had been able to carry openly onto the plane. It was a thumb drive and outwardly no different than a normal device that could be purchased at any computer supply store. This drive, however, carried a number of very sophisticated programs. Bill pulled the cap off the thumb drive and inserted it into one of the USB ports on the side of the computer.

A small blue light in the interior of the thumb drive illuminated to confirm that it was functional. There was an almost imperceptible humming noise. Bill moved the cursor on the screen to the space where the User ID was supposed to be typed in and pressed the return key.

The blue light on the thumb drive began to blink rapidly. Five seconds elapsed. The work "Sahaba" appeared in the space for the User ID. Bill moved the cursor down to space where the password was to be typed in and pressed the return key again.

Once more the blue light on the thumb drive began to blink rapidly. Seconds passed. Seconds became a minute and then two. Bill sat, eyes glued to the screen, listening intently for any sound outside on the breezeway.

Two minutes became three, then five. Unconsciously, Bill began to tap his foot. The geometry of the office that had caused him so much trouble in making an entry now presented itself in reverse. He was inside of the cube. If anyone appeared, he had nowhere to go, nowhere to hide.

The light stopped flashing. In the space for the password, "Surah98:6" appeared briefly and then vanished to be replaced by "X"'s. *How appropriate*, thought Bill. The password was a reference to a passage from the Koran. He did not consider himself to be a

Koranic scholar, but Bill knew this passage well. It was a favorite of Jihadis:

"Truly those who disbelieve in the religion of Islam, the Quran and Prophet Muhammad (Peace be upon him)) from among the people of the Scripture (Jews and Christians) and hypocrites will abide in the Fire of Hell. They are the worst of creatures."

The computer screen in front of Bill went momentarily dark and then came up to Sultan's desktop screen. There were icons on the screen for a variety of programs. Bill held down the control key on the keyboard and then pressed the keys 1, 3, 5, in succession. A command screen for the thumb drive came up as an inset to one side of the computer screen.

Inside the command screen were a number of smaller icons that worked as shortcuts to different programs on the thumb drive. One of them read "Remote Monitoring Installation". Bill clicked on this icon, and the light in the thumb drive began to blink red.

Once installed this program would allow Bill to remotely access Sultan's computer whenever it was connected to the Internet and to download anything on it. That meant he did not have to sit exposed for hours working his way through everything stored on the machine. Still, it would take almost ten minutes for the program to finish installing, and until then he was fixed in time and space.

Bill moved the cursor over to the Skype icon on Sultan's desktop and clicked the mouse. The Skype screen opened and prompted him for another User ID and password. He could use the thumb drive to break the encryption, but that would mean shutting down the install and having to start it all over again. He opted to do it the old fashioned way and to hope that even bad guys got lazy.

For the username, Bill typed in "Sahaba" again. Then he typed in "Surah98:6" for the password and clicked on "log-in". The main control screen for the Skype program appeared. He was in.

At the top of the screen was a list of Sultan's Skype contacts. There were a half-dozen generic Hispanic names and four that jumped out as different: "High Roller," " Akbar", "Addas" and "Sumaya." "High Roller" was Carlos. Bill assumed "Akbar" was a superior based purely on the significance of the name "Akbar" as that of a famous Mughal emperor. He had no idea who the others were.

The red light on the thumb drive was still blinking. Bill changed the screen and began to look at the call log. He saw that there had been calls to most of the contacts every week or two for the last six months.

Bill also noted that there were no calls to "Addas" before a month ago. What that meant he had no idea. He also had no clue what the significance of the name "Addas" might be. It was unlikely to be a true name, but as a name of importance in Islam it rang no bells with him.

According to Bill's watch, he still had a few minutes before the installation of the remote monitoring software was complete.

He decided to use the time to take a look at whatever files might be stored on the computer's hard drive. He backed out of the Skype account, making sure to log out completely, and then brought up a list of documents stored on the hard drive.

Bill began to scan down the long list of documents stored on Sultan's computer, hoping for something to catch his eye. Most of the files looked to be business forms and agreements, things that were connected to Sultan's cover business not his illegal activities. He kept scrolling downward.

Bill froze. Highlighted on the screen were the words "Unit 731". He double-clicked on the title, and the document opened on the screen.

Unit 731 was a secret Japanese organization during the Second World War. Members of the unit conducted experiments on live human subjects – Koreans, Chinese and Allied prisoners of war. They removed organs from conscious subjects without the benefit of anesthesia. They tested flamethrowers on defenseless prisoners. They froze the limbs of live prisoners solid, thawed them out and watched as gangrene set in and the subjects died in agony. They also tested a wide variety of pathogens as possible biological warfare agents.

The "Unit 731" document opened. It was a lengthy compilation of research on the unit. There were photographs of experiments in progress, Unit 731 personnel and its nightmarish commander, Shiro Ishi. There were diagrams of the unit's facility at

Harbin in Manchuria, where over 10,000 people were killed. There were long charts showing the results of efforts to perfect methods for the use of cholera, plague, anthrax and typhoid for biological warfare.

This was not a copy of something that had been published elsewhere. This was the result of dedicated research by someone who had been directed to learn everything they could about Unit 731 and the hideous work it had done. It would take Bill days to digest.

Bill backed out of the document. He would access it later remotely. The red light was still flashing on the drive. He scanned down the list of documents again. His eyes focused on one with the title "Ways to Improve on Unit 731 Biological Agent Distribution Methodologies." His blood ran cold. He was almost afraid to open the document, as if not reading it would somehow make it go away.

The door to the office opened, and the light came on. Sultan stepped in and reached for an attaché case sitting on the desk closest to the door. He had forgotten something.

Bill came to his feet in an instant, knife in hand, chair banging against the wall behind him. Sultan turned suddenly, startled that he was not alone.

"You son of a whore, how did you get in here?" yelled Sultan. He started forward, hand raised as if to strike Bill. Then he stopped, hand still over his head, eyes wide with fear as he saw the knife in Bill's hand.

"Who the hell are you?" said Sultan. He was peddling backward now, trying desperately to keep distance between him and Bill.

Bill came around the desk, knife in hand and advanced steadily. If he could get Sultan before he made it out of the office, he could kill him, shut the door and still hope to keep anyone outside from noticing anything.

"You're an American," stammered Sultan. His mind was trying desperately to catch up with events. Moments before he had been about to discipline a thieving Mayan janitor. Now he was face to face with a mortal enemy. He made it to the doorway and turned to run.

Bill lunged. The war rug went out from under his feet. He fell hard on his left side, halfway through the doorway. Sultan was gone.

"Fuck", grunted Bill. He jumped to his feet and leaned over the railing. Sultan was on the sidewalk below and hustling away in the direction of the market.

Bill ran back in the office. The light had stopped flashing on the thumb drive. He pulled the drive from the machine and logged off. Then he shut off the lights, pulled the door shut, refastened the padlock and locked the door. That took a total of less than twenty seconds.

Five seconds later, Bill was on the sidewalk in front of the office. Sultan had disappeared, but he couldn't be far. Bill stepped off the sidewalk into the street and began to run in the direction in which Sultan had vanished. He had to catch him before he had a chance to alert anyone to what had happened. He had to catch him, and he had to kill him.

CHAPTER NINETEEN

**2055 HOURS, 13 AUGUST 2002.
MUSLIM COMMUNITY CENTER, BALTIMORE, MARYLAND.**

"Thank you," said imam Willy Malik. It was late, but long hours in the service of God were nothing new to him.

"For what?" asked Aphrodite.

"For coming to the rescue of a sometimes overzealous sister," said the imam. He looked pointedly at Afiyah as he spoke. He was seated behind the large, wooden desk in his office at the Muslim Community Center wearing a white linen suit that accented the warm, tea color of his skin. Aphrodite and Afiyah were sitting in two armchairs in front of him.

"Allah protects," said Afiyah.

"And, sometimes a good right hook doesn't hurt either," said Willy.

"I am glad I could help," said Aphrodite.

"And what can we do to help you?" asked the imam. "Tell me about your concerns regarding young Eddie."

"His mother found a business card for the Center in his room," said Aphrodite. "She also talked to some friends of his who said he had been coming here for the last few weeks and that they were worried about him."

"Worried how, sister?" said Willy.

"I think they felt he was becoming very…angry," said Aphrodite. She paused. She was not sure where to go from here.

"You are not from the States, sister, are you?" asked the imam.

"No," said Aphrodite. "I am Greek".

"And what is Islam to a Greek, sister?" asked Willy.

"The enemy of my blood," said Aphrodite.

"But you do not feel that way."

"A lot of things I was taught as a child were lies," said Aphrodite.

"Islam is a religion of peace," said the imam. "But, unfortunately, these days there are more than a few that want to warp it into something hateful."

"The world has no shortage of people who kill in the name of God," said Aphrodite.

"Eddie has opened his eyes to the fact that there are a great many ugly things in the world," said the imam. "And, I understand much of what he is saying. I have been there myself." Willy's smile tightened and he leaned back in his chair a bit. Sometimes, the summer of 1968 seemed a long, long time ago. Other times, it seemed like just yesterday.

"Has he been staying here?" asked Aphrodite.

"Many young brothers and sisters who have lost their way spend time here," said Afiyah. "We give them a place to come to get off the street and get themselves together."

"Eddie has been here off and on for weeks," said the imam. "He was in my office this morning saying he wanted to organize a protest against the American invasion of Afghanistan."

"His mother thinks he may be getting ready to do something violent," said Aphrodite.

"I think he feels betrayed by the world," said the imam sadly. He stretched his long, powerful arms out in front of him for a moment. "He wants to lash out. Thinks that will make it right. Do you understand what I am saying, sister?"

"I do," said Aphrodite. She didn't elaborate. There was a time, on the street in Athens, when hate was the only emotion she'd had.

"Afiyah, can you take this sister up to the bunkhouse where the men are staying and see what you can find out about Eddie and where he might be now?" asked the imam.

"Of course," said Afiyah. She smiled at Aphrodite, reached over and squeezed her hand. "Let's go," she said.

"Thank you," said Aphrodite. She stood and shook Willy's hand.

"Glad to help," said Willy. "Go with God."

Aphrodite and Afiyah stood and walked out of the office, down the wood floored hallway and out of the big, brick building where the Center was housed.

"The bunkhouse for the men is over there," said Afiyah. She pointed to what Aphrodite assumed were the old servant's quarters behind the main house.

"And where do the women stay?" asked Aphrodite.

"Over there," said Afiyah. She pointed toward some ragged row houses in the direction of the park. "It would not be proper for the men and women to stay under the same roof."

"I see," said Aphrodite. She was not sure she did at all.

"You are thinking this is all very strange. You are wondering why a white girl with blue eyes is here, doing this," said Afiyah. She smiled.

"I am trying to understand," said Aphrodite.

"I needed God," said Afiyah. "This is where I found him. As far from meth, Indiana and my father as I could get."

"It is the finding that is important, not the place," said Aphrodite. She couldn't remember the last time she'd talked to God, but she envied those who did.

The two women walked silently across the rough lawn in the darkness. Police sirens were wailing in the distance. From the building in front of them came the sound of Arabic prayer.

"We cannot go inside," said Afiyah when she reached the door to the building. She pressed a doorbell next to the weathered doorframe. There was an audible buzzing sound and then the sound of someone walking heavily on a wood floor. The door squealed open on rusty hinges.

"Yes, sister?" said a large, black man in his twenties with a full, dark beard and a white skull cap.

"I am sorry to disturb you, brother Walid" said Afiyah. "This sister is looking for Eddie. Is he here?"

"Cop?" asked Malik. He kept the door only partially open and looked Aphrodite up and down.

"Does she look like a cop?" asked Afiyah. Aphrodite said nothing. Inside the building the praying continued.

"Eddie's not here," said Malik. "I don't know where he is."

"Guess," said Afiyah.

"Sparrows Point, " said Malik.

"What's Sparrows Point?" asked Aphrodite.

"It's where the Bethlehem steel mill used to be," said Afiyah.

"It's a wasteland," said Malik.

"There's another masjid there," said Afiyah.

"Filled with some very scary boys," said Malik. "They've been getting in Eddie's head a lot recently."

"I need to find this place," said Aphrodite.

"Bad idea," said Malik.

"I'll take you," said Afiyah.

"At least wait for daylight," said Malik.

"First thing in the morning then," said Afiyah.

"Thank you," said Aphrodite.

CHAPTER TWENTY

2055 HOURS, 13 AUGUST 2002.
FELIPE CARILLO PUERTO, MEXICO.

Sultan had the lead, and he knew the area. But, Bill had advantages too. He was in better shape. He was trained to kill with his hands. And, he knew that Sultan dared not call for help. He was a man up to his neck in illegal activities. He was on his own.

Ahead through the traffic and exhaust, Bill saw the lights of the native market, come to life now that the heat of the day had dissipated. A chattering crowd of Mayan women in traditional dress was emptying onto the sidewalk through the tall wooden archway that formed the entrance to the maze of shops and open air stalls. Sultan pushed past them and disappeared inside.

Bill doubled his pace. A bus roared past, so close it almost knocked him down, and someone on board spat at him. A man on the sidewalk yelled for him to get out of the road and then, insufficiently interested to keep yelling, turned back to buying slices of mango from a street vendor.

Sultan was a hundred feet ahead, at the far end of a long, dusty passageway lined with jewelry shops when Bill came through the entrance into the market. Between them were crowds of men and women haggling with shopkeepers over beaded necklaces with large wooden crosses and hair clips decorated with ancient Mayan symbols. The smell of rum, coconut and sweat was heavy in the air.

Bill turned his face downward and shuffled forward. He could see that Sultan was standing where the corridor ahead intersected with another that ran to the left perpendicular to it. Sultan was peering intently in Bill's direction, trying to ascertain if he was being followed, but Bill was betting he had not spotted him in the crowd.

Two fat Mexican men wearing cowboy hats with silver buckles on them pushed past Bill and shoved him hard against the wall. He looked like a down at the heels backpacker, and he was getting the respect that went with that status. Bill resisted the urge to hit back, and continued to shuffle forward.

Just ahead now was the intersection of the two tiled corridors. Sultan was nowhere to be seen. Bill paused and scanned the small shops on either side of the hallway. He did not see Sultan in any of them. It was another hundred feet from the point where the corridors met to the far exit from the market. It did not seem likely that Sultan had covered that distance in so short a time.

Bill made the turn to the left into the other corridor and pressed forward. The crowds were worse here, crushing in on all sides and surging back and forth like a current.

Bill stumbled for a moment, almost lost his balance and realized there was a wooden bench in front of him and that the crowd was parting like the Red Sea to pass around it. Steadying himself on the arm of the bench, Bill scanned the immediate vicinity again. To his left, was the glass window of a jewelry shop and inside of it racks displaying literally hundreds of silver bracelets and earrings. A tall, light-skinned Mexican woman with jet-black hair and Castilian features was standing on the other side of the window admiring a jade ring with the image of a human skull carved into it.

On Bill's other side was a small shop selling drinks and snacks. A couple of scrawny Mayan teenaged boys were leaning against the counter at the front of the shop drinking Coke and talking about girls. A ballad singing the praises of a Guatemalan narco-trafficker named "Oscar" was playing on a boom box on the counter in the shop so loud that it almost drowned out the din of the crowd.

All around, were people, some tall, some short, some Mayan, some with more European blood in their veins, all pushing, shoving, arguing prices and searching for a deal.

Bill stepped up onto the bench and stood on top of it. It wasn't much elevation, but every little bit helped. Instead of staring at a sea of anonymous faces, he now had some perspective.

Fifty feet ahead, the market emptied onto a cross street, and the crowd momentarily broke up. Across the street, Bill could see the narrow entrance to another market filled with vegetable, fruit, spice and food vendors. He could already smell the charcoal and tortillas.

Sultan was standing just on the other side of the crosswalk. He had his back to Bill, and he was looking right and left as if trying to decide which way to go. Bill dropped down off the bench and began to claw his way forward. Sultan paused and went straight ahead into the market between shelves covered with jars of spices and a table stacked with coconuts.

Bill reached the cross street a few moments later. Around him the bodies were thinning and visibility was improving. Sultan was three stalls away, standing next to a melon stand.

Sultan finished examining the melons and headed deeper into the market. Bill made no move to follow. So far, it seemed that Sultan had not noticed him, but his luck could not hold. Sultan had gotten much too good a look at him in the office. Bill needed to change his appearance, and he needed to do it now.

Bill backed out of the market the way he had entered. To the right and running parallel to the corridor down which Sultan was walking was a narrow alley that ran behind the shops. Bill entered the alley and began picking his way forward over trash, empty cardboard boxes and other debris.

Fifty feet into the alley he found what he was looking for, clothes hung out on clotheslines to dry. The first clothesline was hung with a couple of grimy sets of shorts and t-shirts. That was not going to help him look like something else. He kept moving, past women's skirts, and boxer shorts and soggy socks. Halfway down the alley he came across a battered straw cowboy hat, a long white, embroidered shirt and a pair of loose, white cotton pants with a drawstring, all held to a plastic clothesline by cheap plastic clothespins.

The shirt was dingy and fraying along the hem. It obviously belonged to a Mayan peasant without many shirts to spare. Bill did not care. He quickly changed in the shadows, leaving his old attire lying in the filth of the alley next to a stack of boxes filled with pirated CD's.

Bill trotted the rest of the way down the alley until he came out onto the next cross street. Sultan was standing about fifty feet away, using the reflection in a shop window to look behind him for any sign he was being pursued. Ahead of him the next block of the market was filled with clothing, shoes and housewares. Bill tilted the hat forward on his head to help obscure his appearance and walked right behind Sultan, down an aisle between stacks of men's shirts and brightly colored plastic washtubs.

Now it was a game of cat and mouse. Bill knew Sultan would wander through the market for as long as it took for him to be convinced he was clean. Then he would make his move to head for home. For Bill it was matter of staying undetected until then. Until Sultan left the market and moved away from the crowds it was impossible to have an opportunity to finish him.

Bill stood a few stalls into the market making a show of shopping and working hard to keep his face from being too visible. Moments passed. Sultan walked closer, glancing over his shoulder periodically to check for pursuit but taking no interest in Bill who had preceded him into the market. Bill moved forward, staying a stall or two ahead of Sultan and keeping track of him in his peripheral vision instead of succumbing to the temptation to look directly at him.

Minutes passed. The strange, slow motion pas de deux continued, with Bill following by leading, always close enough to ensure he knew where Sultan was, never so close as to attract attention to himself. Sultan, visibly nervous at first, gradually appeared to relax.

At the end of the block there was another side street and a small juice stand set up on the pavement with crude wooden chairs and tiny laminated tables. Bill walked over, sat down and, in rough, guttural Spanish, ordered a glass of mango juice. Sultan stood not thirty feet away, still in the market, taking a long, hard look back the way he had come.

Sultan came out of the market, glanced once at Bill without any apparent recognition, and then turned down the side street and walked briskly in the direction of the next major thoroughfare. Bill let him get a lead of about seventy-five feet and then fell in behind. The mango juice sat untouched on the table behind him.

Sultan reached the intersection of the narrow side street and a broad avenue. To his left was a cabstand with several white taxis with green stripes parked against the curb. The drivers were gathered twenty feet away around a small television set on a rough wooden table. The sounds of the soccer game were almost drowned out by their laughter and joking.

Sultan turned sharply and walked to the last taxi in the line. He glanced through the window, saw keys dangling from the ignition and yanked open the driver's side door. The car's engine roared. The drivers turned and began to yell. The taxi jumped from the curb into traffic.

Bill sprinted to the corner. The drivers were screaming about calling the cops. The owner of the stolen car was cursing. Sultan whipped the taxi he was driving around a truck, in front of a bus and disappeared into the darkness. He was gone.

Bill swiveled his head and scanned the area. Another cab rolled by, and he contemplated flagging it down and telling its driver to follow the car in which Sultan was riding. It worked in all the movies. It would not work here. The only likely result of a stunt like that was that the driver would turn him in to the first cop he saw.

A young Mayan man in a sleeveless white t-shirt and a red motorcycle helmet turned into the alley, stopped his bike and dismounted. He pulled his helmet off and placed it over one of the side view mirrors. His cell phone rang, and he pulled it from his pocket and answered the call. Bill could hear a high-pitched female voice speaking Spanish on the other end of the line.

The keys were still in the ignition of the bike. Bill stepped forward. The Mayan man turned with a questioning look on his face and started to say something. Bill caught him with a fist in the jaw and knocked him flat on his back in the street. The cell phone flew ten feet, hit the ground, bounced and shattered into a dozen pieces.

Bill landed on the bike, discarded the hat and yanked on the helmet in one fluid motion. Someone in front of him was yelling in Maya. The man Bill had hit was getting to his feet. Bill turned the key, started the bike and gunned the engine.

Someone grabbed at Bill's shoulder. Another hand reached for his wrist. A knot of onlookers was appearing around him. He dropped the clutch. He was gone.

The motorcycle exploded into traffic, tearing in front of a truck loaded with bananas and in between two motor scooters carrying entire families. Bill dodged left, then right, then left again.

In front of him was a white cab. Bill pulled level with the vehicle and looked inside. There were three fat women holding a dozen plastic bags stuffed with vegetables and fruit. He hit the gas again and sped forward.

A few hundred meters ahead, the road intersected a divided street that ran east and west through town. A few miles east the road met the main highway that ran north to Cancun and south to Belize. To the west, the road ran deep into the forest and the interior of the Yucatan.

A cab was turning right to head east. Another white car that might have been a cab was turning left and going west. Bill had no time to close the gap to either vehicle before he had to commit. He figured it was a fifty-fifty proposition. He chose right.

Bill took the corner onto the divided street at close to fifty miles an hour, the bike leaned hard over to one side, his knee almost dragging on the ground. The air rushing past was blowing the loose fabric of his long, white shirt out behind him like a sail.

The cab was two hundred meters ahead when Bill came out of the turn. Bill twisted the accelerator and the bike almost stood on its rear wheel. He leaned forward, pressed his chest against the gas tank and gave the bike more gas.

The miles sped by. The taxi still had the lead, but the gap was narrowing. A sign said the intersection with the coast highway was approaching. Bill saw the right turn blinker on the taxi kick on. If he had guessed right, and it was Sultan in the car, then he was making a run for the border with Belize.

The bike shook and bucked. The front tire wobbled. Bill glanced briefly at the gas gauge. It read empty. He hoped it was broken.

The taxi took a right turn onto the coast highway. Bill went with it. A white highway sign with black letters said it was 122 kilometers to the border. Endless black jungle sped by on both sides of the road.

Bill was just off the taxi's rear bumper now. He swung across the centerline of the two-lane highway, pulled even with the car and shot a glance inside. Sultan was behind the wheel. He twisted his head to look Bill directly in the eyes, screamed something unintelligible, and yanked the wheel of the taxi hard to the left.

Bill slammed on the brakes, and the motorcycle twisted violently. The rear wheel skidded hard to the right. Bill leaned sharply into the skid and fought desperately to keep from going down. The taxi shot from right to left, inches in front of him. Loose gravel erupted into the air as the taxi's tires hit the shoulder on the left side of the roadway.

The two vehicles had switched positions now. Bill came out of the skid, wobbling but upright, on the right hand side of the road. Sultan careened back onto the roadway from the shoulder in the left lane. Bill gunned the bike's engine. He was a sitting duck. He needed speed. More than that, he needed a plan. Now that he had found Sultan, he needed to figure out a way to stop him.

Sultan stomped the gas pedal in the taxi. The engine whined. The car shot forward. Bill was only yards away on the other side of the road. There were no other vehicles visible in either direction on the highway.

Sultan pulled even with Bill. Bill twisted the accelerator again. The bike coughed and hiccupped. There was no mistaking that sound. Broken gauge or not, he was running out of gas.

The taxi slid across the centerline. The road curved sharply left. Bill edged right to stay clear of the taxi, but the car kept coming. There were only a few feet left now between Bill's tires and the loose rock on the side of the road. The bike coughed, sputtered and died.

Bill was out of ideas. He was out of time. There was no plan. He was dead.

A horn blasted. Huge, blinding headlights burst into view. A massive cargo truck stacked high with goods from Belize came around the corner steaming north and straddling the centerline.

Bill leaned right and flew off the road, down the embankment and slid to a stop at the edge of the jungle. He was shaken but in one piece. The bike was dead and useless underneath him.

Sultan went left, barely missed the front right fender of the truck and slid off the roadway on the opposite side from Bill. The taxi slapped sideways against a palm tree and came to rest. The truck rumbled on and disappeared into the darkness heading north.

Bill dropped the bike and sprinted across the road to the taxi. Somewhere in the distance, howler monkeys were calling. The road was once again empty and black.

The door to the cab was open when Bill got there. Sultan was gone. Bill stopped, crouched and willed himself to stop gasping for air. He needed to hear what was happening around him.

Birds called on the other side of the road. The leaves of the trees around Bill stirred in a momentary breeze. The monkeys called again. A branch snapped. Something heavy fell. To Bill's right, maybe fifty feet away in the trees there was a muffled curse.

Bill turned in the direction of the voice. Ten feet away, a narrow, but clearly defined trail lead into the jungle. He knew there were Mayan villages throughout the area and that the Yucatan was crisscrossed with trails that led to them. He walked carefully to the point where the trail entered the forest and knelt down again.

Somewhere in the darkness ahead Bill heard more branches breaking. Something thudded against a tree trunk and there was another muffled curse. Sultan might be a dangerous man, but he was out of his element in the jungle.

Bill came to his feet and began to move slowly and evenly down the path. The darkness around him deepened and pooled like ink. Insects buzzed. Leaves rustled. A snake slid over a rotten log and disappeared from view.

The years slipped away. It was the Yucatan. It might have been Panama. Bill was hunting a Pakistani terrorist. He might have been back at Jungle Warfare School. He lifted his feet carefully with each step, eyed the ground in front of him suspiciously and planted each foot with care. He did not so much walk as glide.

Somewhere in the black ahead, Sultan screamed. Then he screamed again. Bill did not need to see to know what had happened. Sultan had brushed against the trunk of a Chechen tree in the dark. Its sap burned like acid. Bill moved toward the sound.

Ahead the trail curved left. On the right hand side was a clearing where scraggly cornstalks were barely visible in the uncertain moonlight. Momentarily, Bill caught a glimpse of Sultan's silhouette. Then he was gone, swallowed by the jungle again, stumbling deeper into the forest.

Bill followed the trail. Every three or four steps he stopped briefly, listened and then pressed ahead. The distance between him and Sultan narrowed steadily.

Several hundred meters into the jungle Bill caught up. Sultan was down on his hands and knees next to a jumble of large stones. The sound of water gurgled in the background from some unseen source. Sultan was gasping for air.

Bill pulled his knife from his pocket and came forward without saying a word. Sultan staggered to his feet cursing and spitting. His eyes were wide with fear and confusion. He brought his arms up in a last desperate attempt to stave off certain death.

Bill's brought his knife hand down. Sultan caught it by the wrist and tried to push it aside. Bill was bigger. He was stronger. He shoved the knife toward Sultan's throat and bore down with all his weight.

Sultan bent backward. His knees buckled. He fell with Bill on top of him and the knife inches from his face.

The ground opened. The dim moonlight vanished. Both men plummeted into thin air.

A second that felt like an eternity passed. Bill plunged head first into cold, black water. The knife came free from his hand and vanished. He flailed and kicked and clawed his way back to the surface of an invisible pool.

Twenty meters above, there was a small window of pale moonlight visible through the hole in the surface into which Bill had fallen. He and Sultan had tumbled unknowingly into the entrance to a cenote, a sinkhole that dropped into an underground river.

Bill snorted to clear his nose of water and rubbed his eyes to clear his vision. He hadn't touched bottom when he fell. He had no idea how deep this pool was. In the darkness he couldn't see its sides either. He was afloat in an infinite sea of ink.

Something slapped against stone to Bill's left. He spun in the direction of the sound, treading water and desperately searching for sensory input in this void. Sultan coughed and wheezed. His fingernails clawed at bare rock. He was trying to get out of the water. He was only meters away. Bill swam.

Sultan was half out of the cenote, hanging on the edge of a great slab of black rock, when Bill found him. The man's sandals were gone, and his ankles were slippery with mud. Bill grabbed them and pulled. Sultan screamed, cursed and clawed desperately in a vain attempt to save his life.

It was wasted effort. Bill pulled him down into the cenote. Sultan spun, spit and flailed. Bill punched him in the throat, smacked his head against the rocks on the side of the pool and then thrust Sultan's head under the water.

Sultan screamed a cloud of bubbles and clawed desperately at Bill's arms and chest. Bill pulled Sultan's head to the surface and smashed it again against the rocks. Then he thrust the man's head back under the water and held it there.

Sultan kicked. His arms twisted and groped and clawed for life. Bill held on. The arms jerked and twitched and stopped moving. A cascade of huge bubbles exploded around Bill in the darkness. Sultan's body went limp. Bill let go.

Nothing moved. The air was filled with the stench of gas from Sultan's intestines. Bill pulled himself up on the black, nearly invisible stone, rolled over and lay still. His breath was coming in huge puffs like a locomotive.

Minutes passed. Bills' breathing slowed. Feeling returned to his limbs. Around him, shapes emerged from the darkness as his eyes adapted to the cave's lack of light.

Bill rolled over, came up on all fours and then stood. Mentally, he took stock of his body. He was covered with scrapes and scratches and bruises. Miraculously, though, he had emerged intact from the night's activity.

Next to Bill there was a jumble of rock that had fallen from the surface when the hole opened above him hundreds of years before. Long tree roots and vines were interlaced with the stone. Bill began to climb. Above him in the distance more howler monkeys called.

Ten minutes later, Bill scrambled through the opening into which he had fallen and staggered to his feet. He turned and looked back into the pit from which he had emerged. The water below was invisible. The opening to the cenote, perhaps five meters across, seemed just another shadow in the jungle.

Something rustled in the darkness behind Bill. He turned. A man stepped forward, then another. There were six of them, all of them small, stocky Mayans in nothing but canvas shorts.

"Why?" said the man closest to Bill. He was speaking Spanish.

"What?" said Bill.

"Why did you kill him?" said the man. The others stood dark and still.

"He was a bad man," said Bill without knowing why. He realized suddenly that there was blood all over his hands.

"Who are you?" said the man.

"Bill," said Bill. Was that the right answer?

"You are American, Bill?"

"Yes."

"Go home to America, then," said the man. "There must be bad men there as well."

Bill looked back at the entrance to the cenote. The smell of death from below seemed suddenly overpowering. He turned back to face the Mayans. They were gone.

In the distance, there was the sound of a truck on the highway. Bill felt suddenly that he was late for something very important.

CHAPTER TWENTY-ONE

1032 HOURS, 14 AUGUST 2002.
ISLAMABAD STATION, ISLAMABAD, PAKISTAN.

"What the fuck is this?" asked Mack Michaels. He hooked a thumb at the screen of his computer and squinted at Andrew. His short gray hair was standing straight up like quills on a porcupine, and his always-ruddy face was a darker shade of red than usual.

"It's an intel report," said Andrew. He was sitting on a couch in front of Mack's desk.

"I can fuckin' see that," said Mack. He was the Chief of Station Islamabad. He was not interested in playing games.

"It's a threat report," said Andrew. "If it's true, it means that there is a pending biological weapons attack on the United States." He leaned back and crossed his legs. He was way past the point in his career when a Chief of Station yelling shook him up.

"Julie!" bellowed Mack. He looked backed at the screen of his computer and scrolled down, reading the text displayed as he went.

"What do you need, boss?" called Darlene. She was the receptionist sitting outside the Chief's office.

"Get me Julie!" yelled Mack.

"You know you can send her an instant message right from the thing on your desk right?" said Darlene. She was already on her feet and walking into the next room, where Julie, the station reports officer sat.

"Just get her," muttered Mack. He finished reading the report and then started all over again.

"I don't understand the problem, boss," said Andrew. He rubbed his hands over his bloodshot eyes and sighed. He'd had maybe five hours sleep in the last two days. He was whipped.

"The problem is that headquarters is going to have a fuckin' cow," said Mack. He looked briefly at Andrew and then went back to reading.

"What's the problem, chief?" asked Julie. She was a petite white woman in her thirties with pale skin, red hair and giant black glasses. She looked like an elementary school librarian.

"Sit down," said Mack.

"Welcome to the inquisition," said Andrew, as Julie sat down primly next to him.

"What is Lashkar-e-Taiba?" asked Mack without looking up.

"Sir?" asked Julie.

"What the fuck is Laskar?" growled Mack.

"Lashkar-e-Taiba," began Julie. "The Army of the Righteous. A Pakistani terrorist group dedicated to the liberation of Kashmir from Indian occupation. Founded by Hafiz Muhammad Saeed..."

"I know all that shit," barked Mack.

"I'm confused," said Julie. She pushed her glasses back up on her nose and looked to Andrew for guidance.

"Here it comes," said Andrew.

"How many goddamn times has Lashkar attacked American targets?" snapped Mack. He stopped reading and glared straight at Julie.

"Sir?" asked Julie.

"None," said Andrew.

"You're damn right, none," said Mack. "Not one blessed time. Everything they have ever done has been directed at the Indians."

"Yes," agreed Julie. "Until now."

"What?" said Mack.

"I read the report before I moved it on to you, chief," said Julie in a strong, even voice. "It sounded credible. "

"And I have the papers," said Andrew. "If this guy Sardar is making this shit up, he went to one hell of a lot of trouble to fake it. Over a hundred pages of English language training manuals. I talked to him for four hours. His story was tight."

"No details," said Mack. "We're telling headquarters that a group that has never attacked the U.S. before has been training English speaking operatives for unspecified activity, which possibly includes the use of biological weapons. But, we're not telling them where it will happen, when it will happen or what targets will be hit."

"Yep," said Andrew.

"Oh, and I almost forget," said Mack as he rubbed the tired muscles in the back of his neck. "Our friends in the Pakistani intelligence service know all about this and are trying to cover it up."

"Yep," said Andrew again.

"You seriously think I should release this?" asked Mack.

"Isn't the whole point of intelligence to tell Washington things it does not know?" said Julie. She was sitting up straight with her hands folded on her plaid skirt.

"And doesn't want to hear," added Andrew.

Mack looked back at the screen and said nothing. He could hear Chief Near East Division bellowing at him over the phone already. He could see the cables expressing "reservations" about the precipitous release of intelligence from an "untested source" with obvious "biases and motivations for fabrication." He could also see the bodies piling up in the streets of Washington and New York if the intelligence was right, and they didn't move in time. He reached over and pressed the button on his keyboard that released the message to be transmitted.

"Thanks, boss," said Andrew.

"Get the fuck back to work," said Mack.

"Yes, sir," said Andrew and Julie in unison as they filed out the door.

"I hope to God it's bullshit," said Mack quietly to himself. He had already moved on to reading the next message in his queue.

CHAPTER TWENTY-TWO

14 AUGUST 2002, 0822 HOURS
BALTIMORE, MARYLAND.

Aphrodite looked at her watch again and thumped the steering wheel in frustration. She was sitting in the car she had borrowed from Irene in front of the Muslim Community center where she and Afiyah had agreed they would meet before going to Sparrows Point together. So far there was no sign of the other woman.

"At eight -thirty I'm going looking for her," said Aphrodite to herself. She reached over and turned on the car's radio. The local news station was broadcasting something about a spate of illnesses in the city.

"Both the University of Maryland and Johns Hopkins hospitals have quarantined portions of their intensive care units. Hospital administrators are characterizing the steps as routine measures employed when dealing with as yet unidentified infectious diseases, but unconfirmed reports suggest that both institutions are struggling to keep up with the number of sick."

Aphrodite looked up from the radio for a moment and watched a couple of men come out of the house where the males of the congregation slept. They were walking across the grass between the men's building and the community center proper. They were coming directly toward the car.

"An anonymous source at Johns Hopkins told our news team late last night that six people had already been confirmed dead and that dozens more had been admitted with a variety of flulike symptoms. According to the source, there is some speculation that the illness may be a form of Legionnaire's Disease. The Mayor will give a press conference on the matter later this morning..." Aphrodite turned off the radio and stepped out of the car.

"Good morning, sister," said one of the two men approaching. It was Malik, the same man she had spoken with the night before.

"Good morning," said Aphrodite.

"Peace be unto you," said the second man. He was much younger, and his beard came in wisps from his chin.

"Have you seen Afiyah?" asked Aphrodite.

"I have not," said Malik. "Just finished breakfast, and now I'm taking this young brother to a job interview downtown."

"Can you tell me which one of those row houses is the women's house?" asked Aphrodite. "Afiyah was going to meet me here at eight, but I haven't seen her."

"Still going to Sparrows Point?" asked Malik.

"Yes," said Aphrodite.

"Still a bad idea," said Malik. "A masjid in an abandoned strip club is no place to hang out."

"We all do what we have to do in this life," said Aphrodite. "Which one is the women's house?"

"The one with the green door," said Malik. "Good luck."

"God be with you, sister," said the younger man. Then he and Malik walked off together in the direction of the bus stop.

Aphrodite walked the other direction down the cracked sidewalk. Ahead of her was a short row of six brick townhouses with wooden front porches and small, weed-infested yards.

The second house in the row had a green door, and the porch was freshly swept. Aphrodite climbed the stone steps and rang the doorbell. There was no sound from inside.

A car drove by slowly on the street in front of the house. It was filled with young black men with bloodshot eyes, and smoke rolled from its windows.

Aphrodite rang the doorbell again. There was a faint sound inside that could have been a footfall. A curtain in one of the front windows overlooking the porch moved slightly, and Aphrodite had a brief glimpse of a small, white face wrapped in a tight, black head covering.

Then nothing.

Aphrodite pressed the doorbell again and deliberately held it down. She was tired of whatever game she was playing.

Nothing. Aphrodite banged on the door with her fist. Still nothing.

"Panagiou mou," said Aphrodite aloud. She wasn't sure whether invoking the Virgin Mary's name in Greek in this setting was appropriate, but she didn't care. "I'll find it myself."

Aphrodite stomped back to the car, started it and pulled away from the curb. She had a basic idea where Sparrows Point was, courtesy of a late night talk with Irene the day before. She'd just have to sort it out from there.

The drive across town took a good forty-five minutes in rush hour traffic. Sparrows Point was a vast industrial site, once home to the largest steel mill in the world. Most of the plant was rubble now, and what was left off it sat on a peninsula east of Baltimore City surrounded by disintegrating housing and boarded up businesses.

Aphrodite pulled up in front of a place called "Shorty's," advertising "home-cooked meals" and "package goods". The gravel parking lot was empty, except for a handful of beat-up pickup trucks and a single tractor-trailer. Behind Shorty's, through a stand of scrub trees and past a rusted chain link fence, was the hulk of an abandoned blast furnace.

Aphrodite walked through the front door of the establishment and stopped briefly to survey the scene. There was a counter against the back wall with a row of stools in front of it. Two young men sat on stools at the counter eating breakfast. Two heavyset women in their forties with big hair and bright lipstick were standing on the other side of the counter discussing somebody's sister who got called in to work the night shift at Johns Hopkins.

The remainder of the room was filled with tables and chairs and some vintage pinball machines. A half-dozen men in their sixties sat around a table against one wall drinking coffee and reading the paper. The guy closest to Aphrodite was holding up a paper so that she could see the headline, "Mystery Illness Hospitalizes Dozens." On a television mounted to the wall above the men's heads, a newscaster on the local news reported a possible problem with the air circulation system at the National Aquarium.

Aphrodite walked to the counter and sat down. A guy with dark, slicked back hair two stools down looked over, eyed her from her black high-heeled boots to her tight t-shirt, and then down again. She ignored him.

"What'll it be, hon?" asked one of the women behind the counter. The nametag on her pink uniform said "Eunice".

"Coffee, please," said Aphrodite. She smiled.

"Comin' right up," said Eunice.

"Hey, baby, where you from?" asked the man with the dark hair. He was wearing a short-sleeved shirt with grease stains on it. Above the left breast pocket on his shirt red stitching said "Dwayne".

"Knock it off, Dwayne," said Eunice. She set a cup of black coffee down in front of Aphrodite and glared at Dwayne. He looked away and went back to eating his grits.

"Thank you," said Aphrodite as she picked up the coffee.

"Cream and sugar, hon?" asked Eunice.

"No thank you," said Aphrodite. She took a big sip of coffee and set the cup down.

"So, what are you doing here, baby?" asked Eunice.

"I'm looking for a strip club actually," said Aphrodite.

"Now we're talking," said Dwayne.

"I'm gonna knock you on your ass, if you keep it up," said Eunice. She didn't even bother to look over at Dwayne as she spoke.

"Actually, I'm looking for a place that used to be a strip club, I guess," said Aphrodite. "I think it's abandoned."

"There were probably six clubs in Sparrows Point, when the mill was really working," said Eunice.

"And you danced at all of 'em back during the Korean War, right Eunice?" asked Dwayne. He grinned, and his buddy sitting next to him fist-bumped him.

"That's the third strike, Dwayne," said Eunice. She reached behind the counter and came up with a long, metal spoon in her hand.

"Ah, come on, Eunice," said Dwayne. He leaned back and eyed the spoon with suspicion. "I'm just having fun."

"This place is supposed to be some kind of mosque now," said Aphrodite.

"Oh," said Eunice. "Mother Juggs".

"Seriously?" asked Aphrodite.

"Ain't nothing subtle about the way men talk about women, darling," said Eunice. "I think you know that." She looked down suggestively at Aphrodite's chest for a moment.

"How do I find it?"

"Drive down Sparrows Point Road, here, hon," said Eunice. She was gesturing vaguely in the air as she spoke. "Follow it around to the left, until it intersects North Shore. It'll be there on the right, next to a boarded up house with shingle siding."

"Thank you so much," said Aphrodite. She dropped a ten-dollar bill on the counter for the coffee.

"What you want with those Muslim boys anyway, hon?" asked Eunice.

"Just looking for a lost soul," said Aphrodite as she stood up and walked out.

"No shortage of those around here these days," said Eunice.

Aphrodite drove down Sparrows Point Road past rows of small, sad, white-framed homes, boarded up businesses and empty weed-filled lots. At the intersection with North Shore, she stopped at a stop sign pockmarked with buckshot holes and looked across the street. Directly in front of her, next to an abandoned home with shingle siding and particle-board nailed over the windows, sat "Mother Juggs".

The yellow brick building had a long red, metal awning. Next to the concrete parking lot on the side of the building was a tall neon sign showing the outline of a topless dancer, complete with big red lights where her nipples were supposed to be. The sign was dark, and the red lights were broken.

Aphrodite pulled Irene's car into the parking lot, got out and locked it. There was one other vehicle in the lot, an Old Chevy van held together with putty and duct tape. There was no sound audible from inside the building.

Aphrodite walked up to the front door under the rusting metal awning and banged on the door. There was no answer. She tried the doorknob, but it didn't turn. She banged again.

"What is with these Muslims?" Aphrodite said aloud. She walked around the side of the building through knee-high weeds and broken glass. There were no windows on this side of the building, but about three-quarters of the way to the rear of the structure was a side door held closed with a rusted hasp and an equally rusted padlock.

Aphrodite looked down on the ground at her feet. In the weeds she saw a rusted piece of metal that looked like it had once been part of a leaf spring. She picked it up, wedged it between the hasp and the door and yanked on it. The rusted metal screws holding the hasp to the doorframe tore out of the rotted wood, and the door swung open.

The interior of the building was dark and smelled of mold and decay. Aphrodite stepped through the doorway and into the shadows pooled inside. A wooden desk layered in dust and bird droppings sat on one side of the room. On the opposite wall were a dartboard and a faded poster advertising the debut of a stripper named "Joos-E".

Aphrodite stood motionless. She slowed her breathing. She closed her eyes. She willed herself to absorb every sound around her.

Something scratched at the wall in the corner of the room. It sounded like a rat. Aphrodite ignored it.

Outside, a truck lumbered past. A horn sounded down the block. There were insects buzzing outside in the weeds. All that meant nothing.

The linoleum in the hallway outside the door cracked. Cloth brushed a wall somewhere nearby. Someone was whispering.

Aphrodite opened her eyes. The first few, angry inches of a shotgun barrel were visible through the door, which lead to the hallway from the office. She slid sideways across the room and crouched against the wall next to the door. The barrel of the shotgun came a few inches deeper into the room and began to swing in her direction.

In an ankle holster on the inside of her right ankle, Aphrodite had a Glock 26 compact semi-automatic Irene had loaned her. Silently, Aphrodite drew the weapon and extended it in front of her with both hands. Her grip was rock solid. The sights of the pistol were trained on the point in a few inches above the barrel of the shotgun where the face of the person carrying it would appear.

Part of a head came into view and then vanished. There was more whispering. Someone said something about "the po-lice".

The head came back through the doorway. It was wrapped in a green and black checked cloth. It began to turn and the face of a young black man came into view. His eyes were wide. He was gripping the shotgun with both hands and searching the gloom for signs of movement.

"Do not move," said Aphrodite in a slow, calm, clear voice. The man froze in his tracks and turned his head right, in the direction of the sound.

"I will kill you where you stand, if you move again," said Aphrodite. She stepped half a pace forward and pressed the barrel of her gun directly against the man's temple. "And, if your friend in the hallway so much as breathes hard, I will blow your brains out and then kill him too."

"In God's name, do not shoot," said the man.

"I want you to throw the shotgun across the room and lie down on your stomach with your hands stretched out in front of you palms up," said Aphrodite.

The man hesitated. A shoe scuffed in the hallway.

"Now," said Aphrodite.

The man in the green and black head cloth threw the shotgun across the room with an awkward, underhand motion and then stretched out on the floor with his arms extended in front of him and his palms up.

"You in the hallway," said Aphrodite. "I want you to back through the door with your hands on your head and your eyes closed."

"You'll shoot me," said a thin, adolescent voice.

"You have ten seconds," said Aphrodite. She had gone to one knee. "After that, I guarantee you that I will shoot you."

A moment passed. Something thudded on the floor in the hallway. A tall, thin white boy with long, stringy black hair came through the door with his hands on his head.

"Where's your gun?" asked Aphrodite

"I left it on the floor outside," said the boy. He was maybe nineteen.

"How many others here now?" asked Aphrodite.

"Nobody else," said the boy. "Just Andre and me."

"Lie down next to your friend with your arms out in front of you and your hands up, like he did," said Aphrodite.

The boy complied. Aphrodite came forward slowly, rounding the corner of the doorway into the hallway inch by inch, cutting it into neat, narrow slices, weapon at the ready, finger on the trigger. The hallway was clear. The building was dead silent.

Across the hallway, Aphrodite could see into another room with counters, sinks and broken mirrors. It was probably the room where the dancers got dressed, or undressed, to perform. There were prayer mats on the floor and someone had spray-painted the word "Mecca" in green on the wall to mark the direction to face when praying. There were what looked like cans of paint stacked in one corner, some gas cans in another and a laptop computer sitting on a stack of cardboard boxes in the center of the room.

Aphrodite glanced down the hallway toward the front of the club. The door was open into what had been the bar. She could see the rusting stripper pole still standing on a small circular stage surrounded by cheap stadium style seats with cup holders.

"Beautiful clubhouse you have here, children," said Aphrodite. The deer rifle the kid had dropped on the floor was lying in the middle of the hallway. Aphrodite pushed it away and up against the far wall with her foot.

"It's a mosque," said the guy in the headdress.

"What's your name?" asked Aphrodite. She came back into the room with her pistol still extended in front of her and her finger still on the trigger.

"Andre Hernandez."

"Very Islamic," said Aphrodite.

"I converted," said Andre. "My parents were infidels."

"How sad for you," said Aphrodite. "No wonder you're leading the revolution now."

"We are restoring the Caliphate," said Hernandez.

"I've got news for you," said Aphrodite. "Your Caliphate is a lie. Your revolution is a lie. All revolutions are a lie. Trust me. I've been to more than one."

"Who are you?" asked the skinny white kid.

"No one," said Aphrodite. "Where's Eddie?"

"He's not here," said the skinny white kid.

"Where is he?" said Aphrodite.

"Gone, bitch", said Andre. He chuckled.

"Wrong answer, donkey-fucker," said Aphrodite. She fired the pistol into the floor about six inches to the right of Andre's head. Fragments of linoleum showered the room. The sound echoed against the walls. Andre squealed like he had been stuck with a hot knife.

"What's your name?" asked Aphrodite. She was standing over the white kid now. Andre was whimpering.

"Dalton," said the kid.

"My name is Eleni," said Aphrodite. "Here are some things you need to know about me. I am not a cop. I am not an American. I killed a man for the first time when I was sixteen. And, it makes no difference to me at all whether you two live or die. Whatever happens in this room, I will sleep well tonight."

Dalton said nothing. He was trembling from head to toe. Urine was running out onto the floor next to his right thigh.

"Do you understand me?" said Aphrodite. She leaned down and pressed the barrel of the pistol against the base of Dalton's skull.

"Yes," squeaked Dalton.

"Where is Eddie?"

"He's down on Clinton Street," said Dalton.

"You're sure?" said Aphrodite.

"Yes," said Dalton. He was almost crying as he spoke. "The harbor. The docks. But, you're too late. It's probably done by now."

"Tell me how to find this place," said Aphrodite.

CHAPTER TWENTY-THREE

1925 HOURS, 14 AUGUST 2002.
RESIDENCE OF GENERAL HAMID ZIA, ISLAMABAD, PAKISTAN.

"Sit down," said General Hamid Zia. He was sitting in an ornate armchair and dressed in a dark suit with a red and yellow striped regimental tie. Colonel Khan sat down on a leather couch across from him. Behind Khan, the orderly who had shown him in closed the door to the wood-paneled study.

"It is good to see you, sir," said Khan. He was sitting up ramrod straight as if at attention. He and Zia had both been formally retired for some time, but the General remained a figure of great respect.

"It is good to see you as well," said Zia. On the walls behind him were photographs of him at various stages in his distinguished career. There was one of him as a young lieutenant in the 1971 war with India. There was another of him standing next to Mullah Omar on the outskirts of Kabul.

"We are ready to begin," said Khan. He understood that the General was, as always, a man who wished to get directly to the point.

"But not without incident," said Zia. He looked down at his manicured hands folded neatly in his lap. His hair was died jet black, his moustache waxed and twisted into two exact points.

"No, sir," said Khan. Despite himself he shifted uncomfortably in his seat. "We have lost contact with Sahaba in Mexico."

"Why?"

"We do not know, sir," said Khan. He had learned long ago on active duty not to attempt to shade the truth with Zia. "He is a man who is engaged in many things that have nothing to do with us. He may have had a problem for reasons that have nothing to do with us."

"Or, he may have been discovered," said Zia. He looked up from his hands and his piercing black eyes locked onto Khan's.

"Yes," admitted Khan. "But, he has done his part already. It is too late."

"Tell me about this Pashtun policeman," said Zia.

"His name is Sardar Ghayur," said Khan. Despite himself, his face colored slightly. This was not the conversation he wanted to have with the man who had been head of the ISI and was still one of the most powerful in Pakistan. "He is nothing. Shah and Bhutto will find him and finish him."

"He has documents?" asked Zia. He looked down at the toes of his brightly polished shoes.

"Yes," said Khan. "We closed one of the camps. It had been in use for some time and was beginning to attract scrutiny. We were moving the trainers to another camp. Someone talked. The safe house was raided. It was just bad luck."

"There is no such thing as bad luck, Colonel," said Zia. His voice was steady and even, but the tone was like a slap in the face. "There are only mistakes. The documents the trainers were carrying are lost, yes?"

"Yes, sir," said Khan simply.

"Has the policeman gone to the Americans?"

"We have no reason to think so," said Khan. It was a question he had not anticipated.

"He has documents clearly designed for the training of operatives. They are in English. He is on the run and desperate. What would you do?" said Zia.

"Yes, sir," said Khan simply.

"The test has been conducted?" asked Zia. He looked down at the razor-sharp creases on his slacks and brushed a stray bit of lint away.

"Yes, sir," said Khan. "Everything worked as planned. "

"If I give the order, you are prepared to execute the operation immediately?" asked Zia. He looked up again and focused his eyes on another picture on the far wall of his study. It was a picture of the World Trade Center towers in flames.

"Immediately, sir," said Khan.

"Khan," said Zia. "Do you understand what we are about to do?"

"We are about to strike back against the Americans, sir," said Khan. "We are about to teach them a lesson they will never forget."

"The Americans are arrogant bastards," said Zia. "They developed the atomic bomb, built the world's largest stockpile of nuclear weapons and then had the audacity to tell us that we were a rogue state for acquiring the bomb ourselves."

"Yes, sir."

"They commit war crimes around the world, and bomb and murder Muslims across the globe and then profess horror and surprise when Islamic warriors strike back against them."

"Yes, sir."

"What we are about to do on behalf of God himself will be the justice they deserve," said Zia. He paused for a moment, then looked down from the picture and directly at Khan again. "It may also mean the destruction of this nation if our role in it is discovered. Do you understand?"

"The Director is dead," said Khan. "We will find the policeman."

"Start the attack now," said Zia firmly. "Tell the American to move. And make sure that nothing remains afterward to connect this to us."

"Yes, sir," said Khan. He felt a lump in his throat. He had known this moment would come, but the enormity of it was overwhelming nonetheless.

"That is all," said Zia. He looked down at his gold watch momentarily. "I must attend a dinner at the President's residence."

"Yes, sir," said Khan. He stood and turned to leave. It was time to unleash the whirlwind.

CHAPTER TWENTY-FOUR

14 AUGUST 2002, 0935 HOURS.
BALTIMORE, MARYLAND.

Aphrodite pulled her car up against the curb just behind a tractor-trailer parked on Clinton Street. Across the street was a rusting metal warehouse surrounded by a chain link fence. On her right was the harbor. Jutting out into the harbor was a long concrete pier with two large, gray U.S. Navy supply vessels tied up to it.

Traffic was light. Ahead, the road was lined with piers and warehouses, but the area seemed virtually deserted. Aphrodite started to open the door and step out of the car. Her cell phone rang. She looked down at the number on the display. It was Bill.

"Hello," said Aphrodite into the phone. "Where are you?"

"Charlotte," said Bill. His voice sounded scratchy and distant.

"Why?" asked Aphrodite. She was watching an old brick warehouse past the two ships as she spoke. Something moved inside one of the broken windows of the abandoned structure.

"I got the first flight out of Cancun this morning," said Bill. "Engine trouble a couple of hours into the trip. We diverted here, because this is where the mechanics are."

"How long?" asked Aphrodite. There was movement again inside the warehouse. There was more than one of them whoever they were.

"Unknown," said Bill.

"Are you done with the job down south?" asked Aphrodite.

"Yes."

"How did it go?" asked Aphrodite.

"Well enough," said Bill.

"There were problems."

"I handled it," said Bill. "How are you?"

"Handling it," said Aphrodite.

"You ok?" asked Bill.

"I'm ok," said Aphrodite. "I may have found the kid."

"Good," said Bill. "Be careful."

"I was careful long before I met you, Tarzan," said Aphrodite. In spite of herself she smiled. It crept up on her sometimes just how much she had let herself need Bill.

"I know," said Bill. He paused. "I love you."

"I love you too, even if you are a donkey sometimes," said Aphrodite. She heard what sounded like voices from inside the brick warehouse drifting on the wind. "But, I have to go."

"I'll be there soon as I can," said Bill.

"I know," said Aphrodite.

"Bye," said Bill.

"Bye," said Aphrodite. She closed her phone and put it into the pocket of her jacket. Then she exited the car, locked it and headed down the street toward the pier, the two ships and the brick warehouse beyond.

Dalton, terrified that he was about to be executed, had told Aphrodite that she would find Eddie on Clinton Street near the pier where the Navy ships were docked. He'd babbled a lot about how she was too late to stop whatever Eddie was involved in. He'd begged for his life. He hadn't made much sense beyond that, and Aphrodite still had no clear idea what she was walking up on or how many other people might be with Eddie. She paused momentarily, drew her pistol and held it in her right hand by her side as she walked.

Something moved again inside one of the windows on the ground floor of the warehouse. There were definitely voices now, but they were too muffled to make out. It sounded like something heavy was being rolled on concrete inside the building.

Aphrodite passed the entrance to the pier on her right. It was closed off with heavy chain link gates held shut with a length of chain and a padlock. Beyond the fence she could see the gangplanks to the two naval vessels. There was no one visible on the pier and no one visible on either one of the ships either. Aphrodite kept moving.

The brick warehouse was just on the other side of the pier and jutted out into the harbor parallel to it. There were big, sliding doors along the side of the warehouse facing the pier like it had once been used to house cargo going on and coming off vessels docked there. Half the windows in the warehouse were broken now, and there was no sign it was being used for anything.

Aphrodite came up to the end of the warehouse that abutted Clinton Street. There was a doorway there with a faded sign overhead that said "Shipping Office". The door was slightly ajar. Parked against the curb about ten feet past the door was an old Chrysler minivan with fake wood paneling, so faded it almost looked white.

Aphrodite squatted down next to the doorway and listened. She could hear water lapping against the pier next to her. Overhead some gulls were screeching. There was not a sound now from inside the warehouse.

Smoothly, Aphrodite came to her feet with the pistol in her right hand. With her left, she pushed the door, and it squealed open on rusting hinges. There was still no sound from inside the warehouse.

Slowly, gun now in front of her in both hands, Aphrodite came around the edge of the doorframe, scanning the interior of the warehouse as she went. There was nothing in sight but shadows, debris and broken glass. Nothing moved.

Aphrodite came through the door, stepping slowly and carefully, heel to toe, so as to make as little sound as possible. A few feet inside the building was an overturned desk lying on its side. Aphrodite went down on one knee next to the desk and sat quietly in the gloom waiting for her eyes to adjust and soaking up the sounds around her.

"Hit it with the sledgehammer!" yelled someone. It sounded like the voice was coming from the other end of the warehouse.

"Shut up," said another voice.

"Just do it already," responded the first voice, who sounded like a young man. There was a series of loud, sharp, banging noises, metal striking metal.

Aphrodite came silently to her feet, weapon locked out in front of her in both hands. In the dim interior ahead, she could see shapes moving. They seemed to be thirty or forty meters away. She thought there were three. She began to advance steadily in their direction.

"Ok," said someone. "It's open." That sounded like a new voice to Aphrodite. If so, she was right, there were at least three of them.

"Get the sprayer," said guy who had first spoken. He wasn't yelling anymore.

There was the sound of metal wheels rolling on a gritty metal track. A door opened on the side of the warehouse facing the ships. Two young white men were clearly visible now in the light streaming in. A third man, who looked African-American, was still standing in the shadows.

Aphrodite continued to move. None of the men gave any indication they had seen her.

"Roll it over here," said one of the white men. He was short and muscular with a wispy, ginger-colored beard and a white skullcap. That was Eddie, thought Aphrodite. She recognized him from a photo Irene had shown her.

"Ok," said the black man. He was the one whose voice Aphrodite had heard first. There was a screeching sound, and then the man came out of the shadows wheeling some kind of big, blue canister mounted on a two-wheeled cart. Long plastic hoses hung in coils on the sides of the canister.

"Let's do this," said the other white man standing next to Eddie. He looked maybe eighteen. His face was pockmarked with acne.

"Hook up the hoses," said the black man. He pushed the cart with the canister on it outside the warehouse onto the dock and left it sitting there. The gray hull of one of the Navy ships was clearly visible on the other side of the pier.

"Got it," said Eddie. He turned and started toward some large metal buckets that were sitting on the ground less than ten meters from where Aphrodite was now. He was looking right at her.

"Freeze," said Aphrodite. She kept advancing.

"What the fuck?" said Eddie. Behind him the two other men dropped what they were doing and turned to see what was happening.

"You're Eddie," said Aphrodite. She was scanning the area and the hands of all three men as she came forward. There were no weapons in sight.

"Yeah," said Eddie. "Who the hell are you?"

"Your Mom sent me," said Aphrodite. She was only a few feet away now. She still had the pistol out in front of her, and she was sweeping back and forth covering all three men as she moved.

"Are you shitting me?" said Eddie.

"Your mom sent somebody to hunt you down?" asked the black guy.

"I'm a grown man," said Eddie.

"I don't give a shit," said Aphrodite. She stopped right in front of Eddie with the barrel of her gun sighted on the bridge of his nose. "You're never old enough to worry your mother."

"Damn," said the black guy. "Fuckin' social worker with a gun."

"What's all this gear for?" asked Aphrodite. She nodded with her head toward the canister on the cart.

"It's a sprayer," said Eddie.

"For spraying what?" asked Aphrodite.

"Paint," said Eddie.

"Paint?" said Aphrodite. She glanced at the metal buckets next to where she and Eddie were now standing. The label on the one closest to her said "Olympic – Fast Hide – Flat".

"We're gonna spray paint graffiti on the ships," said Eddie. "They use them to carry troops and cargo to the Middle East."

"To fight our Muslim brothers," said the guy with the acne in a small, terrified voice. "'Cept right now the ships are in mothballs."

"Graffiti," said Aphrodite. She lowered her weapon to her side and walked over to the canister on the cart. Printed on its side were the words, "Graco Portable Paint Sprayer".

"You still gonna shoot us?" said the black guy.

"Go home," said Aphrodite. She didn't know whether to laugh or cry. All this to stop somebody from spray-painting crap on a ship. "Go home. Get a job. Don't ever come back here."

"Don't have to tell me twice," said the black guy. He headed for the door. The kid with acne jogged after him like he was afraid Aphrodite would change her mind. Eddie started to turn to leave as well.

"Oh no, boy," said Aphrodite to Eddie. "You're going home to Mommy to get your ass whipped."

CHAPTER TWENTY-FIVE

1025 HOURS, 14 AUGUST 2002.
COUNTERTERRORISM CENTER STRATEGIC THREATS TEAM,
CIA HEADQUARTERS, LANGLEY, VIRGINIA.

"That's it," said Spalding, the head of the Strategic Threats Team. He dropped a file folder onto the desk of his administrative assistant, Janice, and smiled.

"Enjoy some time off, sir," said Janice. She was a prim, older women dressed impeccably in a neatly tailored suit.

"I will," said Spalding. He'd come in for a couple of hours to clear the last time sensitive matters from his desk, and now he was off to his cabin in the mountains for some much needed relaxation with his family. "See you in about ten days."

"Keep the cell phone off," said Janice. "The world will survive without you for a little while."

"You got it," said Spalding. He was already heading for the door to the hallway and the elevators.

"Hey, boss," said Rogers. He came bounding out of his office a few doors down from Spalding's and trotted after him. He was wearing his trademark cardigan and penny loafers.

"I am off the clock, Rogers," said Spalding wearily. He stopped and turned. "Really."

"Yeah, I know," said Rogers. He came to a halt in front of Spalding and held up a folder with a Top Secret coversheet stapled to it. "But, you're going to want to read this."

"Off the clock, Rogers."

"Trust me, boss," said Rogers.

Spalding squinted hard at Rogers. His head hurt. His back ached from hunching over a computer. He could already taste the sunshine and fresh air in the mountains. But, Rogers was the best analyst he had. Spalding took the file and began to scan the contents.

"Interesting, huh?" said Rogers after about thirty seconds.

"What do we know about this cop?" asked Spalding. He was still reading.

"He is Pashtun," said Rogers. "Clean as they come. Like he's trying twice as hard just to show that all his people aren't wearing suicide vests and blowing themselves up."

"And he's telling us all this why?" asked Spalding. He flipped to the next page in the file and kept scanning.

"Because he's concerned that what it all means is that Lashkar is launching an attack inside the United States," said Rogers.

"And because he got himself sidewise with ISI, and they want his ass," said Spalding. He was still reading. Behind him Janice was scowling at Rogers.

"He says he thinks ISI is in on this," said Rogers.

"On an attack on the United States," said Spalding. His eyes were blurry. He was tired of reading. He flipped closed the folder and handed it back to Rogers.

"Yes," said Rogers.

"Lashkar, the group that has never attacked Western targets before," said Spalding.

"And whose ideology is virtually indistinguishable from that of AQ," said Rogers.

"What kind of attack are we talking about?" asked Spalding. He glanced down at his watch. He had promised Christine he'd be home by eleven.

"Could be biological," said Rogers.

"Biological," said Spalding.

"Could be," said Rogers. "Some of the training materials seem to indicate that."

"Seem to," said Spalding.

"Seem to," said Rogers.

"Could be," said Spalding.

"Could be," said Rogers.

"Anything else at all in the whole world that supports any of this?" asked Spalding.

"Bunch of people sick, some dead in Baltimore," said Rogers.

"That aquarium thing?" asked Spalding.

"Yes," said Rogers.

"Aren't they saying that's Legionnaire's Disease?" asked Spalding.

"They don't know what it is, boss," said Rogers. "That's just for the public so they don't have to admit they're scratching their heads. I talked to a guy I know at the Centers for Disease Control this morning. He says he thinks it might be the plague."

"The plague. In Baltimore," said Spalding.

"The plague. In Baltimore," said Rogers.

"So, you're telling me that the attack already happened and that all of this was about infecting a few people in Baltimore?" said Spalding. He glanced at his watch again.

"Maybe it was a test," said Rogers.

"Assuming it was the plague, Rogers, how did all these people get it?' asked Spalding.

"My guy says it may have originated with one lady," said Rogers. "Seems like she was patient zero, the one who went down first."

"Isn't the plague spread by fleas?" said Spalding. "How would one lady spread it to other people?"

"You can get it directly from someone else if it is the pneumatic form," said Rogers. "That's what they think happened in Europe in the 1300's with the Black Death."

"And how would you give someone that?" asked Spalding.

"Don't know," said Rogers.

"Does your buddy know?" asked Spalding. He was feeling less sympathetic all the time.

"No," said Rogers.

"Is anybody at CDC listening to your buddy?" asked Spalding.

"Not so far," admitted Rogers.

"Ok, Rogers," said Spalding. "Follow-up on this. Find out what really happened in Baltimore for starters. And pump out some requirements to the field to see if anybody anywhere on the planet can confirm even the smallest portion of what this Pashtun cops says."

"If it was a test, boss," said Rogers. "We may not have a lot of time."

"If," said Spalding.

"If," said Rogers.

"I am not sounding the alarm about a biological terrorist attack on the U.S. by an Islamic group with no history of actions against American targets and supported by the intelligence service of what most people in DC consider a friendly government based on that, Rogers," said Spalding.

"Right," said Rogers.

"If you come up with anything tangible, call me," said Spalding.

"Yes, boss," said Rogers. Janice was still giving him the eye.

"And, Rogers," said Spalding. "If you call me, you'd better have something good." He turned to leave.

"Yes, boss," said Rogers. He tucked the file under his arm and shuffled back toward his office without making eye contact with Janice. He had phone calls to make and messages to send. No matter what the boss said, something was going on.

CHAPTER TWENTY-SIX

1035 HOURS, 14 AUGUST 2002.
FELLS POINT, BALTIMORE, MARYLAND.

"I ought to kick your ass," bellowed Irene. Her face was bright red, and she had a heavy wooden rolling pin in one hand. Eddie was standing across the narrow row house kitchen from her and struggling to keep his distance.

"Don't kill him after I went to all the trouble to find him," said Aphrodite. She was sitting on a counter to one side wincing.

"We were doing what God commanded," said Eddie weakly.

"God commanded you to spray graffiti on a ship?" yelled Irene. "Bullshit!"

"You wouldn't understand," responded Eddie.

"You're right," said Irene. "God, Eleni, can you get through to this boy?"

"I'm out of here," said Eddie. He turned and started toward the kitchen door.

"No," said Aphrodite.

"What?" said Eddie.

"No," repeated Aphrodite. She hopped down off the counter and squared her feet.

"Listen, Eleni, or whatever your name is," said Eddie. "I listened to you. I came here. But this is Groundhog Day. Same shit, all over again. I'm out."

"Shut up," said Aphrodite.

"I've heard it all before," said Eddie.

"Not this," said Aphrodite.

"Listen," said Irene.

"You want to worship God, be my guest," said Aphrodite. "And call him whatever name you want. But, don't worship death."

"You don't know what you're talking about," said Eddie.

"I know exactly what I am talking about," said Aphrodite. "I know, because I worshipped death for years. We called him Marx or Mao or Stalin depending on the year, but it was the same. In the end, it was the same. It was about death."

"It was just graffiti, Eleni," said Eddie.

"Today," said Aphrodite. "Today, games for children. Tomorrow, someone is dead."

"What do you want from me?" asked Eddie.

"Live," said Aphrodite. "Love your mother. Make peace."

"You want me to stay," said Eddie.

"I want you to choose love over hate," said Aphrodite.

Eddie paused. He looked at the door then back to Irene.

"Please," said Irene. She put the rolling pin down next to her on the counter.

"Ok," said Eddie. "Just let me go snag my bike, and I'll be right back."

"Where's your motorcycle?" asked Irene.

"Chained up behind the sisters' house by the Community Center," said Eddie. "I left it there for safekeeping yesterday." He held up a set of keys on a key chain in his right hand.

"I'll go get the bike," said Aphrodite.

"I'll be back," said Eddie.

"Stay here," said Aphrodite. She pushed past Eddie and took the keys out of his hand. Then she went out the door and headed for the street to hail a cab.

◆◆◆

Twenty-five minutes later, the cab dropped Aphrodite in the street in front of the sisters' row house. Aphrodite paid the Nigerian driver and walked down the alley next to the building. She'd had enough of banging on doors and being ignored.

The garbage-strewn alley ended at another alley that ran behind the row of homes, which included the sisters' place. There was an identical row of homes on the other side of the alley facing the other way. Aphrodite turned left and rounded the corner into this new alley. She was right behind the sisters' place now.

There was no motorcycle in the alley. The backyard of the sisters' row house was surrounded with a ragged wooden fence about eight feet in height that blocked Aphrodite's view. There was a gate through the fence that opened on the alley. It was unlocked. Aphrodite pulled it open and stuck her head inside to see if the Eddie had put his motorcycle in the yard.

The backyard of the row house was bare earth, weeds and trash cans overflowing with refuse. Chained to the sagging wooden back porch of the home was a large Japanese racing bike. Aphrodite picked her way across the yard and started fumbling for the lock on the chain.

"Tonight..." It was a voice from somewhere nearby. Aphrodite stopped what she was doing with the bike and looked up. She could hear a voice but not what was being said. It was muffled, like it was coming from inside the row house.

So someone is home, thought Aphrodite. She walked a few feet closer to the row house and then stopped to listen. She could tell it was a woman talking now. It sounded like Afiyah.

In front of Aphrodite were short windows set close to the ground. They appeared to open into the basement of home. Aphrodite squatted down and peered into one of the windows. Facing her was Afiyah, head wrapped tight in a white scarf. She was speaking to someone standing in the shadows. Aphrodite couldn't tell who it was.

Sitting on the floor next to Afiyah was a plastic cooler. Sitting next to the cooler was a cardboard box with something that looked like a small gray box pictured on it. Aphrodite could see the words "Pro Neb" but couldn't make out the rest of the wording.

Afiyah was waving her hands as she spoke. Her face was hard, and there were dark circles under her eyes. She stopped talking and started nodding her head. The other person was talking now.

A rat scurried in the garbage on the ground around the trashcans. A stray cat crouching on the fence above jumped for it. A metal lid fell to the ground and clanged against a discarded cinder block with a sound like a metal gong.

Afiyah looked up, saw Aphrodite and pointed. Aphrodite straightened up and stepped back. Reflexively, the thought of walking away flashed through her mind.

To her right and above, the door onto the raised back porch opened. A woman in a black headscarf Aphrodite had never seen before opened the door. Behind her inside the house there was the sound of running on stairs.

"Who are you?" said the woman in the black headscarf.

"I'm Eleni," said Aphrodite.

"She's a friend," said Afiyah. She pushed past the other woman on the porch and came toward the stairs, which lead down into the back yard.

"Hello," said Aphrodite. "I waited for you this morning."

"I'm sorry," said Afiyah as she came down the steps. "I got tied up with things here." She forced a smile.

"I just wanted to get Eddie's bike," said Aphrodite. "I found him."

"That's great," replied Afiyah. "But come meet the sisters before you leave." She took Aphrodite by the hand and tugged her toward the steps. "Come." She smiled again.

Mechanically, Aphrodite followed Afiyah up the stairs and into the home. Ahead of her she could see a long, narrow hallway. At the other end, in the gloom of the interior, she could see a huddled group of women, all wearing head scarves and long dresses.

Aphrodite stepped inside. To her right was a tiny kitchen that smelled of grease and garlic. To the left was a doorway to a steep stairwell. Aphrodite looked down the stairs. At the bottom she could see a man with blond hair. He was looking up at her. His eyes were a piercing blue.

There was something wrong. No man should be here. The hair on the back of Aphrodite's neck bristled. Her stomach dropped. She started to turn. Too late.

Afiyah hit Aphrodite in the small of her back with her shoulder. Aphrodite stumbled forward and pitched into the stairwell. Her right hand clawed at the banister for a brief instant and then came free. She crashed down the stairs in a tangle of arms and legs. Her head cracked against the cement floor at the bottom. Blood oozed into her curly, blond hair. Her eyes closed.

"Bring me some duct tape," said Anwar. "And, get the sisters ready to move."

CHAPTER TWENTY-SEVEN

1245 HOURS, 14 AUGUST 2002.
FELLS POINT, BALTIMORE, MARYLAND.

The cab pulled to a stop in the street in front of Irene's house. Bill climbed out, tossed cash to the driver, shouldered his backpack and walked to the door. There was a doorbell on the right. He pressed it.

Someone came down the hallway inside. The door opened. A young man wearing a white skullcap and sporting a ginger colored beard was standing inside.

"You're Eddie," said Bill.

"You must be Bill," said Eddie.

"She found you," said Bill.

"Yeah," said Eddie. "I think she would have found me anywhere."

"She would have found you on the dark side of the moon," said Bill. He stepped inside as Eddie moved out of the way. "Where is she?"

"Not sure," said Eddie. Bill was walking ahead of him down the hallway in the direction of the kitchen in the rear of the home. Irene was standing in the kitchen with a cell phone in her hand.

"She's not answering her phone," said Irene.

"Where'd she go?" asked Bill. He dropped his backpack on the floor in the kitchen.

"She went to get Eddie's motorcycle," said Irene. "Up by the Muslim Community Center."

"How long?" asked Bill. He looked at his watch.

"She left two hours ago," said Eddie.

"Maybe she had an accident on the bike," said Irene.

"Not Eleni," said Bill. "She doesn't know how to fall."

"When did you talk to her last?" asked Irene.

"This morning," said Bill. He pulled out his cell phone. "I've been texting her but not getting an answer." He punched in numbers on the phone, held it to his ear for a moment, then flipped it off and shoved it back in his pocket.

"No luck?" asked Irene.

"It's not on," said Bill. His mind was racing.

"Maybe her battery's dead," said Eddie. He shrugged.

"Eleni doesn't forget to charge her phone," said Bill through gritted teeth. The feeling that he was late for something was more intense now. "She doesn't fall. She doesn't make mistakes. "

"Ok," said Eddie.

"Not ok," said Bill. "Take me where she went. Now."

◆◆◆

Twenty minutes later, Bill pulled up in front of the sisters' house in Irene's car. Eddie was strapped in next to him. Irene had stayed behind in case they were wrong, everything was fine, and Aphrodite came back under her own power.

Bill bounded up the stairs onto the front porch of the row house and pressed the bell. Eddie came up the steps behind him and tried the door. It was locked. There was no sound from inside.

"You said she came to get your bike," said Bill. "Where did you leave it?"

"Chained up in the backyard," said Eddie. He pointed around the side of the building.

Bill jumped the railing on the side of the porch and landed running in the alley. Eddie came down the steps and followed.

The gate in the back fence was open. Bill went through at a run and up the stairs onto the back porch.

"That's my bike," yelled Eddie as he came through the gate behind Bill. He pointed at the Japanese racing bike chained to the porch. Bill didn't turn to look. He was cupping his hands around his face and trying to see through the back windows of the house.

"There has to be someone home," said Eddie as he walked up the steps. "There are probably ten sisters that live here." He walked up to the back door of the row house and pounded on it with his fist.

"Yeah?" said Bill. There was no sound from inside the building.

"Maybe not," said Eddie. He pounded on the door again.

"Do these sisters have a vehicle?" asked Bill.

"Yeah," said Eddie. "It's an old Chevy Suburban."

"Where do they park it?" asked Bill.

"Out front," said Eddie.

"Did you see it coming in?" asked Bill. He reached inside his jacket and pulled out the Glock that he had left with Irene for safekeeping when he went to Mexico.

"No," said Eddie.

"Stand back," said Bill. He pushed Eddie to one side and stepped back two paces from the door.

"You can't break in," said Eddie.

"The fuck I can't," said Bill. He rushed forward and kicked the door right next to the doorknob. The doorframe around the latch splintered. The door flew open and slapped against the hallway wall inside.

Bill snapped the Glock out in front of him in a two-hand grip. His eyes scanned the dim interior of the house. Nothing moved.

"Stay directly behind me," said Bill. "Nowhere else."

"Right," said Eddie in small voice.

Bill went through the door smoothly and silently, clearing the space in front of him as he went. His eyes and his weapon worked as one unit. Where his eyes went, the muzzle of the weapon pointed as well.

The kitchen to the right was empty. The hall ahead was clear. To Bill's left was a narrow, wooden stairway into a basement. The wooden banister in the stairwell was ripped loose from the wall at the top and sagging toward the floor. At the bottom of the stairs dark blood was smeared on the concrete floor.

Bill went down the steps one at a time, with his back against the wall on the left and his eyes fixed on what he could see to the right through the open stairwell as he descended. Eddie came two steps behind, almost holding his breath.

Bill knelt at the bottom of the steps and touched the blood on the floor. It was still sticky. There were long, curly, blond hairs matted in it.

"What's the plate on that Suburban?" asked Bill. He stood and looked at Eddie.

"I don't know," said Eddie.

"Who does?" asked Bill.

"The imam," said Eddie. "Why?"

"Because they're gone," said Bill. "And, they took Eleni with them."

CHAPTER TWENTY-EIGHT

1259 HOURS, 14 AUGUST 2002.
ANNE ARUNDEL COUNTY, MARYLAND.

Aphrodite opened her eyes and lifted her head. She was sitting upright in a straight-backed wooden chair. Her vision was blurry. She blinked her eyes, and it cleared slightly.

It was cold and damp. The wall in front of Aphrodite was bare cinder block. The floor of the room in which she was sitting was cement. No lights were on, but Aphrodite could make out the outlines of her surroundings in the uncertain light that filtered down a wooden staircase about twenty feet away.

Aphrodite looked down. Her bare arms were duct taped to the arms of the wooden chair. Her legs were duct taped to the legs of the chair. Her clothes were gone. She was dressed only in her black bra and panties.

There were occasional footsteps above her. People were walking around. It sounded like there were several of them at least.

Aphrodite swiveled her head to survey her surroundings. Her skull felt like it had been shattered. There was blood matted in her hair. Her neck was stiff and sore. She walled the pain out and scanned the area around her.

The room seemed empty of furniture except for a long wooden workbench set next to one wall. There was no sign of a door. On one side of the room high in the wall were three small cellar windows. They seemed to have been papered over with something, but light was leaking in around the edges.

The room was unfinished. Above Aphrodite, the ceiling was unfinished as well. Water pipes and electrical lines were dimly visible. She could hear water rushing when someone elsewhere in the house flushed a toilet or ran water.

Aphrodite added up the facts at her disposal. She was apparently in the basement of a home. She had no idea where. It was still light outside, so she had probably been unconscious for only a matter of hours. That did not help much. In that time she could have been moved 150 miles.

The door at the top of the stairs opened. Light flooded down the rough, wooden steps. Someone began to descend. Then another person followed.

The man with the blond hair came down the steps and flipped a light switch on the wall. Fluorescent lights hanging from the ceiling kicked on. The man came across the basement floor and stopped directly in front of Aphrodite. Afiyah followed him and stood on his right.

"I am Anwar," said the man.

"Fuck you," said Aphrodite. She looked from Anwar to Afiyah and then back again.

"A woman should refrain from the use of profane language," said Anwar.

"Where are my fucking clothes?" said Aphrodite.

"We removed them to make sure you were not carrying any kind of tracking device," said Afiyah. She pursed her lips slightly.

"Really," said Aphrodite. "Not to turn on Brother Anwar here?" She sneered.

"It is unfortunate for you that you had to show up when you did," said Anwar.

"I have no idea what the hell you are talking about," said Aphrodite.

"We could not let you go," continued Anwar.

"You're still babbling," said Aphrodite. She looked at Afiyah. Her eyes seemed focused on some distant object, rather than on what was happening in front of her.

"You have no idea what kind of trouble you have bought yourself," said Aphrodite. "Bill will find me, and he will kill you."

"I have no idea who Bill is," said Anwar. "But nothing he can do will possibly make any difference." He turned to Afiyah. "Bring down the sisters."

"Yes, brother," said Afiyah. She turned and ascended the stairs. Anwar walked to the long wooden workbench. Aphrodite could see now that sitting on the bench were the cooler and the box she had seen before. Anwar stood facing her and began to take things out of both the cooler and the box and arrange them in front of him.

The door at the top of the stairs opened again. People began to descend into the basement. They were all women, the same ones Aphrodite had seen in the row house. There were a total of eight of them not counting Afiyah. They lined up in front of the workbench facing Anwar.

"Do you know what the Black Death was?" asked Anwar. He was looking past the women to Aphrodite.

"Eat shit," said Aphrodite.

"It began in Italy," said Anwar. "And then it swept across all of Europe. Entire towns died. People barricaded themselves in their homes and prayed to God. But your God did not save them. They died by the millions."

"Fascinating," said Aphrodite.

"Historians still argue over how many died," said Anwar. "Some say a third of the population. Others say half. The dead lay unburied in piles in the streets." He reached down, picked up a white facemask like doctors wore and put it on.

"We are ready, brother," said Afiyah.

"Then let us begin," said Anwar. In front of him was the gray machine that Aphrodite had seen pictured on the box in the row house. Anwar took some sort of plastic receptacle form the top of it and opened a lid it its top. Then he took a tube from the cooler and poured some sort of thick, yellowish slush out of the tube into the receptacle.

"Who is first?" asked Anwar as if he were handing out candy to children.

"Pick me," said several of the women at once.

"Choose Sister Bobbie," said Afiyah. "She has always been the first to complete her chores."

"Very good," said Anwar. He put the tube back in the cooler and snapped the receptacle back into the gray box. Then he connected a long, clear plastic tube to the box. On the end of the tube was a plastic facemask with an elastic band on it.

"I am ready," said Sister Bobbie. She was a large, square white woman with her head wrapped tight in a black head cloth.

"Place this over your face, sister," said Anwar. He helped Bobbie pull the elastic over her head and seat the mask on her face.

"God is great," said Afiyah. He eyes were cast heavenward.

"God is great," said the sisters in unison.

"Yes, he is," said Anwar. "Now breathe deeply, sister Bobbie." He reached down and flipped a switch on the side of gray box. A motor kicked on, and a fan began to blow. A thin, yellow mist filled the hose and the mask on Bobbie's face.

"There are three forms of the plague, the disease that caused the Black Death," said Anwar. He was talking to Aphrodite again. "Two of them are spread by fleas which bite infected individuals and then bite individuals not yet infected. The third kind, pneumonic plague, is more interesting. It infects the lungs. And it spreads by breath itself."

"You are a sick bastard," said Aphrodite.

"That is enough," said Anwar to Sister Bobbie. He turned off the machine, removed the mask from Bobbie's face and then placed it on the woman next to her. Then he took another tube from the cooler and refilled the receptacle.

"God is great," said the sisters again. Anwar flipped the switch. The machine began to whir. The woman wearing the mask gulped down the yellow mist.

Aphrodite looked down at her feet. The duct tape was wrapped a quarter inch thick around her arms and legs. The chair was duct taped just as heavily to a wooden support post behind it. She could not move. She closed her eyes and tried to shut out the madness around her. One by one the sisters took their turns swallowing death, with Anwar refilling the receptacle for each.

Finally the last woman was done. Anwar turned off the machine. The sisters began to file back upstairs. Aphrodite looked up. Anwar and Afiyah were standing in front of her. Anwar was holding the gray box with the facemask attached in his hands. A long extension cord ran from the back of the box to a socket in the wall.

"Hold her head," said Anwar. He nodded his head to Afiyah who walked around behind Aphrodite and grabbed her head in both arms.

"Fuck you!" screamed Aphrodite. She twisted her head back and forth violently, but her muscles were tired and sore, and Afiyah had her in a tight headlock.

"I am giving you the chance to die in the service of the true faith," said Anwar. "You should thank me." He pushed the mask over Aphrodite's face and flipped the switch on the box. The machine turned on. The fan began to blow.

Aphrodite closed her eyes and her mouth and threw her head from side to side. Afiyah tightened her grip. Anwar crushed the mask over Aphrodite's mouth and nose and held it there.

There was a warm mist blowing against Aphrodite's face. It felt like a light spray of Vaseline, sticking to her skin and oozing into her nostrils and the corners of her mouth. Her lungs were beginning to burn. The pain in her head screamed for relief.

"Breathe," said Anwar.

Aphrodite's lungs were on fire. She did not care. She clamped her jaws tighter together. She refused to submit.

"Breathe," hissed Afiyah in her ear.

Aphrodite's lungs screamed with pain. She willed herself to hold on, and her will failed. Her mouth opened. She sucked for air. Huge, sticky, warm gasps of the yellowish mist filled her lungs.

"Good," said Anwar. He turned off the machine and took away the mask. Afiyah released her hold.

"He will find me, you bastard," screamed Aphrodite.

"Maybe," said Anwar. "But, whoever he is, he will find you dead." He turned and walked toward the stairs.

"He has given you a chance to die in the service of God," said Afiyah. She was standing in front of Aphrodite now. "You really should thank him." She turned and followed Anwar up the stairs. The light went out. The darkness returned.

CHAPTER TWENTY-NINE

1303 HOURS, 14 AUGUST 2002.
BALTIMORE, MARYLAND.

"What's the plate on the Suburban the Center owns?" said Bill as he strode into the imam's office.

"Who are you?" said the imam. He looked up over his reading glasses through bloodshot eyes. His desk was awash in grant applications, tax bills and requests from members of the congregation for assistance.

"We need to find the sisters," said Eddie. He came through the door and stepped up beside Bill in front of the imam's desk.

"Eddie, you're found," said the imam. He took off his glasses, tossed them onto the clutter on his big desk and stood up.

"I need to know the license plate on the Suburban the sisters use," said Bill. "It's an emergency."

"Is there a problem?" said Mrs. LaRooche. She was standing in the doorway of the imam's office with worry in her pale, gray eyes.

"I'm sure we'll be fine," said the imam. He smiled reassuringly at Mrs. LaRooche, who nodded her gray head and went back to her desk and her bookkeeping in the office across the hall.

"The sisters have disappeared, imam," said Eddie.

"And, they have taken my wife with them," said Bill through clenched teeth. He stole a look at his watch. They were losing time. Every five minutes meant a minimum of one more mile added to the radius of the area they would have to search.

"Who are you?" repeated the imam.

"Bill Boyle," said Bill.

"And just what in the name of God are you two talking about, Mr. Boyle?" asked the imam.

"My wife was here," said Bill. "Blond, Greek."

"I remember her," said the imam. "As I recall she came here with Sister Afiyah."

"She found me," said Eddie.

"Ok," said the imam. "And?"

"And she went back to the sisters' house to get my bike," said Eddie.

"And never returned," said Bill.

"Have you gone to the house?" asked the imam.

"You're not listening," said Bill. He stepped forward and slapped the imam's desk with the palm of his hand. "We went to the house. We went inside. There's blood at the bottom of the basement stairs with my wife's hair matted in it. All the sisters are gone. Every one. And the car."

"Maybe your wife got hurt, and they took her to the hospital," said the imam.

"All of them?" said Bill.

"Their clothes are gone," said Eddie.

"You think the sisters abducted your wife," said the imam.

"Yes," said Bill.

"Why?" asked the imam.

"No idea," said Bill. "I'll let you know when I find her."

"You're out of your cotton-pickin' mind," said the imam. "Sister Afiyah has done nothing since she has been here, but take in other women who had lost their way and give them a place to live and worship."

"What is the license plate number?" barked Bill.

"I'm calling the cops," said the imam. He reached for the phone.

"Imam!" yelled Jimmy Owens. He was standing in the doorway holding a basketball. The other members of the mosque basketball team were clustered behind him.

"What now?" said the imam.

"Tyrell just came up from Pigtown, and he says the sisters' Suburban is sitting under the Jones Falls burnin'," said Jimmy. His bushy Afro was quivering with excitement. Behind him Tyrell, the team center, shook his dreadlocks in the affirmative.

"Where?" said Bill.

"I'll drive," said the imam.

◆ ◆ ◆

They made it from the Center to the spot under the expressway in a little over ten minutes, with the imam at the wheel of his old midnight black Cadillac and Tyrell folded into the backseat to give directions. Bill checked his watch impatiently in the front passenger's seat the whole way, and Eddie tried not to get crushed by Tyrell in the back seat as they squealed around each corner.

They found the Suburban sitting amidst the concrete piers holding up Interstate 83, the Jones Falls expressway. Behind the Suburban and amidst the supports, what remained of the Jones Falls River crept through a trash strewn concrete trough. Across a narrow blacktopped road from the Suburban were the abandoned brick shells of the old cotton mills that once lined the river's banks. Black smoke from the burning Suburban drifted heavily toward downtown.

Bill was out of the vehicle and moving before the Cadillac came to a complete stop. There was a lone Baltimore City cop leaning on the hood of his patrol car to one side talking into his

246

radio and looking bored. Bill ignored him and made a beeline for the burning vehicle.

The Suburban had been burning for some time, and the fire had almost died out. A few orange flames licked out from under the hood periodically, but otherwise the hulk was blackened and smoking. The windows were gone. The rubber tires were melted and the metal rims exposed.

Bill walked around the vehicle and looked into the interior through the oily haze and heat. There was no one visible inside nor were there any suitcases or other personal belongings. The only exception was what looked to be an old bowling bag on the floor in the front seat. It was blackened and partially melted, but still recognizable.

"That your car?" yelled the cop.

"No," responded Bill without turning around. He reached out and tried pulling open the front passenger's side door, but the handle was too hot to grip.

"It was stolen," said the imam. He walked toward the cop.

"You'll have to file that report at the station," said the cop. "I'm just waiting till the fire department and the tow truck show up."

Bill walked over to the edge of a cluster of scraggly trees and bushes at the edge of the broken blacktop and picked up a couple of empty cardboard six pack beer carriers. He tore the carriers apart and wrapped his hands in flat strips of cardboard. Then we walked back to the Suburban, grabbed the door handle and yanked the door open.

The stench of burning plastic and insulation from inside the Suburban was intense. Bill leaned in, grabbed the smoking bowling bag and tossed it clear of the vehicle. Then, without closing the door, he walked over to the bag, squatted down and pried it open.

In the bottom of the bag was what looked like it had been some sort of electronic device. Using his cardboard mitts, Bill reached in, grabbed the object and dropped it onto the pavement next to the bag.

It wasn't a device. It was several, partially melted and fused together now by the heat of the fire. By Bill's count there were at least ten of them, all cell phones. All but one looked to be some sort of cheap flip phone. The tenth was a red Blackberry.

"What's that?" said Eddie. He had come up behind Bill and was watching him poke at the melted mass of phones.

"They've gone off the grid," said Bill.

"I'm lost," said Eddie.

"They've destroyed all of their cell phones," said Bill. He stood. "That means they don't want anyone to be able to track them by identifying where on the system the phones are."

"That's bad," said Eddie.

"It gets worse," said Bill. "That red Blackberry belonged to Eleni. I bought it for her about a month ago."

"This makes no sense, " said the imam. He had finished talking to the cop and walked over to where Bill and Eddie were standing. "We're talking about Sister Afiyah and eight sisters who have dedicated their lives to God. They wouldn't hurt anyone."

"Blond man with them." The voice came from somewhere in the direction of the trees where Bill had scrounged the cardboard. All three men turned to look.

"White boy," added the man who had spoken. He was a tall, white man in an old olive drab Army jacket. His long hair and beard were matted and almost covered his face. He was standing in the brush a few feet from the road.

"What did you say?" asked Bill. He moved slowly in the direction of the man while checking the area to see who else might be about to materialize.

"I saw them," said the man. "From my camp." He pointed up into the trees toward a ragged blue tarp and a rusted shopping cart.

"You live here?" asked the imam.

"Since I lost my job," said the man. He reached up and scratched at the tangle of fur on his face.

"What did you see?" asked Bill.

"You got anything to drink?" asked the man. He squinted at Bill to see what reaction his words might provoke.

"No," said Bill. "But, if you tell me what you saw I'll give you twenty to buy some."

"Forty," said the man.

"Done," said Bill.

"Show me the money," said the man. He walked down out of the brush and out onto the blacktop.

Bill reached in his wallet, pulled out two twenties and held them up in the air. The man scurried forward, snapped the bills out of Bill's hand and then stepped back quickly.

"Talk to me," said Bill.

"They got out of the Suburban and into an old minivan that was sittin' here," said the man.

"Who brought the van?" asked Bill.

"I don't know," said the man. "I ain't seen it before. I went over by the supermarket to go through the dumpsters for a few hours. When I got back it was sitting there."

"How many people?" asked Bill.

"There was nine women in headscarves," said the man. "Like they was Muslims 'cept they weren't Arab. And one guy with blond hair. White boy, like I said. Young. They had bags with clothes and stuff and a couple of boxes."

"How about a lady with blond hair?" asked Bill.

"They was carrying a lady like that," said the man. "Like she was real sick or something, like she couldn't walk."

"Shit," said Bill.

"This is impossible," said the imam. He put his hands over his face and then ran them back through his short, graying hair.

"And then right after they got the last thing out, the cooler, they set the car on fire and drove away," said the man.

"What did you say?" asked Eddie.

"A cooler?" said Bill.

"Yeah," said the man. "A cooler. The last thing the white kid did before he torched the Suburban was to get this plastic cooler out of the front seat and carry it to the van. Carried like it was filled with gold or something too."

"Christ," said Bill. He looked heavenward and closed his eyes. He felt the world starting to spin around him.

"What?" said Eddie. "What do you thinks in the cooler?"

"The end of the world," said Bill. His eyes were still closed.

"You're not making any sense," said the imam.

"I'll explain while you drive," said Bill.

"Where are we going?" asked the imam.

"To call in the cavalry," said Bill.

CHAPTER THIRTY

1657 HOURS, 14 AUGUST 2002.
ANNE ARUNDEL COUNTY, MARYLAND.

At some point Aphrodite had blacked out. She didn't know when. She lifted her head and blinked her eyes to clear away the crust that had gathered on them. Her face felt sticky and tight. Her neck was knotted in pain.

Above her in the house Aphrodite could hear voices and the creaking of floorboards as people moved about. There was still light leaking in around the paper over the basement windows. Outside there was the occasional sound of a car or a truck passing by.

Aphrodite craned her neck to see as much of the room as possible. In the dim light she saw nothing but bare floor and the work bench on which Anwar had set his machine of death. Somewhere in the darkness something small moved.

Aphrodite looked down at her arms and legs and the tape that bound them to the chair. She strained as hard as she could, but the tape did not budge. She could feel that her hands and feet were going slightly numb, because her bindings had been wrapped so tightly. Her ass throbbed from sitting on the hard wooden chair.

Behind Aphrodite the chair was bound with more tape to a wooden post. She forced her head around to one side as far as she could to take a look at it. Her neck screamed with pain. She ignored it. She had no clear idea of how fast the plague worked, but she knew enough to understand her time was short. If she stayed where she was, she was already dead.

The post was a standard six by six. Its edges were sharp and regular. In the cold the tape around the post seemed to have lost some of its adhesiveness. It looked stiff and seemed to be separating slightly from the wood around which it had been wrapped.

Aphrodite turned her head back to the front and closed her eyes for a moment to ease the pain. Tears were forming in the corners of her eyes, and she felt all the more frustrated that she could not wipe them away. She wanted to scream, but stifled the urge. Above her the footsteps continued, as did the low murmur of voices.

Aphrodite leaned back hard against the chair and sat as straight as she could. Then she pushed with both feet against the concrete floor as if to stand. Nothing. The chair did not move. She pushed again. Still nothing. Her legs ached, and the small of her back tensed like a taught rubber band.

Three more times, Aphrodite repeated the attempt. Each time she failed. She was a strong woman, with long, lean muscles in her legs and arms. It did not matter. She could not move the chair.

Something scratched again in the corner. Someone ran water upstairs. Aphrodite closed her eyes and tried to wall out the madness and the despair. Her defiance to Anwar aside, she understood exactly what her chances were.

No one knew where she was. No rescue was coming. The invisible microbes already at work inside of her would literally eat her alive, as she sat alone in the darkness, vomiting blood and raging with fever.

The temptation to quit was overwhelming. Outside of a few brief intervals with Bill, she had known nothing in her life but pain and struggle. It might be a relief to accept defeat.

Something moved up Aphrodite's bare right leg. She looked down. A black spider the size of a silver dollar was climbing over her knee.

Aphrodite closed her eyes. She willed herself to shut out her surroundings. She teetered on the edge of the abyss. She dreamt without sleeping.

◆ ◆ ◆

She was in Athens sitting cross-legged on a filthy concrete floor in front of a smoking kerosene heater. Around her were others, grubby and drawn like she was, eyes hollow from life on the street. She was sixteen, and she was homeless.

Across from her sat Pavlos. He was twenty, bearded and three times her size. He stank of ouzo and pot. Next to her was Nikos, the boy she had come to the apartment with. It was chilly outside. Winter was coming. Athens was damp and gray.

"Who's the bitch?" said Pavlos. He was talking about Aphrodite but he was talking to Nikos as if she wasn't there. Aphrodite looked at Nikos. He stared at an imaginary spot on the dirty floor and picked at dirt under his fingernails. He didn't lift his head. He didn't answer Pavlos. He was a coward.

"Do you fuck, bitch?" said Pavlos. He laughed, took a big swallow of ouzo from a greasy bottle in his right hand and looked at the other men in the circle around the heater as if he had said something of note. They grunted in support. He laughed again.

"Not pigs like you," said Aphrodite. She was maybe a hundred pounds. She was not a coward.

"You do if I say you do," said Pavlos. He took another swallow of ouzo, set the bottle down on the floor and stood. Nikos studied his fingernails. Aphrodite scrambled to her feet.

Pavlos' first punch knocked her off her feet and against the far wall. She staggered up. He hit her again. She went down, and the room went dark momentarily. She regained consciousness, as she was being dragged by her ankles into the next room and thrown onto a filthy mattress on the floor.

"Now you'll fuck," said Pavlos. He kicked the door closed, turned back to Aphrodite and started fumbling with his trousers.

"If you touch me, you're a dead man," said Aphrodite. She was on her feet in the center of the thin mattress with the crude knife she had stolen from a fisherman in Piraeus in her hand.

"I'll shove that knife up your ass, bitch," said Pavlos. He stumbled forward on uncertain feet. Aphrodite danced left. Pavlos tried to turn. He was too late.

Blood jumped across the room. Pavlos grabbed at the gash on the side of his neck. Aphrodite slashed at him again. He stumbled and fell. There was more blood now. She ran.

It was two days before she heard that he had died.

◆ ◆ ◆

Aphrodite opened her eyes. She was back in the chair in the basement. The spider was moving across her bare stomach toward her breasts. She closed her eyes and walled out the world again.

◆ ◆ ◆

Bill was lying on the bottom bunk of the tiny cabin in a Greek car ferry. Aphrodite was sitting on the side of the bunk, dressed only in a t-shirt, hair still damp from the shower. They were on their way to Santorini. It was the night before Takis died.

"You have no idea what I'm talking about, do you?" said Aphrodite.

"I understand, lady. I just don't have time for that right now," said Bill. His voiced cracked. He looked like he would cry.

"If you have time for nothing else, you have time for this," said Aphrodite. She leaned down and kissed Bill, and he pulled her into him. They made love for the first time.

◆ ◆ ◆

Aphrodite's eyes opened. She was sitting in the wooden chair. She was still bound. She was no longer contemplating surrender. She had fought her way out of hell to the chance of a life with the man she loved. Surrender now was not an option.

Aphrodite pushed with both legs as hard as she could and then relaxed. She pushed again, then relaxed. Ten, fifteen, twenty times she repeated the motion. She arched her back. She rocked from side to side.

The chair moved. The spider jumped to the floor.

Aphrodite forced her head around and strained to see out of the corners of her eyes. The tape had moved against the sharp edge of the post. Ever so slightly it was cut. The tear was maybe an eighth of an inch in length now. It did not matter. If she could cut the tape, everything else was a matter of time.

Aphrodite relaxed her legs and rested her muscles for a moment. Excitement and hope flooded back into her. She did not know how long it would take or what she would do when the chair was free, but she was no longer helpless and bound.

With a massive effort with both legs, Aphrodite pushed. The chair slid up the post. She relaxed and the chair dropped. She did it again. The chair moved more. She began to try to calculate her next moves.

The door opened at the top of the stairs. Aphrodite froze. Someone started down the steps.

CHAPTER THIRTY-ONE

1859 HOURS, 14 AUGUST 2002.
ANNE ARUNDEL COUNTY, MARYLAND.

The light came on. Afiyah was standing at the bottom of the stairs. She looked at Aphrodite and then walked over to her slowly.

"What do you want?" said Aphrodite.

"It is time for you to embrace your fate," said Afiyah. She walked from one side of the chair to the other examining the tape that held Aphrodite to the chair. She did not walk around behind the chair to look at the post.

"I need to go to the bathroom," said Aphrodite.

"Really," said Afiyah. She formed her thin, bloodless lips into an approximation of a smile.

"I've been tied up for hours," said Aphrodite. "Either you take me to the bathroom, or I piss on the floor."

"I am not a fool," said Afiyah.

"Your choice," said Aphrodite. "One way or the other, I am going to go."

Afiyah paused. She looked over Aphrodite's head for a moment at something on the other side of the room and then back at Aphrodite. Without saying anything she turned and went back up the stairs. She did not turn out the light.

Time passed. There were loud voices upstairs. One of them was male. Then there were footsteps on the stairs.

Afiyah came to the bottom of the steps and walked over to Aphrodite. Behind her were two other sisters, one a stout white woman, the other a tall, thin black woman. The white woman had a metal softball bat. The black woman had a piece of rusting pipe. In Afiyah's right hand was a box cutter. In her left was a fresh roll of duct tape.

"I am going to cut you free," said Afiyah. She had squatted down in front of Aphrodite and was cutting at the tape on her ankles. "If you give us any trouble, these sisters will kick your ass."

"Of course," said Aphrodite. "Spreading God's word with a baseball bat. Beautiful."

Afiyah did not respond. She finished cutting the tape free of Aphrodite's ankles and then moved on to her wrists. When she was done she stepped back with the knife at her side and the roll of tape on the floor in front of her.

Aphrodite stood. She was stiff and sore. Maybe it was her imagination or the damp in the basement, but her throat felt scratchy and her chest tight. She hoped the plague did not act so quickly.

"Behind you," said Afiyah. She gestured vaguely past Aphrodite's head toward the other side of the room.

Aphrodite turned. On the far side of the basement were two doors. One had a deadbolt on it and seemed to lead to an outside stairwell. The other was partially open. Through the doorway, Aphrodite could see a toilet and a sink.

"Hurry up," said the black woman. She had a dark, hairy mole on one cheek of her tightly wrapped face.

Aphrodite walked around the post and shuffled toward the bathroom. Her back was tense, and there were goose bumps up and down her arms and legs from the chill.

The bathroom door squealed as Aphrodite pushed it open and stepped inside. She stopped, turned, flipped on the light switch and then moved to close the door behind her.

"Leave it open," said Afiyah. She and the other two sisters had followed Aphrodite across the room and were standing in a half circle directly outside the bathroom door.

"Whatever turns you on," said Aphrodite. She pulled down her panties, sat and began to urinate.

"Hurry," said the black woman. She squinted her eyes and slapped the metal pipe against the palm of her hand.

"Kiss my ass," said Aphrodite without looking up.

Aphrodite finished. There was no toilet paper. It did not seem like a big issue under the circumstances. She stood, pulled up her panties and flushed the toilet.

"Back to the chair," said Afiyah. She was still holding the box cutter.

"Where else would I go?" asked Aphrodite. She stepped out of the bathroom.

"Shut up and move," said the black woman. She was standing on Aphrodite's right. She reached out with the pipe and poked Aphrodite in the side with its rough, rusted end.

"What's her problem?" said Aphrodite. She turned her head to the left and smiled mockingly at the white sister. Then she spun, swept her right leg out and up and delivered a round kick to the side of the black woman's head. The woman flew back and smacked against the concrete block wall behind her. The pipe skittered across the floor.

Afiyah rushed forward swinging the box cutter in wide, awkward arcs. Aphrodite danced back, caught Afiyah's arm by the wrist and twisted it violently, first sideways and then up tight behind Afiyah's back. Something snapped in Afiyah's shoulder. The box cutter fell.

Aphrodite ducked. The metal softball bat went by over her head, and the heavy set white woman stumbled to one side trying to regain her footing. Aphrodite came upright, released her grip on Afiyah's arm and stepped away.

The big woman spun around with the bat in both hands and wound up for another roundhouse swing. Aphrodite didn't wait. She went forward at full speed, ducked under the bat and rammed the woman in the stomach with her shoulder. The sister staggered back, gasping for air. The bat was down now, held loosely in one hand.

Aphrodite stepped in. She punched the woman in the face. Blood spurted from her broken nose. Aphrodite hit her again, this time in the throat. The woman went down on both knees. Aphrodite kneed her in the face. The woman collapsed screaming.

Afiyah was trying to get to her feet. The black woman was on all fours clutching at the pipe. Aphrodite ran to the basement door and fumbled with the bolt. It was locked, and the key was not there.

To Aphrodite's right were two of the windows, which had been papered over. She stepped to the first window and tore the paper from it. It was a simple pane of glass set in a wooden frame.

Aphrodite turned. The baseball bat was lying on the concrete floor a few feet away. She grabbed it and slammed it against the window. The glass shattered. She swung again and again.

There were still small, ragged pieces of glass protruding from the frame. The window was barely big enough for Aphrodite to fit through. It was her only chance. She dropped the bat, jumped, caught the edge of the frame and dragged herself into the narrow opening.

The window opened directly on the lawn outside. Aphrodite dug her fingers into the dirt and turf and pulled. Her arms and shoulders came free. She turned her head and looked around. She could see another small, suburban home only thirty or forty feet away. It looked like there was a road of some kind to her left.

Sharp glass teeth cut at Aphrodite's stomach. She could feel blood running into her crotch and down her legs. She gritted her teeth and pulled. Her ass came through the window. She was almost free.

Behind her Aphrodite heard movement. Someone grabbed one of her feet. She kicked violently, and whoever it was let go. She drove her elbows into the lawn and wiggled from side to side. Her knees came through, then her feet. She came up on all fours on the grass.

Aphrodite started to stand. Her head spun. She settled down on one knee for a moment and wiped at something wet on her face. Her hand came away covered in bright, red blood. It was running from her nose. She struggled to her feet.

Above Aphrodite were the branches of a wide oak tree. She looked up at them, and they began to spin. The house behind her shifted and rolled. Her face felt suddenly hard and hot, like it had been baked in an oven.

Aphrodite looked down from the tree and tried to focus her eyes. Anwar was walking toward her across the lawn. His long, blond hair was hanging in his face. He had a syringe in his hands. Aphrodite tried to raise her arms, but they did not move.

"You can't leave. God has plans for you," said Anwar. He jabbed the syringe into the side of Aphrodite's neck and jammed the plunger down. Aphrodite's eyelids slammed shut. The world went dark. She crumpled to the ground.

CHAPTER THIRTY-TWO

1944 HOURS, 14 AUGUST 2002.
NEAR BERKLEY SPRINGS, WEST VIRGINIA.

"I'll get you another glass of wine," said Spalding. He stood up from his chair on the cabin deck overlooking the creek below.

"Don't you dare check your cell phone, baby," said Christine. She looked up and smiled and then went back to watching the kids splashing in the water. Her long black hair hung down the back of her chair and glistened in the setting sun of another hot August day in the country.

Spalding opened the screen door between the porch and the interior of the cabin, stepped inside and pulled the door shut behind him. To his left was an open living room with a stone fireplace. Ahead of him was the kitchen with all steel appliances and a granite-topped island counter. He and Christine had been putting money into this place for years, and they were finally getting it the way they wanted.

The half empty bottle of Prosecco was sitting in a brass ice bucket on the counter. Spalding took the bottle from the bucket, pulled the cork and began to refill both his and Christine's glasses.

Soft jazz music was playing in the background. *Maybe I'll just never go back to the office*, he thought.

Outside something moved on the deck. He couldn't see it, but Spalding heard it brush against the side of the house briefly. There was a pistol on the top shelf of the cabinet in front of him. As a precaution, he reached up and opened the cabinet door. He was on vacation, but he was still a spy.

Spalding finished filling the glasses, put the cork back in the bottle and placed the bottle back in the ice bucket. The sliding screen door to the back stairs whispered on its steel track. Spalding glanced up at the butt of the pistol barely visible at the edge of the shelf above him. He calculated mentally how long it would take him to grab it, jack a round in the chamber and turn to fire.

The floor creaked about eight feet behind Spalding. That was the spot where he had replaced several water-damaged floorboards two winters ago. Without turning he glanced out of the corner of his eye and caught a fuzzy, familiar reflection in the polished surface of the refrigerator door.

"Ever hear of telephones?" said Spalding. He closed the cabinet door, picked up the two glasses of Prosecco and turned around slowly.

"Your cell phone is off," said Bill. He was standing a few feet away on the other side of the kitchen island. He was unshaven, and his eyes had dark, sooty circles under them.

"You look like hell," said Spalding. He was still holding the glasses. Behind Bill, he could see Christine beginning to get up from her chair.

"Eleni's missing," said Bill.

"How'd you get here?" asked Spalding.

"I parked down the road, and walked through the woods," said Bill. "Didn't know who else might be here. Wanted to scope the place before I came in. "

"I'm on vacation," said Spalding.

"That's what your neighbor told me," said Bill.

"Nobody here but the family," said Spalding.

"Bill?" said Christine. She was standing at the screen door and slid it open as she spoke.

"Hey," said Bill. He turned and attempted a smile.

"How are you?" said Christine. She came forward, hugged him warmly and shot a quizzical look at Spalding as she did so.

"Okay," said Bill.

"I was bringing the wine," said Spalding. He handed one of the glasses to Christine.

"I know," said Christine. "I just thought I might make us something to snack on."

"Can you give us a few minutes?" asked Spalding. He set the other glass down on the counter untouched.

"Sure," said Christine. "Good to see you after all this time, Bill." Christine walked back out to the deck and then down the stairs toward the creek below. In the background, the children were squealing and splashing.

"Eleni has been kidnapped," said Bill when Christine was out of earshot. He ran both hands through his hair and exhaled heavily.

"By whom?" said Spalding. He leaned back against the counter and crossed his arms.

"Not sure," said Bill. There were bar stools on his side of the kitchen counter. He pulled one of them out and sat down.

"Not tracking," said Spalding.

"She was helping a friend," said Bill. "Jimmy's daughter. Her kid was mixed up with some half-assed wanna-be jihadi types. Eleni went to find him and sort it out."

"Where were you?" asked Spalding.

"Mexico," said Bill. "Paying a debt."

"You think the folks the kid was mixed up with grabbed Eleni," said Spalding.

"I know they grabbed her," said Bill. "She's gone."

"Have you talked to the cops?" asked Spalding. "Finding people in the U.S. isn't exactly CIA's gig."

"Fuck the cops," said Bill. He snapped to his feet and strode around the counter to within a couple of feet of Spalding. "We don't have time to dick around with filling out missing person reports."

"Why?"

"Because they'll be way out of their league on this," said Bill. His face was red now, and the crimson was spreading to the tips of his ears.

"What the hell does that mean, Bill?" said Spalding.

"It means she stumbled into something a hell of a lot uglier than what she thought it was. She went down a hole looking for a lost kid and ended up in the middle of a plot to stage a biological weapons attack in the U.S."

"Bio," said Spalding slowly. "Like the plague?"

"Yes," said Bill. "Exactly like the plague."

"Where was Eleni when she disappeared?" said Spalding. He reached for his phone and turned it on.

"Baltimore," said Bill.

"Goddamn it," muttered Spalding. He punched in a number and held the phone to his head.

"Who are you calling?" asked Bill.

"Rogers," said Spalding. "I think this attack already started."

CHAPTER THIRTY-THREE

0947 HOURS, 15 AUGUST 2002.
PANERA BREAD RESTAURANT,
ANNE ARUNDEL COUNTY, MARYLAND.

"I'll have one of those," said Anwar. He pointed to one of the blueberry muffins in the glass display case in front of him. He would be dead soon, and he hadn't had a blueberry muffin since he left home for Pakistan.

"Anything else?" asked the teenage girl working the counter as she picked up the muffin with a sheet of wax paper and placed it on a plate.

"And a large, black coffee too please," said Anwar. He smiled and brushed his long, blond hair from his eyes.

"Absolutely," said the girl as she turned to the coffee urns.

While he waited, Anwar scanned the restaurant. There was nothing remarkable to see. At one table a group of elderly men in running shoes and Bermuda shorts were talking about the day the Colts moved to Indianapolis. At another, a couple of businesswomen were haggling over the price of office copiers. Otherwise the place was empty.

"Here you go," said the girl behind the counter. She handed Anwar his coffee, took his money and handed him his change. Anwar took the muffin and the coffee and walked to a booth in the back of the restaurant. He sat down facing the entrance, so he could see everyone coming and going. Then he pulled his laptop from his backpack, placed it on the table in front of him and turned it on.

While the computer powered up, Anwar checked his watch. It was still a few minutes until his communications window. He was right on time.

The computer screen came to life and automatically brought up the Skype log-in screen. Anwar keyed in his password and pressed the "enter" key. His computer chirped to signal that Skype was now active.

The old men at the table toward the front of the restaurant raised their voices. One of them opined authoritatively that Johnny Unitas was the greatest quarterback that ever lived. Another argued that Unitas would never have been able to handle the speed of the modern game. A middle-aged white man with a shaved head and a paunch walked into the store and sat down at a table behind Anwar without ordering. The waitress stopped making time with the young man who made the sandwiches and picked up the phone.

Anwar's computer chirped again. He looked down. Akbar had gone active on his screen. There was a pause. A text message appeared.

"Report status," it said.

"We are ready to execute," typed Anwar. "The sisters have taken their medicine."

"Have you encountered any problems?" came the response.

Anwar paused. He wondered if he should bother Akbar with the news of his kidnapping of the blond woman called Eleni. It seemed unnecessary. Nothing was going to matter very soon. On the other hand, he had been taught to report everything fully and completely.

"There was an intruder at Sumaya's house," typed Anwar. "A woman. She saw too much. We have her."

"Intelligence?" came the response.

"It is unclear," typed Anwar. "She says she was helping a friend find her son. This may be true. But, I could not take the chance of letting her go."

A minute passed. The cursor blinked at the bottom of the spring where the window for text messages was. Anwar waited.

"Kill her," came the response.

"She is already dead," said Anwar. "I gave her the same medicine I gave to all the sisters. She is showing the signs."

Tires screeched outside on the pavement. Anwar looked up. Two policemen were climbing from a patrol car that had skidded to a stop at the entrance to the restaurant. The girl from the counter met them a few steps inside and gestured emphatically in Anwar's direction. Anwar swallowed hard and closed his computer.

The first cop was a tall, thin white guy. The black cop behind him was taller and heavier. They plowed their way through the tables and chairs with the girl from the counter in tow. The old men stopped arguing. The businesswomen stopped talking prices.

"Stay right there," barked the white cop. He had his hand on his holster, but he hadn't drawn his weapon.

"We're gonna have a little talk, buddy," chimed in the black cop.

Anwar closed his eyes. There was nowhere to run. He wasn't going to fight his way out of this situation. He was done.

"Put your hands behind your back," said the white cop. The voice came from somewhere behind Anwar toward the restrooms.

"What's going on?" It was a thin, whining voice.

Anwar opened his eyes and turned his head. The white man with the shaved head was handcuffed and up against the wall in the rear of the store. He looked like he was going to cry.

"You're a pervert, that's what," said the black cop. "Let's go." He steered the white man in the direction of the entrance and the patrol car.

"Slimeball," said the girl from the counter. She was standing next to Anwar's table watching the bald man be lead away. "Comes in here and sneaks into the women's restroom with his cell phone to take pictures of ladies on the toilet."

"Sick," said Anwar.

"Real sick," said the girl. "Glad the cops were right around the corner this time."

"Makes you wonder what this country is coming to," said Anwar.

"You got that right," said the girl. "Psychos everywhere." She smiled at Anwar and then walked back in the direction of the counter.

Anwar exhaled slowly and opened his computer. The Skype screen was still illuminated. There was a message from Akbar in the text box.

"When do you move to the targets?"

"Tomorrow morning," typed Anwar. His fingers were still shaking.

"Change bed down locations today," came the response. Anwar froze. He looked up, scanned the room again and bit his lower lip. He looked back down, read the message again and began to type.

"What has changed?"

"We have lost contact with Sahaba. We do not know why. "

"The Americans?" typed Anwar.

"We do not know. A Pashtun policeman here went to them with some information he acquired when some of our brothers were arrested. He did not know much, but it may have been enough to cause problems."

"What kind of pig works against his own people?" typed Anwar.

"We will take care of him," typed Akbar. "You focus on your mission. Move immediately. Proceed as planned tomorrow."

"As God wishes," typed Anwar. "It will be done."

"God is great," responded Akbar. The indicator next to his name on Anwar's Skype screen went off. The conversation was ended.

Anwar shut down Skype and closed his computer. He checked his watch one more time, slurped briefly at his coffee and got to his feet. The muffin sat untouched on the table in front of him, but he gave it no mind. He had not come this far to be caught at the last minute. It was time to move.

CHAPTER THIRTY-FOUR

1013 HOURS, 15 AUGUST 2002.
MARYLAND JOINT TERRORISM TASK FORCE, CANTON, BALTIMORE, MARYLAND.

"Prairie dogs?" said Bill.

"Prairie dogs," said Spalding. They were standing in the center of the small command center on the ground floor of the Task Force building, a converted firehouse. In the front of the room was a bank of flat screen televisions. Arrayed around them in a semicircle were chairs and desks with computer monitors. Most of the chairs were empty. The flat screens were showing a mix of the news and sports.

"It's not as crazy as it sounds," said Rogers. He was standing next to Spalding wearing a cranberry colored cardigan.

"Yes, it is," said Bill.

"There are a handful of cases of the plague in the United States every year," continued Rogers. "Almost all of them occur in the Southwest and are traced to flea bites. The fleas live on prairie dogs, and prairie dog populations carry the plague."

"This is Baltimore," said Bill. He shot a glance at Spalding, who was staring at his feet and waiting for Rogers to finish.

"People travel," said Rogers. He shrugged his shoulders.

"The bottom line is that we've taken one step forward and two back," said Spalding. "CDC agrees now that at least some of the cases of people who got sick at the aquarium are the plague. They haven't signed onto the idea that it is terrorism. They think maybe all of this can be traced back to somebody who was out in New Mexico or Arizona and brought the plague back with them."

"What about the source reporting out of Pakistan?" said Bill. "What about the files on the computer in Mexico?"

"Headquarters has caveated the hell out of the Islamabad reports," said Spalding.

"Because they don't want to believe it," said Bill.

"Because if we accept it, we are damn close to saying that Pakistan is a state sponsor of terrorism," responded Spalding.

"So, if we pretend it ain't happening, we don't have to face the implications," said Bill.

"This is Washington. That's the way it works," said Spalding. He sighed heavily.

"And the computer?" said Bill.

"Headquarters isn't making any judgment about any of that until we see what we pull off the hard drive using your thumb drive and the software you uploaded," said Spalding.

"And, that's going to take a while," said Bill.

"With some luck, maybe later today we'll start seeing some results," said Spalding.

"The WMD experts in the community are just flat out skeptical that a plague attack is viable," said Rogers.

"Really," said Bill. He wondered how many times in his life he had heard that "experts" in Northern Virginia were "skeptical". He wondered when the last time was he had slept.

"The plague is normally spread by fleas," said Rogers. "And, if you were trying to spread it in some aerosol form, you would face all sorts of obstacles. How would you do it? A ventilation system? How would you dispense it?"

"So, you think this is all bullshit?" asked Bill. "You think we're chasing our tails?"

"Hey, I'm on your side, Bill," said Rogers. "I'm just explaining the issues."

"I don't care about the issues," growled Bill. "I care about finding my wife and taking jihadi nut jobs off the street."

"Headquarters is working on accessing the computer in Mexico," said Spalding. "CDC is investigating the aquarium illnesses. Downtown, they're chewing on the possibility that Pakistan is on the other side in this fight."

"And in the meantime, we're on our own," said Bill. He'd paced the floor at Spalding's home all night. He stank. His hair felt greasy and pasted to his head.

"In the meantime, there is no official terrorism investigation," admitted Spalding. "And whatever we're going to get from these guys is going to be in the way of a favor." He nodded in the direction of two individuals who were walking toward them. One was a forty something woman in creased khaki slacks and a dark blue polo shirt with the words "Maryland State Police" sewn over the pocket. The other was a muscular white man in his twenties, with gold hoop earrings in both ears and long blond hair. He was wearing a Metallica t-shirt and faded jeans.

"Good to see you again," said the woman. She shook Spalding's hand. "Welcome to my center."

"Captain Maloney is in charge of this command center," said Spalding. "Captain, I think you know Rogers."

"I do," said the Captain.

"And this is Bill Boyle," said Spalding. He pointed to Bill as he spoke. "Bill's a former CIA officer and does some work with us from time to time. It's his wife that is missing."

"Pleased to meet you, Captain," said Bill. He reached out and shook Maloney's hand. He noticed as he did so that her grip was firm, her nails were unpainted, and she wore no perfume. This lady was all business.

"Good to meet you," said the Captain. "And this guy with the hair and the jewelry is Sergeant Yards, the head of the State Police Fugitive Capture Unit.

"Hey," said Yards. He shook hands all around and smiled.

"I can't formally do much of anything on this until somebody tells me we are looking at terrorism," said Maloney. "But, in the meantime, unofficially, we will do whatever we can."

"Appreciated," said Bill.

"Your wife was looking to find some kid who ran off with some jihadis?" asked Yards. He was talking to Bill.

"A kid named Eddie," said Bill. "Son of the owner of the Full Moon Saloon. It's a long story, but she's the daughter of an old friend who was killed. Eleni and I went to look her up and stumbled into this thing."

"Your wife's not the lady who took out the Hun with a bottle of vodka is she?" asked Yards. He cocked his head to one side and smiled.

"Yeah, that'd be her," said Bill.

"Well, shit, Captain," said Yards. "We got to find this lady just so I can shake her hand."

"I'm assuming that Mr. Boyle here still has a security clearance," said Maloney.

"I have taken care of that," said Spalding. "He's current."

"Good enough for me," said Maloney.

"Clearance?" said Bill. He squinted at Spalding to signal his lack of comprehension. "When did that happen?"

"When you went into Iraq for us," said Spalding. "I left it active just in case we might be seeing each other again."

"You son of a bitch," said Bill. He shook his head and smiled briefly.

"Yards will be your P.O.C. on this," said Maloney. "Despite the jewelry and the hair, he's the best we've got."

"Ah, damn, boss, now you're getting all mushy on me," said Yards. He put his arm around Maloney and grinned. Maloney seemed to stiffen all the more.

"Thanks," said Spalding.

"Yes, ma'am, thank you," said Bill.

"I'm headed downtown to a meeting with the Baltimore Police Commissioner," said Maloney. "I'll check back in with you when I return." She turned and walked crisply back to her office.

"What's the next step?" asked Bill. He looked around the room briefly. There was a guy behind him doing a crossword puzzle at his desk. Another guy across the room was watching Wheel of Fortune on the big screen in front of him. It was hard to feel like they were gathering much momentum.

"Let me go check with Chuckles," said Yards. He pointed across the room to a short, round man in a short-sleeved button-down shirt who was staring intently at the computer screen in front of him. "When the Captain gave me the quick and dirty on this thing this morning, I asked him to rummage through incoming reports and the police blotter and see what he might be able to dredge up."

"Chuckles?" said Bill, but Yards was already walking away.

"I'm going to go find a secure phone and call Headquarters," said Rogers. "Want to make sure they're really focused on getting into that computer down in Mexico." He wandered off in the same direction the Captain had gone.

"Okay," said Spalding. He looked at Bill.

"Not sure sitting in here is going to get Eleni back," said Bill. He could not remember feeling this helpless since the day his first wife was killed in front of him on the streets of Athens.

"Before you hit the street, you need some clue where to start looking," said Spalding.

"Yeah," said Bill. Maybe I'll just start by rattling some cages at the mosque, he thought.

"Hey!" yelled Yards. Bill and Spalding turned. Yards was standing next to the short, round man and waving them over.

"This is Chuckles," said Yards as Bill and Spalding approached. "Best friggin' analyst we've got here."

"O'Brien," said the man. He rolled his eyes to make sure Spalding and Bill understand that the joy of being referred to as "Chuckles" had long since worn off.

"Good to meet you," said Bill.

"Thanks for your help," said Spalding.

"Chuckles has pulled up something very interesting," said Yards. "Some guy phoned into Anne Arundel County cops this morning. Works nights as a security guard at a warehouse. Got home this morning, and his wife told him that she saw some lady in her underwear crawling out the basement window of the house next door around seven last night."

"What did she look like?" asked Bill.

"Blond hair, white, thirties maybe," said Yards. He was leaning over reading off O'Brien's computer screen. "The wife wasn't sure what was going on, because the house had been sitting vacant, and I guess she didn't even know anybody had moved in. She went to get her glasses, so she could see more clearly. When she got back to the window, the lady was gone."

"Anything else?" asked Bill.

"The guy told the cops that the basement window that his wife says the lady crawled out of is definitely broken. He also said that he saw two ladies in headscarves standing on the front porch of the house this morning."

"When did this call come in?" asked Bill.

"At 0837," said O'Brien.

"Anne Arundel cops responded yet?" asked Spalding. He checked his watch. It had been almost two hours since the call had come in.

"Not yet," said Yards. "Probably not at the top of their list."

"How fast can we can get there?" asked Bill. The blood was pounding in his head. They had a scent.

"Shit, man," said Yards. "With me driving, we're already there."

CHAPTER THIRTY-FIVE

1109 HOURS, 15 AUGUST 2002.
ANNE ARUNDEL COUNTY, MARYLAND.

"The Captain wants me to knock on the door and ask permission to search," said Yards. He was behind the wheel of his cherry red Ford F-150 pickup truck.

"Bad idea," said Bill. He was sitting in the front passenger seat of the truck. Spalding was directly behind him. Rogers was sitting next to Spalding in the back seat.

"I agree," said Yards.

"So, what's the plan?" asked Bill.

"The plan is we go in hot," said Yards. He grinned from ear to ear. His wrap around mirrored shades were flashing reflections of passing cars and road signs, as they rocketed down the street toward their destination.

"Suits me fine," said Bill. He had the Mossberg 500 with an extended magazine that Yards had given him pointed at the floorboards in front of him and a tight grip on it with both hands. Between Yards and him there was a sixteen-pound sledge. Behind him, he heard Rogers swallow hard.

"This is it," said Yards. The truck's tires screamed as he turned off Route 3 and down a narrow side street lined with small one-story homes and weed-infested yards. A stray dog streaked across the street. Yards didn't touch the brakes.

"Ready," said Bill. His mind had gone stone cold. The terror of helplessness had been replaced by the necessity to focus on the task at hand.

"No knock," said Yards. He yanked the steering wheel hard over and slammed to a stop in the crumbling blacktop driveway of a rundown home with broken shutters and a sagging roof. "We go in strong."

"Roger," said Bill. They were both moving, Yards in front with the sledgehammer and his Beretta PX4 on his hip, Bill behind covering the front windows of the house with the shotgun. Behind them both, Spalding had another shotgun to his shoulder. Rogers trailed, overwhelmed.

Yards went up the concrete steps to the front door. The storm door was hanging off its hinges to one side. He took a wide stance, swung the hammer sidearm and smacked the front door just beside the latch. It flew open and slammed against the wall to the right.

"Moving," said Bill. He went through the door with the shotgun up against his right shoulder. The short hallway directly ahead was clear. He swung right through a doorway and into a small bedroom. There were a half-dozen old mattresses on the molding carpet. The door to the small closet was open. "Clear," yelled Bill.

"Clear," yelled Yards. He had dropped the sledge, pulled his pistol and gone left into the living room, kitchen area.

"Holding the hallway," said Spalding. He had advanced through the front door and was standing with his shotgun pointed straight ahead. A real SWAT team, trained to work together, would not need to communicate so much verbally. Yards, Boyle and Spalding were doing this ad hoc, and they weren't taking any chances.

"Let's move," said Yards. Spalding started down the hallway. Bill and Yards fell in behind. Nothing stirred in the house. There was no sound other than their tense breathing and the muffled sound of their shoes on the bare floors.

Halfway down the hallway was a door to a bathroom. It was ajar, and the room was empty. Spalding glanced quickly, saw the room was clear and kept moving.

At the end of the hallway were an open passage to the left to the kitchen and two doors to the right. Spalding went through the first door on the right into another bedroom with an attached bath. There were mattresses on the floor here too, but otherwise the rooms were bare. "Clear," he yelled.

"I'm going down," said Bill quietly. He was standing the second doorway, and he could see that it lead to a set of wooden stairs into what seemed to be a basement.

"Roger, right behind you," whispered Yards.

Bill stepped down two short steps onto a landing. The stairs went to the right from here in a long flight into what seemed to be a bare concrete room. He advanced slowly, and smoothly with the shotgun at the ready and his finger on the trigger. A dim light was on. He could hear nothing over the pounding in his chest. He was terrified, not of being confronted or shot, but of being too late.

Bill reached the bottom of the stairs and swung right. The room opened in front of him. To his left front was a wooden workbench. In front of him, in the center of the room, was a wooden chair duct taped to a wooden support post. There was a bathroom on the far side of the room. The door was open. No one was inside. A few feet to the right of the bathroom was a door that looked like it lead to an outdoor stairwell. It was closed. There was no one in sight.

"Clear," yelled Bill.

"Roger," yelled Yards. He came down the stairs and stepped up beside Bill. The two men could hear Spalding and Rogers walking around on the floor above.

"That's the window," said Bill. He walked over to one of three small basement windows set into the wall of the room. Two of the windows were covered in brown paper. The third, the closest to the outside door, was uncovered and broken out. Pieces of brown paper were lying around the room. A few small shards of glass crunched under Bill's feet.

"Yeah," said Yards. He walked over to the window. His pistol was back in the holster on his hip. "Broken from the inside."

"She did that," said Bill. He stood on his tiptoes and peaked out the window onto the grass outside. Big chunks of broken glass were scattered across the lawn. The windowsill was stained dark with blood.

"Tough girl," said Yards.

"She is that," said Bill. He shuddered at the thought of Eleni dragging herself through the window while the glass still embedded in the frame cut into her legs and stomach.

Bill turned and scanned the room. The chair was taped to the post. There was also tape on the arms and legs, but it had been cut. On the floor next to the chair was a roll of duct tape.

"They were holding her here," said Yards. There were footsteps on the stairs. Spalding and Rogers were coming down.

"And, then they cut her loose," said Bill.

", she talked them into cutting her loose," said Yards. He was standing over near the bathroom now. There was blood smeared against the wall of the basement several feet away and long strands of dark hair stuck in it.

"Somebody's head hit the wall pretty hard," said Bill. He came up next to Yards.

"Your girl's blond right?" said Yards.

"Yeah," said Bill.

"Well, then, looks to me like she kicked some ass," said Yards. He grinned.

"Not enough," said Bill. He looked back at the window.

"Nothing upstairs," said Spalding as he came down the stairs and into the room. Rogers came down right behind him, stepped over to the workbench and stopped to look around.

"They boogied," agreed Yards.

"Why's she still alive?" asked Bill.

"Let's just be happy she is," said Spalding.

"I'm not wishing her dead, bro," said Bill. He had the shotgun hanging at his side in one hand now. "I'm just saying, why? They didn't know she was coming. She stumbled on this crazy plot of theirs. Why not just end her and skip the trouble of keeping her under control?"

"Good point," said Yards. "Not like they've got a problem with killing obviously."

"Did you see this?" asked Rogers. He was standing on the far side of the workbench from the other men. He knelt down for a minute and then stood back up with a small black and white pamphlet in his hand. It had a picture of some sort of rectangular object on it.

"What's that?" asked Spalding. He laid his shotgun on the workbench and then walked around to the side where Rogers was standing to get a better look.

"It's really bad news," said Rogers. He handed the pamphlet to Spalding and then looked up at Bill.

"What?" said Bill. He set his gun down too.

"Fuck," said Spalding. He handed the pamphlet to Bill.

Bill looked down at the sheets of paper in his hand. The first page said something about a nebulizer. On the second page there was a sketch of someone holding a facemask over his mouth and nose. The facemask was connected by a hose to a box.

Bill looked up. He said nothing. He knew what the pamphlet meant, but he didn't want to accept it.

"They are killing her," said Rogers in a low, reluctant voice. "They're just doing it in the slowest, cruelest way they can."

"I'm lost," said Yards. He was standing next to Bill looking at the pamphlet. It meant nothing to him.

"That's how they're going to spread the plague," said Spalding. He was staring into space. He couldn't bear to look at Bill. "They're inhaling the bacteria directly into their lungs. They're breathing the shit."

"Fuck," said Yards. "And you think they made Bill's wife breathe it too."

"I guarantee it," said Bill. His face was gray stone.

"I'm sorry," said Rogers.

"How long?" said Bill. He looked down at his watch as if that would somehow help him sort this all out.

"Hard to know," said Rogers weakly.

"Guess," growled Bill.

"Two to three days max," said Rogers. "Maybe a lot less. After that, even if we find her, it's too late."

"They've had her a day already," said Spalding.

"Then, we better find her fast," said Bill. He picked up his shotgun and headed for the stairs.

CHAPTER THIRTY-SIX

1323 HOURS, 15 AUGUST 2002.
STAR SPANGLED BANNER HOTEL, HOWARD COUNTY, MARYLAND.

"How many rooms?" said the desk clerk. He was a short, pockmarked white man in his forties with a long, graying ponytail and a tattoo of a topless hula dancer on his right forearm.

"Three," said Anwar. He smiled. The desk clerk leaned to one side and looked past him out the dirty windows of the motel office at the van filled with women in headscarves parked against the curb.

"All with you?" asked the desk clerk. Behind him a small color television was showing the Jerry Springer show. Some heavy set black woman was screaming at an equally big black man and, for no discernible reason, tearing off her blouse to expose her bra.

"Yes," said Anwar. "Church group." He smiled again.

"Pentecostals?" said the desk clerk. He was punching buttons on his computer keyboard.

"Same kind of thing," said Anwar. He put a credit card and a driver's license on the counter and made a show of watching the television. The big woman was threatening to take off her pants, and Jerry was reacting in mock horror.

"Here you go," said the desk clerk after a few moments. He handed Anwar three sets of metal keys on oversized plastic key chains. "Checkout is at eleven."

"We'll be gone well before then," said Anwar. "Thank you." He took the keys and returned to the van.

"Any problems?" asked Afiyah, as Anwar climbed into the van and started it up. She was sitting in the front passenger seat. Behind her, the van was filled with women coughing and wheezing.

"None," said Anwar.

"No questions about who we were?"

"He could care less," said Anwar as he backed up the van and then began to pull around to where their rooms were. "On any given night this place is filled with junkies, whores and felons. We're the least of his concerns."

The three rooms that Anwar had rented sat side by side on the back of the old style motel. All the rooms opened directly into the parking lot. A rusting, metal stairway led to a second story catwalk and an identical line of gray, metal doors to motel rooms.

Anwar pulled the van into a parking space in front of the center room, turned off the engine and climbed out. Behind him the women hacked and choked their way out of the van and began to drag their few bags toward the room doors. Two them half carried Eleni from the van. Her eyes were closed, and there was blood crusted under her nose.

"Take these keys and get the sisters settled. Then come see me in my room," said Anwar. He handed two sets of keys to Afiyah and then used the third set to enter the remaining room. Behind him he could hear one of the sisters start to cry. He closed the door, lay down on one of the beds and closed his eyes.

A few minutes later there came a knock at the door. Anwar stood and opened it. Afiyah was standing there. Her face was gray and pinched.

"Come in," said Anwar. Afiyah walked to a chair in the corner next to the television set and sat down. Anwar closed the door behind her. Then he took a small pill bottle from his backpack, shook some pills into his hand and walked over to Afiyah.

"Take these," said Anwar. He put two pills in the palm of Afiyah's hand, then walked to the bathroom sink and filled the two small plastic cups sitting on the counter with water.

"What are they?" asked Afiyah as Anwar returned and handed her one of the two glasses.

"Medicine," said Anwar. He walked to his backpack, took another two pills from the bottle and popped them in his mouth.

"What kind of medicine?" asked Afiyah.

"Ciprofloxacin," said Anwar. He took a drink of water from the other glass and swallowed.

"For the plague?" asked Afiyah. Her palm was open in her lap with the two pills sitting in its center. She was staring straight ahead.

"For the plague," said Anwar. He sat down on one of the two double beds in the dark, faux wood-paneled room. Next to him there was a cigarette hole burned in the cheap nylon bedspread.

"Why for us?" said Afiyah. She looked down at the pills in her hand.

"We have to ensure that they others get to their targets," said Anwar. "To do that we have to stay healthy. We cannot avoid being infected when we are this close to them all day."

"Sister Denise is terrified," said Afiyah.

"Take the pills, sister," said Anwar softly. "This is what God needs of you now. And do not despair about the suffering of the sisters. By this time tomorrow it will all be over, and they will be with God forever."

Afiyah looked up at Anwar for a moment. Her eyes were hot and wet. Her lips quivered. Then she popped the pills in her mouth and drank the water.

"How is the blond woman?" asked Anwar.

"Unconscious," said Afiyah. She set the glass down on the chipped laminate surface of the table on which the television sat. "In and out. Burning with fever."

"She will live long enough," said Anwar. He checked his watch. "In a little while I will need to go and get the tickets. If we wait until the morning, we may not get seats."

"Okay," said Afiyah. She looked past Anwar at the far wall of the room. There was a print in a plastic frame on the wall. It showed the British fleet bombarding Fort McHenry in the War of 1812. A giant American flag was flying over the fort in the picture. The frame was hanging crooked on the wall. "I understand."

Someone knocked at the door. Anwar got up, opened it and stood to one side. Sister Bobbie, the one who had been the first to use the nebulizer, came in. Anwar shut the door behind her.

"What is it, sister?" asked Afiyah. She was still sitting.

"Sister Denise wants to go to a hospital," said Sister Bobbie. She had her hands crossed in front of her. Her eyes were sunken deep into her fat, white face.

"Impossible," said Afiyah.

"She is crying," said Bobbie. "She has swelling under her armpits and...down there." She looked away, as if humiliated by having to make a reference to a woman's private parts.

"The other sisters are trying to calm her?" asked Anwar.

"Yes, brother," said Bobbie. "She is saying she wants to live. She is threatening to go on her own."

"I will speak to her," said Afiyah. She started to stand.

"Bring her here," said Anwar to Bobbie. He motioned to Afiyah to stay seated.

"Yes, brother," said Bobbie. She left the room pulling the door shut behind her. Anwar took the pill bottle that he was still holding in his hand and placed it back in his backpack. Then he took something else from the bag, slipped it into his pocket and sat down.

"Tomorrow morning, before we leave, I will give you more medicine," he said.

"What are you going to do about Denise?" asked Afiyah.

"What God commands," said Anwar. "Turn on the television."

"To what channel?" asked Afiyah.

"It does not matter," said Anwar. He stood. The television flickered to life. There was a knock at the door.

"Here she is," said Bobbie as Anwar opened the door. She shoved Sister Denise, a petite Filipina, in front of her into the room. Denise was coughing heavily into a towel. It was red with blood.

"Thank you," said Anwar. He smiled reassuringly at Sister Bobbie. "We'll talk to her alone for a while."

"The blond woman threw up on the shirt she was wearing," said Bobbie. She sounded like a big sister telling on a sibling. "We won't be able to take her anywhere in that now."

"Wash it if you can, sister," said Afiyah softly. "Or, look for something in one of the sisters' bags that she can wear."

"Yes, Sister Afiyah," said Sister Bobbie. She stepped back out onto the sidewalk in front of the room and pulled the door shut behind her.

"I am sorry, brother," said Sister Denise when the door had closed. "I cannot do this."

"I understand," said Anwar. He put his hand on her shoulder and guided her toward the bathroom. "Let's get a look at you in the light."

"I know I am failing you, brother," said Denise quietly. She shuffled to the bathroom on unsteady feet. "But, my children need a mother."

"God loves you, Sister Denise," said Anwar. He looked at Afiyah standing in front of the television with the remote in her hand and mouthed the words "turn it up".

"I think I am going to be sick," said Denise. She stepped into the bathroom and looked at her small, yellowing face in the mirror. Behind her the weathermen on the television had started screaming about thunderstorms over the next few days.

"It's all fine now, sister," said Anwar. He stepped into the bathroom, grabbed Denise by her hair through the headscarf she was wearing with his left hand and yanked her head back. Then he drove the slender blade of the switchblade that had appeared in his right hand into the side of Denise's neck just behind the hinge of her jaw.

Blood shot from Denise's neck and spattered across the bathroom counter and against the wall. Her carotid artery was severed. Anwar yanked Denise's head to the left and shoved her forward into the bathtub against the far wall. She toppled in on her face with her hands clutching spasmodically at the gaping hole in her neck.

"Brother, what have you done?" said Afiyah in horror. She was standing in the doorway behind Anwar with her hands to her face.

"What God requires," said Anwar. He stepped forward, lifted his foot and then stomped on Denise's head, smashing it against the bottom of the tub. Blood poured down the drain. Denise gurgled and twisted and finally lay still.

"Don't bother cleaning it up," said Anwar. He stepped back out of the tub and looked at Afiyah who was still standing with her hands pressed over her face. "We'll use the bathroom in one of the other rooms until we leave tomorrow."

CHAPTER THIRTY-SEVEN

**2352 HOURS, 15 AUGUST 2002.
ISLAMABAD, PAKISTAN.**

"Here," said Andrew. He reached inside of his jacket, pulled out a thick envelope and handed it to Sardar, who was sitting next to him in the front passenger's seat of the cramped Toyota sedan. They were parked on the outskirts of Islamabad, on the side of a rough dirt track that lead into the hills surrounding the city.

"Thank you, my brother," said Sardar. He did not open the envelope or count the money. He knew the cash was the key to making a new future for his family, but he still felt uncomfortable taking payment from the Americans.

"When will you leave?" asked Andrew. He looked over the steering wheel in front of him into the darkness.

"In the morning," said Sardar as he shoved the envelope filled with cash inside of his shirt. "By train to Karachi. Then by boat from there."

"Still planning on making it to Dubai?" asked Andrew.

"Yes. My cousin is expecting us there," said Sardar. "He runs security for a big hotel. He will put us up and help me find work."

"It will be hard starting over," said Andrew. "But, I know you will do well."

"The family will be together. We will be safe," said Sardar. "If we stay here, the ISI will never stop looking for us."

"Agreed," said Andrew. "And, again, thank you, my friend for what you have done. You may have saved many lives."

"I hope so, my friend. Be well," said Sardar. He shook Andrew's hand, opened the car door, climbed out and shut the door behind him.

Andrew started the car and drove off without switching on his headlights. Sardar waited and listened. The sound of the car engine faded into the distance. A herd of wild boar snorted in the brush somewhere uphill behind him. Otherwise, the night was still. Sardar retrieved his motorcycle from the bushes where he had hidden it, climbed on and headed for home.

Forty-five minutes later, Sardar bumped the bike down a washboard dirt road into a slum area on the edge of Rawalpindi and pulled up in front of the tiny, concrete block home where his family was hiding. Across the narrow, unpaved street in front of a row of crude one-story stone houses with tin roofs, a group of young men was huddled together talking about the cock fight they had just left. Otherwise, the street was empty.

Sardar chained the motorcycle to a metal drainpipe on the outside of the building, took off his helmet and walked to the front door of the building. The stench of raw sewage running in the street mixed with the smell of rotting garbage from the vacant lot next door. He gagged and coughed as he fumbled with the lock on the metal door and went inside.

On the inside of the metal entrance door was a tiny vestibule with a rough concrete floor. On the right, another locked metal door led to the ground floor apartment where the landlord lived. On the left, a narrow, dusty concrete stairway went upstairs to the second floor where Sardar had left his family. The power was out and there were no windows, so Sardar made his way up the steps by feel and memory. Somewhere in the darkness, rats scurried and chewed.

At the top of the stairs was a metal door bolted shut from the inside. Sardar knocked softly on the door hoping to attract Warda's attention without waking Zakia. A minute passed. He knocked again. Something moved inside. Another few moments passed. The bolt slid back, and the door opened.

"How long have you been standing out here?" asked Warda sleepily. She was wearing a pink nightgown, and her hair was half-covering her face.

"Just a few moments," said Sardar. He stepped through the metal door and bolted it closed behind him. Then he turned and kissed Warda on the forehead.

"Did you get the money?" asked Warda sleepily as she walked across the tiny kitchen with its two-burner kerosene stove toward the single bedroom in the apartment.

"I got the money, wife," said Sardar. "Now, let's sleep. Tomorrow will be a very long day."

"Walk lightly," said Warda. "It took me forever to get her to bed." She pushed open the door to the bedroom. The room was bare except for a mattress on the floor. Zakia was curled in a ball toward the bottom of the mattress, swaddled in a pink blanket and hugging a stuffed Sponge Bob toy.

Sardar knelt down, kissed his daughter on the cheek and fussed with the blanket in which she was wrapped for a moment. Then he walked around to the other side of the mattress, next to the suitcases that were sitting on the bare concrete floor. Dim light filtered through the small dirty window in the bedroom wall.

"We need to be on the train at eight in the morning," whispered Sardar. He began to slowly undress.

"I set the alarm," said Warda. She knelt down and then carefully stretched out on the mattress ,so as not to wake Zakia.

"By tomorrow night we'll be on the boat," said Sardar. "And, in a few days, we'll be with my cousin, in a real apartment again." He tried to sound encouraging. He knew how hard it had been on Warda to leave everything behind so suddenly.

"And, then we can have my mother come visit us there," whispered Warda.

"If she will come," said Sardar. "You know how she hates to travel." He smiled to himself at the thought of Warda's mother, who hated to leave her village for the town five miles away, getting on a plane.

"She will come," said Warda softly. "She promised."

Sardar froze. His blood ran like ice in his veins. He turned slowly to look toward Warda in the dim light. "What do you mean she promised?" he asked.

"Don't be angry," said Warda in a thin, almost invisible voice.

"When did you talk to her?" said Sardar. He had just unbuckled his belt and was about to take his pistol from the holster on his hip. He stopped and began to buckle his belt again.

"Today," said Warda. She rolled up to a sitting position on the far side of the mattress facing the door to the kitchen. "I know you told me no phone calls. I had to speak to my mother before we left, husband."

"How?" said Sardar. His pistol was in his hand. He was moving toward the door. "When?" His mind was suddenly full of the details of the men in the street talking about the cock fight. He did not remember seeing any of them before.

"From the store at the end of the block," said Warda. She tucked her knees into her chest and wrapped her arms around them.

"Pick up Zakia," said Sardar as he opened the bedroom door. "Get her dressed."

It was too late.

Sardar was halfway across the kitchen when the breaching charge went off. There was a blinding flash of hot, electric-white light and a simultaneous thunderclap of ear-crushing noise. The blast wave smashed him against the back wall. The door, twisted and warped beyond repair, rocketed past him, across the bedroom and crashed into the far wall.

Men came through the door. Sardar couldn't tell how many in the dark and the smoke. He struggled to raise his arm to shoot. His arm did not respond. He looked down. His pistol was nowhere to be seen. His arm was twisted like a corkscrew to one side. Bone was protruding through the flesh.

"Sardar!" screamed Warda. She came through the bedroom door with Zakia in her arms. Her face was contorted with fear, panic and the certain knowledge of impending death.

Sardar turned his head toward his wife. Bullets were smacking the wall behind him. Something was tugging at his shirt.

He looked down absently. There was blood soaking through the fabric. He was bleeding. He had been shot. He had no idea how many times. His head felt light, and the room began to spin. He collapsed.

Above Sardar a man appeared with an AK-47. He was one of the men from the street. He was smiling. He pointed the AK at Sardar and then swiveled to look past him.

Sardar rolled his head to one side to follow the man's gaze. Warda was down on her knees with Zakia clutched to her chest. She was screaming, but strangely Sardar could not hear her. The man with the AK-47 shut Warda three times in the face. She fell backward and lay still. The man shot Zakia in the head.

Then he turned back to Sardar.

"Who wants to kill this Pashtun fucker?" said the man.

"Me," said another of the men in the room. He stepped up, pointed a shotgun at Sardar's head and pulled the trigger. Sardar never heard the blast.

CHAPTER THIRTY-EIGHT

0923 HOURS, 16 AUGUST 2002.
STAR SPANGLED BANNER HOTEL, HOWARD COUNTY, MARYLAND.

"The maid found her about forty-five minutes ago," said Yards. He looked down at the contorted body of the dead Filipina in the tub and then back at Bill who was standing in the doorway of the bathroom.

"How long has she been dead?" asked Bill.

"Since sometime yesterday I would bet," said Yards. "We'll know for sure when the medical examiner gets a look at her."

"Why?" said Spalding. He was standing behind Bill looking over his shoulder.

"I would guess she got cold feet," said Yards. "Agreed?" He looked back at Bill.

"Yeah," said Bill. "But that's not the worst part of it."

"What's that mean?" asked Spalding.

"The worst part is they didn't try to hide the body," said Bill. "They just left her. They had to know she'd be found. They had to know that would mean cops, and anytime you invite scrutiny there's a chance something gets found, that you give something away."

"So," said Spalding.

"So, they didn't care," said Yards. He looked back at the sad, twisted body in the tub.

"They don't plan on us having the time to exploit anything we find here," said Bill. He closed his eyes and tried to push away the images of a bound, dying Aphrodite that were crowding his mind.

"It's game time," said Yards.

"Fuck," said Spalding.

"Hey, boss."

Spalding turned. Rogers was standing on the sidewalk outside the open motel room door. He had some papers in a file folder in his hand.

"Talk to me," said Spalding. "Give me some good news." He stepped out onto the sidewalk next to Rogers, and Yards and Bill followed close behind.

"I just drove over from Headquarters," said Rogers. He opened the file and looked down as he spoke. "So, this is the scoop as of about an hour ago. Cyber Ops got into the computer in Mexico. Confirmed what Bill already told us. Lots of stuff on biological weapons and a Skype account in contact with the identified players."

"Tell me you got more than what I already had days ago," growled Bill.

"Based on the files on the computer looks like they are referring to this op by the codename Caffa," said Rogers.

"Fabulous," said Bill.

"What the hell is Caffa?" asked Yards.

"It's a city in the Crimean," said Bill. He looked at the ground, took a deep breath and closed his eyes for a moment before continuing. "Was a city in the Crimean. Besieged by a Muslim army in the 1300's. The plague began to run through the besieging army. Thousands were dying. So, the Muslims catapulted the bodies of their dead over the city walls. They used their own dead soldiers to spread the plague to the Christians holding the city. It worked. The plague spread like wildfire."

"And the survivors fled to Italy and brought the plague with them," said Rogers quietly. "That began the Black Death."

"That killed a huge chunk of the population of the entire continent of Europe," said Spalding.

"Tell me something I can use," said Bill. He looked Roger s hard in the eyes.

"This guy, Sultan Rashid," said Rogers. "Not a whole lot on him, but what there is says, in addition to being a major scumbag and a crook, he's also tied in to some big boys in Lashkar-e-Taiba back in Pakistan."

"That fits with what Islamabad Station's source said about an LeT plot," said Spalding.

"Also, that Akbar Skype account is tied to communications from LeT in Pakistan to some of the boys who carried out the attack on the Indian Parliament building in Delhi in December of 2001. So, whoever is using it is a major player."

"Roger, how about something that helps me find my wife before she's dead," said Bill.

"In addition to Sultan, two of the other Skype accounts on his computer have also been talking to Akbar back in Pakistan. One is Sumaya, whoever that is. The other is Addas. That's the one that popped up only recently."

"Saying what?" asked Bill.

"We don't know," said Rogers. "It doesn't work like that. We're not pulling the content, just the connections."

"I'm still waiting for the good news," said Bill.

"We don't know the names of the people using these accounts, but we have identified their computers," said Rogers. He closed the file and looked up. The next time they come up on the net, we will know immediately, and we will be able to jump on them."

"Yeah," said Bill. "All we have to do now is hope they decide to surf the net one last time before they head off to Paradise."

He turned, leaned against the wall of the motel and hung his head for a moment.

"CDC?" asked Spalding.

"Oh, yeah," said Rogers. "CDC is starting to clue in. They have confirmed over 450 cases of the plague now, Maryland, Delaware, Pennsylvania and D.C. Something like four dozen dead."

"At least it sounds like something we may be able to contain," said Spalding.

"Maybe, boss," said Rogers. "Depends on where we are on the curve."

"What curve?" asked Spalding.

"It's all about a race between how fast we are finding, quarantining and treating people and how fast the disease is spreading," said Rogers. He grimaced. "Right now we might be breaking even. That's keeping up with what one lady at the aquarium started. Imagine what happens when we start talking about eight or ten more Patient Zeros out there letting this shit loose."

"Does the lady at the aquarium take us anywhere?" asked Spalding.

"No ID on her," said Rogers. "Scrubbed clean. Not talking. Out of her mind with fever most of the time. Dead end."

"You're a real ray of sunshine, you know that?" said Yards.

"On the good news front, they sent a report to the NSC," said Rogers. "There will be a Principals meeting tonight or tomorrow morning to consider labeling this a terrorist attack."

"What did you say?" asked Bill. He turned and looked hard at Rogers again.

"A Principals meeting..." began Rogers.

"By tonight or tomorrow this whole thing may be a done deal," barked Bill. "By tonight or tomorrow Eleni may be dead."

"Sergeant Yards."

Yards turned to look in the direction of the voice. One of the Anne Arundel County cops who had been posted at the motel to control access to the rooms rented by the group was walking toward him. "We found something you might want to see in this other room," said the officer. Overhead there was the dull thump of the rotors of a State Police helicopter circling the motel.

"Okay" said Yards. "Coming." He followed the police officer in the direction of a room two doors down. Bill and Spalding fell in behind.

"I'm going to make a quick secure call to Headquarters and see if they have any updates," said Rogers. He walked back toward his car in the parking lot.

Yards, Bill and Spalding followed the cop into the motel room. It was a dismal, carbon copy of the room where they had found the dead woman. The beds were a mess, and there were damp towels on the floor in piles.

"Over here," said the cop. He pointed to the floor next to the bathroom door. There was a t-shirt stained with blood wadded up there.

"It's hers," said Bill. He knelt down, picked it up and opened it so he could see the blood soaked into it.

"Might not want to tamper with that," said the cop.

"It's my wife's," snarled Bill.

"It's okay, officer," said Yards. "Thanks." The cop nodded and walked out of the room.

"No holes," said Yards.

"She's vomiting blood," said Bill. He held the shirt down to his side and turned to look both Yards and Spalding in the face.

"And they changed her," said Spalding.

"Because wherever they are going, they are taking her with them," said Bill. "They're not just killing her. They're making her part of the attack."

"Jesus Christ," said Yards.

"We need to start on Cipro," said Spalding. "All of us." He looked at the shirt and then around the room. "Otherwise we're going to be casualties ourselves."

"Rogers is back," said Bill. He motioned past Spalding toward the door. The shirt was still in his hand.

"Anything?" said Spalding. Rogers was walking toward him with a look of excitement on his face.

"Finally," said Rogers. "A break."

"Spill it," said Spalding.

"Cyber says Addas's computer was up on the net last night," said Rogers. "Logged on from a Kinko's down the road about a mile from here. Got on the Amtrak site and bought tickets."

"Bought how?" said Spalding.

"Credit card," said Rogers. He looked down briefly at an index card covered in hasty scribbling in his right hand. "Name of Michael P. Smyth. We're running the name now."

"Tickets to where?" asked Bill.

"New York City," said Rogers. "Leaving from the rail terminal at BWI airport at 0657 this morning. Arriving Penn Station 0953."

"Shit," said Spalding.

"It's 0939," said Bill looking at his watch. "They're almost there."

CHAPTER THIRTY-NINE

0951 HOURS, 16 AUGUST 2002.
JERSEY CITY, NEW JERSEY.

The train came to a sudden and unexpected stop. There was no announcement or explanation. There was no station visible. On either side of the car were railroad tracks, lines of parked rail cars and warehouses.

"What do you suppose this is all about?" said the little lady with blue hair sitting next to Afiyah. She looked up from her reading and squinted her nose over her bifocals.

"No idea," said Afiyah. She leaned out of her seat and looked up the aisle toward the front of the passenger car and the other sisters. A big, burly, black conductor blew past her heading for the front of the train. He looked confused.

"What's happening?" said a man several seats in front of Afiyah as the conductor passed.

"Just single tracking into Penn Station, I guess," said the conductor.

"You guess?" said the man. The conductor breezed past without further comment.

Sister Bobbie was seated across the aisle and two rows in front of Afiyah. She stood, walked back to Afiyah's seat and knelt down. Despite the heavy doses of cold medicine she and all the other sisters had taken to mask their symptoms on the train, her eyes were sunken and her face pale.

"What do you think, sister?" whispered Bobbie.

"I am sure it is nothing, sister," said Afiyah. She was conscious that the woman sitting next to her had stopped reading and had cocked her head to listen. "Just a temporary delay. We'll start moving again soon." She reached out and patted Bobbie's meaty hand in reassurance. Her shoulder still ached from where Aphrodite had wrenched it during the struggle in the basement.

"I hope it's not something else," said Bobbie. She closed her eyes as if to compose herself for a moment, and swallowed hard. "I think the medicine is wearing off."

"Go back to your seat and rest, sister," said Afiyah. She arched her eyebrows to emphasize that Bobbie should keep quiet.

"Yes, sister," said Bobbie. She stood on uncertain legs and walked back to her seat.

"Are you with a church?" asked the woman next to Afiyah.

"Yes," said Afiyah. "Going to New York for a service."

"Your friend looks ill," said the woman. Bobbie was doubled over coughing with a handkerchief pressed over her mouth and nose.

"Just a cold," said Afiyah. "She'll be better soon."

"Are you sure?" asked the woman.

"By the end of the day, she will be fine," said Afiyah. *And, everyone on this train will be on their way to hell*, she thought.

"Ladies and gentlemen," blared the overhead speaker in the train compartment. "We apologize for the delay. Due to some temporary construction delays in the tunnel ahead, we will be held here for a short period of time. We will be rolling forward now and onto a siding. Please remain seated. We will advise you of developments as we obtain additional information."

The speaker cut off. The train car began to buzz with conversation amongst the passengers. There was a loud hiss as the train's brakes were released, and it began to roll forward at a crawl.

Out the window to Afiyah's right she could see a succession of black metal rail and road bridges over the Hackensack River. In the distance, almost close enough to touch, but still on the other side of the Hudson, she could see the skyscrapers of Manhattan. The train lurched to the right, drifted several hundred meters down a vacant siding and squealed to a halt.

Afiyah leaned out of her seat and looked down the aisle toward the front of the train again. Bobbie was still coughing. The other sisters were hunched over in their seats, scarves tied tightly around their heads. Afiyah knew they were coming close to the end. Medicine that masked their symptoms temporarily did nothing to stop the relentless progress of the disease. It was time to strike their targets.

Behind her, Afiyah heard some hushed conversation and a mention of the police. She twisted her head to see down the aisle behind her. Standing in a cluster inside the flexible gangway that connected her car to the one behind it was a tight knot of conductors. They had their heads together and were engaged in some sort of animated discussion. They looked worried.

Afiyah turned back around and looked out the window again. There was a narrow, gravel road that ran along the siding on the right hand side. As she watched, a black and white police car marked, "Jersey City Police," rushed past toward the front of the train.

Afiyah stood. The group of conductors in the gangway was listening to something on a radio that one of them had taken from his belt. Afiyah could not hear what it was. She turned, looked at Sister Bobbie, who was eyeing her intently, and nodded her head.

Bobbie wobbled to her feet and walked over to Afiyah.

"I am worried, sister," whispered Bobbie.

"Get the others," said Afiyah. "We go now."

Bobbie started to turn and head for the front of the car. The door to the gangway at the rear of the car opened. The big conductor who had pushed past them earlier came down the aisle toward them.

"Please step aside, ladies," said the conductor. He shoved past in a rush, walked to the middle of the car and stopped. "Ladies and gentlemen," he said.

Afiyah leaned over and peered out the window. In the distance on a raised expressway, she could see another police car heading their direction with the lights on.

"Oh, my Lord," said the blue-haired woman. She was looking at the police car too.

"Your Lord is a lie," said Afiyah to the woman. The lady's eyes grew large, and she shrank back against the wall of the car. "And he cannot help you now."

"Ladies and gentlemen," continued the conductor. "We have a police emergency."

"Sister," hissed Bobbie. Afiyah turned. "They know."

"Move," said Afiyah. She took one last look past the conductor toward the others. There was no way to reach them now.

"Where?" said Bobbie.

"Go," said Afiyah. She pushed Bobbie toward the back of the train and the gangway.

"Ladies," called the conductor. "Please have a seat. "

Afiyah and Bobbie kept moving. The automatic door to the gangway opened and closed behind them. They were in the flexible connection between cars. On either side were exit doors. Afiyah glanced back. The conductor moved toward them. He was saying something into his handheld radio.

Afiyah stepped to the door on the right side of the train and tried the handle. It did not move. The door was locked. She looked back through the glass window from the gangway into the car they had just left. The conductor was only feet away.

On the wall to left of the door was an emergency release button. Afiyah hit it. The door shot open. Maybe ten feet away and a few feet below them was the gravel road on which the police car had driven.

"Go," said Afiyah. She shoved Sister Bobbie, and the big woman went tumbling out. Afiyah followed, slid, staggered and stumbled but managed to retain her footing. Bobbie came up off the ground, coughing and wheezing and doubled over. Bright, red, bloody spit was flying from her lips.

"Run!" yelled Afiyah. She grabbed Bobbie by the elbow and pulled her up onto the roadway. On the other side of the road stretched lines of tracks filled with stationary freight and tanker cars.

"Hey!" yelled the conductor. He was standing in the doorway of the train. "Hey, you can't get off here!"

Afiyah didn't turn. On the other side of the Hackensack River, maybe a mile away, she could see homes and cars moving on busy streets.

"I can't," huffed Bobbie. Blood was dribbling from her nose.

"God will give you the strength, sister," said Afiyah. "And then he will take you home." Together the two women headed for the lines of graffiti covered rail cars ahead.

CHAPTER FORTY

1037 HOURS, 16 AUGUST 2002.
OVER ELIZABETH, NEW JERSEY.

"How fast does this thing go?" said Bill into the microphone mounted on his helmet. He was seated in the rear of the Maryland State Police twin-engine Eurocopter. To his left was Spalding, and on the other side of Spalding was Yards. Rogers had stayed in D.C.

"It's rated for 190 miles an hour," said the co-pilot, via the aircraft's intercom.

"And, we're doing over 200 now," said the pilot. "Whatever you do, don't tell the Captain. She'll have our ass."

"Getting something from the ground," said the co-pilot. "Hold on." He switched his mike over from the intercom to the radio, and Bill could see his lips moving as he talked to whoever was contacting him.

They were cruising at a little over a thousand feet. Out the windows to his right, Bill could see miles of warehouses, chemical plants and roads sliding by. Ahead in the distance was the skyline of Manhattan. He pressed his face against the glass and strained with bloodshot eyes to make out figures on the ground. He prayed they were not too late.

"Okay," said the co-pilot as he came back on the intercom, "Here's the latest. They stopped the train before it got in the tunnel. It's on a siding just west of Jersey City. The local cops are responding."

"Good news," said Spalding.

"There's more," said the co-pilot.

"There always is," said Bill.

"One of the conductor's on the train says he saw two ladies in headscarves jump off and head off toward the Hackensack River," said the co-pilot.

"Description?" asked Bill.

"Nothing worth shit," said the co-pilot. "Both white. One larger than the other."

"Wow," said Bill. "That narrows it down."

"What about the train?" asked Spalding. "How many are still on the train?"

"They haven't boarded the train yet," said the co-pilot. "They're waiting for the FBI and a National Guard Chem-Bio unit to show up with moon suits and other protective gear."

"How many people on the train?" asked Yards.

"Figure close to three hundred," said Spalding.

"And they're all going into quarantine," said Yards.

"Yep," said Spalding.

"What's the search area?" asked Bill.

"They've got Jersey City cops and State Police working the sidings east of where the train is stopped," said the co-pilot. He pointed out the windshield of the aircraft dead ahead. "You can see the sidings in the distance now. Maybe a thousand rail cars out there on a dozen tracks. They are going car by car now. Could take hours to finish that job."

"They're not in the cars," said Bill.

"How do you know where they are?" asked Spalding.

"They're dying," said Bill. He looked out the broad side window again. In the distance, past the railroad sidings and the Hackensack River on the other side, he could see trees, grass and baseball fields. Beyond that were miles of homes and tree-lined streets. "They're out of time."

"Where do you think they are?" asked Yards.

"What's on the other side of the river?" asked Bill.

"Jersey City," said the co-pilot.

"That's where they're going," said Bill. He thumped the glass for emphasis. "They're not going to go out hiding in a box car surrounded by rats. They're going to end this surrounded by as many victims as they can find."

"What do you want to do?" asked the pilot.

"Take us there," said Bill. "As fast as you can."

"Roger," said the pilot. The nose of the aircraft dipped suddenly, and the engine whined even louder. The ground came up fast below them. They were in a dive.

Ahead, on their left, the Amtrak train was now clearly visible, surrounded by multiple police cars with flashing lights. Other official vehicles could be seen scattered around the sidings next to the train, and individual police officers were now distinguishable.

"What bridge would they have to use to cross the river?" asked Bill. He unbuckled the harness that held him into his seat and squatted down next to the big side window in the sliding access door, so he could see better.

"They could walk the highway bridges," said the co-pilot. He gestured out the front of the aircraft again. "But, they'd be seen."

"And that's not the way they were headed when they left the train," said Spalding.

"What's that?" asked Bill. He pointed out the side window to a black, metal bridge a couple of miles away on their right.

"That's a railroad bridge," said the co-pilot craning his head. "No roadway."

"I bet there's a walkway," said Bill.

"Roger," said the pilot. "Let's take a look." The nose of the helicopter dipped again. They turned hard right, dropped down to a hundred feet off the deck and sped toward the bridge. The river was on their left now. On the other side was a broad park filled with baseball diamonds and soccer fields. There were half a dozen games in progress and what looked to be thousands of people watching from the bleachers.

"There are people on the bridge," said the co-pilot. Bill leaned hard against the glass window on the side of the aircraft and caught a flash of two women in headscarves struggling down a narrow wooden walkway along the side of the bridge as the aircraft passed over.

"Take us back," yelled Bill into the intercom. "Bring us down over top them."

"Roger," said the pilot. He spun the helicopter into a tight turn. The nose went up. The speed dropped away. The sound of the engine shifted from a high-pitched whine to a dull thump.

"There they are!" yelled the co-pilot. He pointed out the front of the aircraft. The two women were almost at the end of the bridge now. It looked like the smaller one was almost dragging the larger one forward.

"Put this thing on the ground," said Bill. He hit the release latch for the door, and it slid open. Hot, muggy air hit him in the face.

"I can't land here," said the pilot. Below them at the end of the bridge were railroad tracks lined on one side with trees and on the other side with telephone poles.

"Put us down," screamed Bill. He held onto a handle next to the door and leaned out into the prop wash from the rotors above. The two women were off the bridge. They were heading for a hole in the fence that ringed the park. They were no more than a hundred meters now from the first of the baseball diamonds he had seen from the air.

"I can't put this aircraft down here," said the pilot. He had leveled off about twenty-five feet in the air. The air from the rotors was driving leaves and debris on the ground in all directions. "Too much chance of a blade strike."

"Roger," said Bill. "It's your bird." He took his headset off and tossed it onto the floor of the helicopter. Then he reached up and pulled the shotgun out of the ready rack on the bulkhead in front of him.

"Whoa!" yelled Yards.

"What the hell are you doing?" bellowed Spalding.

Bill was already out the door.

CHAPTER FORTY-ONE

1050 HOURS, 16 AUGUST 2002.
LINCOLN PARK, JERSEY CITY, NEW JERSEY.

Bill hit the ground with his feet together and his knees bent, just the way he had been taught years before at airborne school at Fort Benning. He collapsed onto his side, rolled over and came back to his feet with the shotgun held tightly in both hands. The noise of the rotor blades above him was deafening. The two women were nowhere in sight.

Between the railroad tracks and the trees surrounding the park was grass about waist high. It was littered with broken beer bottles, used condoms and plastic grocery bags. Bill crouched and moved forward in the direction of the park. Above him, the helicopter ascended and slid away toward the baseball fields and Jersey City.

The noise of the rotors receded and vanished. Somewhere in the distance, spectators at one of the baseball games in the park were cheering. Around Bill, insects buzzed. There was no other sound.

Bill waded through the tall grass to a chest high chain link fence that marked the boundary of the park. The fence had been torn away from one of the fence poles, and the resulting gap in the fence was big enough for a person to wedge through. The grass was worn away here from foot traffic. There were flecks of bright, red blood on the ground.

Bill shoved through the hole in the fence and past some brush on the other side. He stepped out of the shade into sudden sunshine. The brush had given way to well-manicured grass. Twenty feet in front of him were the two women in headscarves. Another twenty feet past them was a boy of ten in a white baseball uniform with blue pinstripes playing centerfield.

Bill jacked the slide on the shotgun and chambered a round. The two women turned suddenly toward him. So did the boy.

"On your knees," said Bill. He put the shotgun to his shoulder and began to slowly advance.

"I have a bomb," said Afiyah. She held her right hand away from her body. It looked like she was gripping some kind of switch. With her left hand she lifted the long-sleeved t-shirt she was wearing to show sheets of explosives packed with ball bearings wrapped around her waist.

"Where is she?" said Bill. He kept moving.

"Run, sister," said Afiyah. She pushed Bobbie toward the little boy and the other players beyond him. Then she stepped forward, so that she was directly between Bobbie and Bill.

"Where is Eleni?" said Bill.

"Stop," said Afiyah. She glanced back over her shoulder to the bleachers packed with children and parents. They were less than fifty yards away. Play had stopped in the game. People in the stands were coming to their feet. She looked back at Bill and raised both of her arms above her head and away from her body.

Bill stopped. The shotgun was still to his shoulder. He computed the odds and the angles. They were standing on a Little League field. That meant it was a sixty-foot diamond and a fraction of the size of a major league field. Afiyah's suicide vest looked like it was holding something like ten pounds of plastic explosive. Everybody standing on the field was going to get hit when that thing detonated.

Bobbie stumbled toward the little boy, who seemed frozen in place. Behind him the other children in the outfield were running toward home plate. A man in a coach's uniform was waving his arms and yelling. People were spilling from the stands onto the field and scooping up the children in their baseball uniforms.

Bill circled left, without taking his eyes off Afiyah. Her face was blank, like someone had wiped all the life and humanity out of it. Her eyes seemed focused a million miles away. Bill could see Bobbie and the boy out of the corner of his left eye as he moved.

"Hurry, sister," yelled Afiyah. She closed her eyes for a moment and then opened them again. She was looking straight through Bill. She was looking for the face of God.

"I am trying, sister," said Bobbie. She was less than ten feet from the boy now. Bloody drool was running down her chin. She stumbled again and then fell forward on her knees.

"God loves you, sister," yelled Afiyah. "He will give you strength." She turned again toward Bobbie.

Bill pulled the trigger, jacked another shell in the shotgun and fired a second time. Both rounds were slugs. The first one hit Afiyah in her left temple, punched a hole the size of a roll of quarters through her skull and knocked most of the frontal lobe of her brain — the portion that controlled voluntary muscle movements — onto the ground behind her. The second one hit just below the hinge of her jaw and severed her spinal column.

Afiyah crumpled to the ground. Her fingers did not close on the switch in her hand. Bill spun left and put his sights on Bobbie.

The boy was standing frozen. The coach sprinted forward, scooped him up and carried him off at a trot toward the other children and spectators who were streaming away in the direction of their parked cars. Bill circled Bobbie with his sights fixed on her head. She was still on her knees.

"Where is she?" yelled Bill.

"Who?" coughed Bobbie. She was staring at the grass in front of her, stained red now with bloody spittle.

"Eleni," bellowed Bill. "Where the hell is she?"

"You mean the blond woman," wheezed Bobbie. Her arms hung like dead weight at her side.

"Yes, you bitch," growled Bill. "The blond woman. My wife."

"Dead," frothed Bobbie. "Or, she will be soon." She collapsed onto her side on the turf and vomited dark, red blood onto the green grass of centerfield.

Above Bill, and away to his left the dull thump of rotor blades began. The State Police chopper crawled into view a few meters above the tall trees that lined the parking lot beyond the baseball diamond. Briefly, there was the sound of a police siren, and then it was drowned out by the growing blast of the rotor wash.

Bill looked up briefly at the helicopter and then turned his back to it to shield his eyes and face from the dust and debris being driven toward him by the blades. Bobbie twitched spasmodically. Her breathing came in slow, shallow wheezes. The helicopter settled to the ground on the other side of the pitcher's mound.

Spalding jumped down out of the chopper, trotted across the grass and came up beside Bill. Bobbie had stopped moving. Afiyah lay dead a few feet away.

"They boarded the train!" yelled Spalding, so Bill could hear him over the whine of the helicopter's turbines.

"What about Eleni?" responded Bill. He had he shotgun at his side in his right hand.

"There were only two others on the train," responded Spalding.

"Where's Eleni?" yelled Bill.

"Not there, brother," said Spalding. "Neither are the rest of them."

"What the fuck are you saying?" yelled Bill.

"I'm saying there's another team," said Spalding.

CHAPTER FORTY-TWO

1057 HOURS, 16 AUGUST 2002.
FORT WASHINGTON, MARYLAND.

Eleni opened her eyes, rolled onto her back and strained to see what she could of her surroundings through the windows above her. She was lying on the floor in the cargo compartment of a rented Chevy Suburban driven by Anwar. She was bound at the ankles and wrists with duct tape. She didn't know how long she had been asleep. In the back of her mind there was a dim recollection of having been injected with something again. Her eyes were crusty, and her breathing labored and shallow.

The sun was out. There were broad trees visible. The sound of the tires on the roadway had changed. They weren't on a highway anymore. They were driving slowly on some kind of narrow roadway. Briefly, she heard children laughing and squealing, and then they were gone. The sound of a swing set faded into the distance.

The Suburban slowed, turned and came to a stop. Doors opened and slammed. Anwar and the women were talking outside. Someone coughed and gagged. Several people walked off on what sounded like a path covered in mulch or wood shavings. Other footsteps approached the back of the car. The hatch opened.

Eleni blinked and twisted her head away from the light. It was almost blinding after the shade in the back of the vehicle. Anwar was standing outside the car looking at her. Behind him were two of the sisters. Their faces were marred by purple blotches and dark circles, like pools of blood, under their eyes.

"I want to show you something," said Anwar. He bent down, opened a zipper on a bag that Eleni could not see and then held up a suicide vest, like he was showing off a new sweater. It was made of sheets of yellowish plastic explosive and packed with thousands of pellets the size of buckshot.

"Very nice," said Eleni. "Make it yourself?" She smirked and tried to project defiance.

"It was made by the brothers in Pakistan," said Anwar. He put down his shirt. "I brought two. Sister Afiyah has the other."

"You are a sick bastard, you know that?" said Eleni. She scanned the area behind Anwar looking for any sign of passersby. There were none. They seemed to be in parking lot in an otherwise deserted area of a park.

"What are you?" asked Anwar. "You're not an American."

"I'm Greek. '

"This isn't even your fight," said Anwar.

"Really? You're talking to a Greek about jihad and spreading Islam and you don't think this is old history to me? Ever been to Constantinople?"

"Constantinople doesn't exist anymore," said Anwar.

"Exactly," said Aphrodite.

"Who is Bill?" asked Anwar.

"My husband. The man who is going to kill you."

"You pray for the wrong things," said Anwar.

"I'm not praying," said Aphrodite. "Just waiting."

"You will be dead soon. You need to begin to make your peace with God."

"Don't talk to me about God. You're ridiculous. A pampered white boy pretending to be a prophet."

"You know nothing about God. You're an unbeliever."

"I know enough about God to know he would never want this," said Eleni.

"This is all God's plan. The only way to make this right is to burn down the filth and the smut and the rot."

"You're sad, and you're pathetic," said Eleni. "What's the matter? Did Mommy and Daddy not kiss your ass enough when you were a boy? Is that what this is all about? One big, pathetic tantrum?"

"I found God," said Anwar. His face had gone pink, and the tips of his ears were glowing red. "I realized the truth. I rejected Satan."

"You found nothing," said Eleni. "Nothing a million other psychos before you haven't found. An excuse to commit evil."

Anwar paused and looked at his feet for a moment. The sisters behind him shifted listlessly from side to side as if they thought they should be doing something. Birds called. The silence lingered. Anwar looked up. His face was composed, and the color was receding.

"We are going to Washington soon," said Anwar. "You are coming with us."

"I am not," said Eleni.

"You are," said Anwar. "And you will follow the instructions I give you. Because there will be a great many people, and if you do not behave, I will detonate this."

"Blow yourself up? I don't think you have the balls."

"Not me," smiled Anwar. "You."

"I'll die before you get that thing on me," snarled Aphrodite.

"We will put it on you, and then you will die," said Anwar. He set down the vest and rustled around in the unseen bag again. When he straightened up he had a syringe in his hand.

CHAPTER FORTY-THREE

Bill looked down at his shoes and the grass under them. The sun was hot on the back of his neck. He felt drained of every bit of energy and motivation. He felt used up. Eleni was dead or dying. He had failed.

"Let's get some water and something to eat," said Spalding. He was standing a few feet away, watching Bill closely in the way you might watch a guy standing on the side of a bridge getting ready to jump. Behind him, the bodies of Afiyah and Bobbie were still sprawled on the ground. A few Jersey City cops were standing around them and talking about how long it would take the technicians to show up and process the scene.

"How did I let this happen?" asked Bill. He looked up at Spalding. His head was pounding with pain and fatigue.

"This isn't on you, bro," said Spalding. "She got caught up in something nobody could have seen coming."

"I could have been here," said Bill. "I could have been anywhere but running around the goddamn jungle saving the world. I could have been doing my real job, taking care of the home front."

"Kicking yourself for something you couldn't have prevented isn't going to help anyone. She needs you."

"If she's still alive."

"Don't think that," said Spalding.

"That one vomited blood and died right in front of me, man," said Bill. He gestured toward Bobbie's body. "Eleni's had that crap inside of her just as long."

"She's stronger than that," said Spalding. "You know that."

"I won't make it without her," said Bill. Despite his best efforts his eyes were getting moist and his voice was cracking.

"She's not gone," said Spalding.

"I've been to hell once," said Bill. "I've looked into that pit. She's the only reason I made it back."

"Bro, we don't have time for this," said Spalding. He walked over and put his hand on Bill's shoulder. "You don't have time for this. Put the Superman suit back on."

"I'm hanging on by my fingernails, brother," whispered Bill. "I swear to God I am."

"She's out there, Bill," said Spalding. "She's out there, and you're going to find her."

"Spalding!" yelled Yards. He was standing about twenty meters away next to the helicopter. The aircraft's engines were off, and its doors wide open.

"Yeah," responded Spalding.

"Rogers is on the phone for you," answered Yards. "Says he has some new info."

"Okay, we're coming," said Spalding. He turned back to Bill and grabbed him by the arm. "Time to get back on the horse, cowboy," he said.

Bill and Spalding walked in silence to the helicopter. Yards was sitting in the back of the aircraft. The pilot was standing some distance away, talking to the Jersey City emergency rescue personnel who had just rolled up. The co-pilot was sitting in his seat in the front of the aircraft with the door on his side open.

"We've got it on speaker, so everyone can hear," said Yards. It's a cellular signal, so it's a two way real time conversation." He pointed to the speaker mounted in the ceiling of the helicopter as he spoke.

"Go ahead, Rogers," said Spalding. "Boyle and I are here now."

"Yes, sir," said Rogers. His voice was distant and mechanical but clear. "I'm at the State Police command post in Baltimore. We're getting information here from Headquarters and from the cops on the train up where you are. I've also got Dr. Ahmed Baluchi here. He's my contact at the CDC."

"Okay," said Spalding. "Bring us up to speed."

"There were two women on the train. One named Anne Marie Stone and one named Jennifer Lynn Blaine. They were both holding tickets purchased by Michael P. Smyth. They were also both holding tickets to a Springsteen concert this afternoon at Madison Square Garden."

"Shit," said Bill.

"I bet you'll find the same on the bodies of the two you took out up there," said Rogers.

"I bet you're right," said Spalding.

"Both the women on the train are showing symptoms of advanced pneumonic plague," said Rogers. "They are going to be treated, but the prognosis isn't good."

"While we're on that subject," said Spalding. "Where do we stand with the woman from the aquarium?'

"She went into a coma about twenty-four hours ago, and died early this morning," said Rogers.

"I thought Cipro could cure this crap," growled Bill.

"Depends on when you catch it," said Rogers. "But, I'll defer to Dr. Baluchi on that kind of detail."

"Okay, doc," said Spalding. 'Talk to us. What kind of trouble are we in? How fast is this stuff going to spread?"

"The Threshold Theorem of Epidemiology says that the spread of an epidemic can be predicted if three things are known: initial number of susceptible people (S(0)), the infection rate (K), and the removal rate (by quarantine or cure) (Q), " said Dr. Baluchi. He had a high, young voice and a pronounced Scottish accent.

"The spread of the epidemic is indicated by the percentage of susceptible individuals who become infected. Diseases that are easily transmitted spread quickly unless measures are taken to quarantine or cure infected individuals rapidly."

"English please, doc," said Bill.

There was a pause and then the sound of the doctor clearing his throat. "Okay. Think of a forest fire. If you catch it early and act aggressively, you have a decent chance of containing it and keeping it behind firebreaks. If you don't, if you're too late, and it gets too big, you're done. It just jumps the firebreaks. At some point, you are reduced to letting it burn itself out. With a forest fire, that could be weeks. With an epidemic that could be years."

"How close are we to having this thing jump the fire breaks?" asked Bill.

"We are on the razor's edge already," said Baluchi. "We have hundreds of people infected from the aquarium incident. Keep in mind, we find out people are infected when they show up at hospitals. That's anywhere from a day to two days after infection, so we are always running behind. Now, we have a train full of people, who may be infected, plus everyone who got on and off the train during the trip, plus everyone who passed through the train station while the infected team was there. Oh, and let's not forget about everyone else who may have come in contact with any of the infected individuals since they inhaled the bacteria."

"What happens if this second team makes it to a crowded venue, something on the scale of Madison Square Garden where the first team was headed?" asked Bill.

"Game over," said the doctor. "Every single one of these people right now is at their peak as far as their capacity to infect others. Every time they breathe out they are expelling clouds of millions of plague bacteria. If you put several of these people into a crowded venue, especially one where the air is moist and warm, and let them circulate, you are talking thousands, maybe tens of thousands of new cases. And, every one of those infected people will rapidly begin to infect others."

"But, we can treat them," said Spalding. "What about antibiotics?"

"You are not hearing me," said Baluchi. "We are up against the limits of the system already. There are only so many doctors and only so many hospitals. Oh, and by the way, in the whole damn country there's maybe enough Cipro to treat a few hundred thousand cases."

"If they make it to the kind of target we think they are after, we're in a world of hurt," said Spalding.

"If they make it to the kind of target you are talking about, you are back in the 13th century. We'll be talking casualty rates in the tens of millions," said Dr. Baluchi.

"Okay, well, Rogers, I hope you have some kind of lead to where the rest of these psychos are," said Spalding. "Because it sounds to me like we are just about out of time."

"We're running down all the names we have so far. No idea how long that will take. We've gone back to the imam at the mosque in Baltimore. He doesn't know the names of the rest of the women. Seems this Afiyah lady handled all that and decided who would stay at the house."

"She was the recruiter," said Spalding.

"Looks like it," said Rogers.

"Well, she ain't talkin'," said Bill. The Jersey City crime scene technicians had only just showed up and were beginning to take photos of the bodies on the baseball field.

"Michael P. Smyth?" asked Spalding.

"Suburban, white kid, Silver Spring," said Rogers. "Cops are talking to the parents now. Dad's a lawyer. Mom's a banker. Divorced. Dad's on this second wife. Mom's living with a guy ten years younger than her. They haven't seen Michael in years. As a kid he was clean cut, kind of a nerd but no real issues, then seems like he went off the deep end, got enamored of Islam and eventually ran away from home. They don't seem to have any idea where he has been since then."

"So, we're hosed," said Spalding.

"Hold on, boss," said Rogers. "Give me a second." Rogers stopped speaking but there was the muffled sound of shuffling papers and hurried conversation in the background.

"We don't have time for a dragnet," said Bill.

"I know," said Spalding. "We've got to have something to help us catch up."

"Boss," said Rogers. He was back on the phone. His voice was hurried and excited. "I've got something."

"What is it?" asked Spalding.

"Two things actually," said Rogers.

"Go," barked Spalding.

"Cyber boys just pulled another Michael P. Smyth credit card transaction. He rented a Chevy Suburban in Laurel this morning. I can send you plates and description. We're talking to the rental car company. They have their vehicles fitted with tracking devices, so they can recover them. Last hit seems to be in the vicinity of Fort Washington in Maryland. That was less than an hour ago."

"Just across the river from D.C.," said Spalding.

"What's happening in D.C. today?' asked Bill. "Where would this nut case go to find a crowd?"

"There's a concert on the mall," said Rogers. "Part of the Celebrate America country music tour. It's a build-up to the celebrations on the first anniversary of 9/11."

"How many people?" asked Spalding.

"Maybe a quarter of a million," said Rogers.

"Get the word out," barked Spalding. "We're saddling up and heading that way."

"I just hope this guy doesn't know we stopped the train," said Bill. "We need to catch him off guard."

CHAPTER FORTY-FOUR

1140 HOURS, 16 AUGUST 2002.
SILESIA, MARYLAND.

"We need water, brother," said Sister Agnes. She was a rail thin black woman with her head wrapped in a white head scarf. She was sitting in the passenger's seat, next to Anwar. The other sisters were in the back with Eleni wedged in between two of them. Eleni's mouth was covered with duct tape and her wrists taped together in front of her.

"I will stop," said Anwar. "But, only for a moment. We need to keep moving." They had only left the park a few moments before, and it was less than thirty minutes to their target.

"Thank you, brother," said Sister Agnes. "The sisters are brave but they are near the end, and they need water to make it the rest of the way." Behind her in the car there was a chorus of coughing and wheezing. One of the sisters looked like she might be unconscious. Another was tilting her head back and holding a cloth against her nose to stop the bleeding.

Ahead on the small country road, Anwar spotted a small building and a sign for the Silesia Country Store. He pulled into the gravel parking lot in front of the establishment, parked and got out.

"I will bring you all water, and then I will give you more medicine to help you make the final part of the journey, sisters," said Anwar. "Courage. You will be with God soon." Then he closed the door and walked into the tiny country store.

"Hello," said a short, gray-haired woman with thick glasses standing behind a counter inside. Behind her on the wall was a sign advertising soft drinks, milkshakes and sandwiches. In front of her were a few low shelves with canned goods and snacks.

"Hello," said Anwar. He walked to a cooler at the end of the store and began to take out bottles of water. Behind him, he could hear the sound of a television playing.

"Oh, Lord," said the woman. Anwar finished filling his arms with bottles of water and walked back to the counter. The woman was looking up at a television mounted near the ceiling in one corner of the room. The set was tuned to a news channel showing aerial photos of a train stopped on a railroad siding.

"Oh, Lord," said the woman again.

"What's going on?" asked Anwar. He set the bottles of water down on the counter and then looked up at the television. At the bottom of the screen, it said "Train Stopped in New Jersey, Possible Terrorist Attack."

"I don't know what this world is coming to," said the woman. She looked back briefly at Anwar and then back at the screen. "They're saying there might be some kind of terrorist attack in New Jersey. Police stopped this train and won't let anyone off."

"Wow," said Anwar. His stomach fell, and his knees felt weak, but he fought to maintain composure.

The picture on the television switched to a newsroom. An anchorman behind a desk was looking into the camera. The banner at the bottom of the screen scrolled the words "Breaking News".

"We're getting reports now of multiple cell phone calls placed by passengers on the train," said the anchor. "For more on that let's go to Candie Crawford, live from Jersey City."

The picture on the set switched again. A young, blond woman holding a microphone was standing next to what looked like a chemical plant. Barely visible in the background was the train.

"Thanks, Brett. Behind me, you can see the Amtrak train that has been stopped and pulled onto a siding just outside Jersey City," said the blond woman.

"We still have no official word on why, and we are not being allowed any closer by police, but we are hearing from individuals who have been called by friends and family on the train. They are reporting that they were initially told that the train was being stopped because Amtrak was single-tracking into Manhattan. However, now the train has been boarded by military personnel dressed in protective gear, like that used to protect against chemical and biological agents. And the passengers have been told that they will be taken to some sort of quarantine facility."

"This is terrible," said Anwar.

"Horrible," said the gray-haired woman. She began to ring up Anwar's purchase.

"Things are still very fluid here, and we have yet to get any official word on what is happening, but, if the word coming out via cell phone is accurate, we could be looking at some sort of terrorist attack, perhaps even one using a biological weapon," continued the blond woman on the television.

"Thank you," said Anwar. He paid for the water and took the bag into which the dark-haired woman had placed the bottles. He turned and walked slowly out of the store. Behind him he heard the anchorman on the television come back on and begin to recap events so far.

Anwar climbed into the Suburban, handed the bag of water bottles to Agnes and started the engine. He did not shift the vehicle into gear. He stared blankly out at the parking lot in front of him and the road beyond.

"Is something wrong, brother?" asked Agnes. She took a bottle of water for herself and then handed the others back to the sisters in the rear of the vehicle.

"They know," said Anwar.

"They know what?" asked Agnes. The other sisters grew suddenly silent.

"They stopped the train with the others on it," said Anwar quietly.

"Somehow they found out."

"How?" asked Agnes.

"It doesn't matter how," said Anwar. "What matters is that if they found out about the train and the others, they probably know about us as well."

"But, they don't know where we are," said Agnes. "Even if the sisters are still alive, they would not talk. And, we are very close."

"Yes, sister," said Anwar. "But, they probably know what we are driving, and with that it is only a matter of time until they find us and stop us."

"We have come too far, brother," said Agnes. "What should we do?"

"We should find another car," said Anwar." He shifted the Suburban into gear, pulled out onto the road and turned back the way they had come, toward the water.

"Fast."

CHAPTER FORTY-FIVE

1152 HOURS, 16 AUGUST 2002.
CHAPEL POINT PARK, MARYLAND.

Anwar drove east past Indian Head Highway, then south and away from Washington, D.C. He wasn't going far, but he needed to buy time, and he figured the police would focus on the routes into D.C. first, if they really had been alerted. Suburbia dropped away. On both sides of the road were scattered homes, forest and swamp. He was in old Maryland, the Maryland that existed before the federal government and bedroom communities for bureaucrats swallowed it whole.

Thirty minutes later, he came to a brown, wooden sign for Chapel Point State Park. He slowed and turned in, watching his rearview mirror the whole time, as he had since leaving the general store, to see if he had picked up a tail. No one made the turn with him.

A few hundred meters past the entrance to the park was an intersection. A sign pointed right to a nature trail. Another pointed left to a boat launch. Anwar turned left.

Two minutes later Anwar came to the end of the road. There was a small, blacktop parking area on the right. Straight ahead was a boat ramp. Beyond it was the Port Tobacco River, bounded here on both sides by marsh and forest.

There were several vehicles in the parking lot. All but one had an empty boat trailer attached to it. The lone exception was a red Ford F-150 crew cab with a USMC bumper sticker on it.

Next to the boat ramp was a short wooden pier. Sitting at the end of the pier was an elderly black man with a cane fishing pole. Next to him was a small boy of about six. Anwar parked the van in the lot and opened the door to get out.

"Sisters," said Anwar. "Stay here and stay out of sight. But, be ready to move. We will be leaving here in a few moments, and we will be leaving quickly. Make your final preparations now."

"We will be ready," said Sister Agnes.

Anwar got out of the vehicle and closed the door. A car came down the road to the boat ramp, turned around and drove away. Inside were two teenage boys. Loud rock music banged from the windows. Anwar made a show of checking the tires on the Suburban until the car was gone. Then he walked toward the pier.

"Catching anything?" asked Anwar as he walked up to the old man and the boy at the end of the pier.

"Nothing," said the man. He looked up at Anwar, then back at the boy. "But, our luck is going to change any minute now, isn't it, Willy?"

"Yep, Grandpa," said the boy. He looked up at Anwar and smiled for a moment. He was missing both his front teeth.

"What do you catch here, mostly?" asked Anwar. He put his hands in his pockets and tried to look nonchalant.

"Perch usually," said the man. "But, we got a late start today. Water's warm. They bite better in the morning and toward sundown." He reeled in the line and then cast it out again. The red and white bobber plunked into the brown water and sent out tiny ripples in all directions.

"That your truck?" asked Anwar.

"The red one?" asked the man without turning around.

"Yes," said Anwar. He looked back over his shoulder to make sure no other vehicles were coming down the ramp.

"Nope," said the man. "Belongs to my son. He's on float in the Middle East right now. That's why I'm helping out with watching Willy here, cuz he's a whole handful for his Momma to take care of all alone."

"Nice truck," said Anwar.

"Thanks," said the man.

"Your son's a Marine?" asked Anwar.

"Marine infantry," said the man. He tapped a "USMC" tattoo on his left wrist. "Just like me. 1972, Mekong Delta."

"A crusader pig," hissed Anwar.

"Here, hold this a minute," said the man after a moment's hesitation. He leaned over and gave the fishing pole to Willy. Then he turned around, came up on one knee and started to stand. Behind him on the far bank of the river a blue heron was wading through the reeds at the water's edge.

"You got something you want to say to me, mister?" asked the man as he came to his feet. His eyes were squinted and his mouth pursed.

"Your son's a baby killer," said Anwar. He smiled, turned one last time to look over his shoulder and then swung the knife blade palmed in his right hand back across the man's throat.

"Jesus, lord," hissed the man as blood cascaded from the gash in his throat down his chest and onto his coveralls. He fell to his knees, grasping at his throat and blowing bloody bubbles from his mouth.

"Grandpa!" screamed the boy. He dropped the fishing pole into the water and came to his feet at the end of the dock. His eyes were wide with fear and his tiny hands clenched in front of him like he was suddenly freezing.

"Grandpa's gone," said Anwar.

"Jesus, lord," sputtered the man again. Blood was pooling around him and dripping through the boards of the dock into the water below.

"Grandpa!" screamed the boy again.

"Enough," said Anwar. He stepped over the body of the bleeding man toward the boy. The boy stepped backward and stopped right at the end of the dock. Behind him the brown water of the river was flowing briskly toward the Chesapeake Bay. It was ebb tide.

"Grandpa's dead," said Anwar.

"No!" screamed the boy. Blood was dripping off the knife in Anwar's hand. Behind him, Grandpa was growing still.

"Yes," said Anwar. He shoved the boy backward into the swirling water.

The boy bobbed to the surface, gasped, spit and called out, then went under again. The water was over his head. He could not swim. Anwar turned around without saying a word.

"Help!" called the boy as he came to the surface a second time. He was further from the dock now, caught in the current and being swept away. Anwar did not turn. He knelt down and began to go through the old man's pockets, searching for his keys. The man was not moving, but there was a long, low, sinking sound coming from his chest.

"Help," said the boy one last time. His voice was weak and muffled by the water in his throat and lungs. He sank below the surface of the river, his coffee-colored face barely visible in the brown river, and drifted away.

"God be praised," said Anwar. He pulled a pair of keys on a Ford key ring out of the old man's pocket and stuffed them in his own. Then, he wiped his knife blade on one leg of the man's coveralls, closed the knife and put it back in his pocket. Finally, he grabbed the fabric on the coveralls with both hands, rolled the man over and pushed him off the side of the wooden dock into the water.

The old man sank briefly, then bobbed momentarily back to the surface. His face was up. His wide, shock white eyes were staring straight at Anwar. Then the old man sank back under the water, with his eyes still wide open, and his body slid slowly away from the dock in the direction that boy's had gone.

Anwar walked off the dock and across the parking lot to the red Ford pickup. He opened the doors and checked quickly inside to make sure there were no surprises. Then, he walked back to the Suburban and opened the driver's side front door.

"It is time, sisters," said Anwar. "Quickly. All of you into the truck."

"We are ready," said Sister Agnes. She had removed her headscarf. She was wearing an "I Love New York" t-shirt and a baseball cap with an American flag on it. Behind her in the vehicle, all the other sisters had changed their appearances as well.

"God is waiting," said Anwar. He closed the door and walked back toward the truck. Behind him, the sisters, pulling Aphrodite with them, piled out of the Suburban and followed.

CHAPTER FORTY-SIX

1335 HOURS, 16 AUGUST 2002.
WASHINGTON, D.C.

The State Police helicopter swung wide over the Potomac River and banked hard right for a landing on the Polo Field just west of the Tidal Basin. Bill's face was glued to the window in the door on the starboard side of the aircraft. What he saw was terrifying.

The entire National Mall from the Capitol Building to the Lincoln Memorial was a sea of humanity. The grass of the mall itself was almost invisible, buried beneath an avalanche of blankets, picnic baskets, Bermuda shorts and baseball caps. At the Capitol Hill end of the mall there was a raised stage with a red, white and blue awning over it. At the other end of the mall, in front of the Lincoln Memorial, was another stage covered in an identical awning. Country bands were playing on both stages, and people near the stages were dancing and singing.

"Jesus, help us," said Bill.

"I hope he's listening, bro," said Spalding. He was hunched over next to Bill with his head in his hands.

The helicopter touched down, Bill slid open the door, unharnessed and jumped out. Spalding and Yards followed, and the bird lifted off again almost immediately. The aircraft was low on fuel, and the pilots didn't want to take any chances with getting back to their base in Baltimore.

A hundred feet away parked on the field itself was a huge blue and white RV with the words "Mobile Command Post" written on it. Next to it were a cluster of support vehicles, a generator and several large antennas. Bill, Spalding and Yards ran for the vehicle. The temperature and humidity were suffocating.

Next to the entrance to the Command Post, a cluster of Metropolitan Police, Capitol Police and Park Police officers was engaged in animated conversation. Bill pushed past with the others in tow, bounded up the steps into the vehicle and stopped to survey the scene.

The interior of the vehicle was broken up into small cubicles and jammed with workstations, computers, radios and white boards. The noise was deafening and the heat unbearable. In the rear of the vehicle was a small conference table. Standing next to it, beside a tall, uniformed D.C. police officer, was Rogers.

"Back here!" yelled Rogers over the din. He motioned to Bill to come his way.

"Coming through," barked Bill. He pushed his way through the crowd of police officers and technicians in the Command Post and came up beside Rogers in the rear of the vehicle. Spalding and

Yards followed suit and wedged themselves into the claustrophobic space around the table.

"This is M.P.D. Captain Ferrell," said Rogers. He pointed to a muscular black gentleman next to him wearing a uniform with shoulder boards on it. "He's in charge of the security for the concert."

"Good to meet you," said Bill, Spalding and Yards in unison.

"Likewise," said Ferrell. His head was shaved clean, and his face grim. Behind him on the wall a live video feed of the crowd on the mall from a helicopter overhead was playing on a flat screen TV.

"Where are we, Rogers?" asked Spalding.

"Here's what we know," said Rogers. "Charles County cops found the Suburban where the GPS said it was, at Chapel Point State Park. It was abandoned. Nobody inside. Nobody in the vicinity of it who looked remotely like the scumbags we are chasing."

"Great," said Spalding.

"Inside the cops found head scarves, bags, skirts and long sleeved shirts," continued Rogers.

"They left naked?" said Yards.

"They changed," said Bill. "Time to blend in."

"Yep," said Rogers. "Looks like. And the bags on the train in New Jersey had normal street clothes in them too. T-shirts, shorts, etc. Guess those ladies up there just never got a chance to put on their concert clothes."

"Any idea how they left the scene?" asked Yards.

"None," said Rogers. "Cops found blood on a dock at the park, but no bodies. Without knowing who's missing, we can't start trying to identify what vehicle may have been stolen."

"You won't find the bodies," said Bill. "Least not any time soon."

"They left one before," said Spalding.

"When they thought they were black," said Bill. He was staring at the tens of thousands of people visible on the flat screen. "They know we're on to them. They saw the news. That's why they ditched the Suburban. They took the bodies with them. They dumped them in the river. They threw them in a ditch. Whatever would buy them time."

"More bad news," said Rogers. He was looking at some notes he had scribbled on index cards as he talked. "Dr. Baluchi says that the conditions here are just about optimal from the bad guys' standpoint. The temperature is just under 102 degrees. Humidity is close to 100 percent. There's no wind. And, we have something like 250,000 people out there."

"It's a freakin' petri dish," said Yards.

"And, this is just the opening act," said Rogers. "There are concerts tomorrow and Sunday as well. People are coming in from all over the country. Any microbe you turn loose out there now will be spread by car, rail and airplane to the entire nation by Monday."

"Cancel the concert," said Bill. "Send them home now." He was still staring at the television.

"Impossible," said Ferrell.

"Why?" asked Bill. He turned his head to look at Ferrell.

"First, I don't have authorization to do that," said Ferrell. "That would be the Mayor, and he already said no."

"I'm lost," said Bill. He surveyed the faces around him and then looked back at Ferrell. "We are talking jet fuel and a match here. If these psychos get into that crowd and start spitting bacteria into every face around them, we are back in the Dark Ages."

"You're preaching to the choir," said Ferrell.

"Captain Ferrell spent the last half hour on the phone with the Mayor, the FBI and the Secret Service," said Rogers. "He's been trying to shut this down since he was briefed on the situation."

"So, what's the problem?" asked Bill. "Shut it down."

"The Mayor won't act without a clear read from the White House," said Rogers. "Says this is national security, and if somebody is going to make the call to shut down this party and throw 250,000 tourists off the lawn, it's going to be the White House."

"And, let me guess," said Bill. "We're still waiting for the NSC to meet and make a call." His eyes were glowing with heat.

"The President's in the air flying back from Camp David early," said Rogers. He was staring at his feet. "We hope to have a meeting this afternoon."

"Do they know thousands of people are going to die, because they need to have a goddamn meeting?" barked Bill.

"We're coming up on the one year anniversary of 9/11," said Spalding quietly. "The whole country's being told that we have the bad guys on the run. Last thing anyone wants to do right now is sound an alarm and tell the nation that terrorists are inside the wire."

"I'm doing what I can," said Ferrell. He smiled weakly. "I have put the word out to all officers in the area. We are checking people going onto the Mall to control for alcohol and weapons, and I have told the officers at those checkpoints to be alert for anyone who seems to be seriously ill or acting suspiciously."

"You're looking for people we can't identify," said Bill. "No faces, no names."

"Who may already be here," said Spalding. "May already be there." He pointed at the television screen. The camera in the helicopter zoomed in momentarily on the stage and the crowd pressed up against the temporary picket fence in front of it. There were five thousand people visible in that shot alone.

"What else do you have, Rogers?" asked Bill.

"What do you mean?" responded Rogers.

"I mean, what else do you have?" said Bill. He enunciated each word slowly and carefully as he spoke. "What you've given us so far leaves us nowhere. That's unacceptable."

"It's not his fault," said Spalding. He reached out to put his hand on Bill's arm, and Bill jerked away.

"I don't care," growled Bill. "I don't care about fault. I don't care about meetings, and protocol and all this other happy horseshit. My wife is out there. She is dying. And, any minute now thousands of others are going to be infected."

"We all know this," said Spalding. "What do you want us to do?"

"In any moment of decision, the best thing you can do is the right thing, the next best thing is the wrong thing, and the worst thing you can do is nothing," said Bill.

"Theodore Roosevelt," said Rogers quietly.

"Yards, let's go," said Bill. He turned and headed for the door. "I'm going to need that badge of yours."

"What the hell are you going to do?" yelled Spalding as Bill pushed his way through the crowd in the Command Center.

"Something," said Bill. He stepped out the door, and Yards jumped out behind him. "Anything."

CHAPTER FORTY-SEVEN

1342 HOURS, 16 AUGUST 2002.
WASHINGTON, D.C.

"Be ready," said Anwar to Sister Agnes seated next to him. "You and Sister Bernice will be the first to get out. Then, after you, Katherine and Lucinda." The car in front of them in traffic inched forward slightly, and Anwar eased up on the brakes, let the truck roll a few feet and then brought it to a stop again. On the left a DUKW, a WWII-era amphibious truck used for tours, rolled past filled with visitors in sun visors and covered in sunscreen.

"Yes, brother," croaked Agnes. Her throat was dry, and her voice increasingly weak. Her skin looked like old wax. Next to her, wedged in between her and Anwar in the front seat, Sister Bernice was unconscious. Her head was lolled over on her shoulder, her breath shallow and labored.

"This is it," said Anwar. He pulled the truck over to the side of the road. To the right, past some trees and on the other side of a blacktop walkway and a temporary security fence, were the silent figures of the Korean War Memorial. Beyond them, barely visible through the foliage was the Lincoln Memorial. All around were people in shorts, tank tops and ball caps swarming toward the mall and the concert.

"Let's go, sister," said Agnes. She reached over and shook the shoulder of Sister Bernice, next to her. Bernice, a coal-black Nigerian, opened her eyes and coughed.

"Hurry, sisters," said Anwar. He was only partially out of the roadway. As soon as the traffic in front of him moved, he was going to have to move as well.

"It is time, sister," said Agnes. She shook Bernice again and looked for signs of recognition in her eyes.

Bernice sat forward. She coughed. She coughed again, and then grabbed at her chest.

"Eternal rest awaits," said Agnes softly. "Just a few more steps on your journey to Paradise."

Bernice doubled over with her arms across her stomach and moaned. Then she rocked back against the seat, eyes wide open with fear and vomited a geyser of brownish, half-digested blood across the windshield and dash of the truck.

"Sister Bernice!" screamed Agnes. She recoiled in horror against the passenger's side door of the truck.

"She's gone," said Anwar. Bernice's eyes slammed shut, and she crashed forward as dead weight against the dash without making a sound. Blood, spittle and tissue coated the instrument panel in front of her and went halfway up the glass on the windshield. The cab filled with the smell of rancid meat.

Sisters Lucinda and Katherine in the back seat began to scream. Anwar looked in the rearview mirror. Aphrodite was still wedged in between the two sisters. Her eyes were closed. It was hard to tell if she was alive or dead.

"God protect us," whispered Agnes. Her eyes were shut tight against the horror in front of her.

Anwar looked up and out the windshield in front of him. A group of tourists on the sidewalk had stopped and was staring at the blood splattered on the truck's windshield. A little girl was crying and pointing. Another group of people stopped and began to point.

"Sisters!" yelled Anwar. "Shut up." The wailing continued.

Several of the tourists on the sidewalk pulled out cell phones. One of them looked like he was making a call. Anwar checked his rear view mirror. Fifty meters behind him, Anwar saw a Park Police officer on a horse moving slowly in his direction. One of the tourists next to the truck began to run toward the cop.

"You need help?" Someone banged on the passenger's side window. Anwar turned. There was a middle-aged white man looking through the glass at Sister Bernice and shading his eyes against the sun. He was bright red with sunburn and wearing a t-shirt for an auto parts store in Des Moines.

Anwar made no response. The sisters in the back seat were still howling.

"Call 911!" screamed someone in the crowd.

"Hey, buddy, you need help?" repeated the man in the t-shirt. He banged on the glass next to Agnes' head again.

Anwar checked his mirror again to locate the mounted Park Police officer. He was stopped on the side of the road about twenty-five meters away. Several people were clustered around him, gesturing and pointing in Anwar's direction.

It was time to move.

"Out of the truck!" screamed Anwar. He pushed open the driver's side door and stepped out into the street.

"Hey, buddy, what the hell are you doing?" screamed someone in a nearby car. Anwar ignored the comment. He walked back to the driver's side rear door, yanked it open and pulled Sister Katherine, a short, olive-skinned woman, out onto the pavement.

"Move!" yelled Anwar. He looked back down the street in the direction from which they had come. The mounted police officer had a radio in his hand and was holding it to his mouth.

"What about the truck?" said Agnes. She was standing on the other side of the bed looking toward Anwar. Dark, black pools of blood had settled under the skin beneath her eyes.

"Forget the truck," said Anwar. "Get them out, and get them moving."

"Yes, brother," said Agnes. She opened the rear door on her side. Sister Lucinda, a muscular, red-haired woman, climbed out and pulled Aphrodite out with her. Lucinda's breath was coming in raspy gasps.

"Move," barked Anwar. There were people standing and staring on the sidewalk right behind Agnes, Aphrodite and Lucinda. One of them was the man who had been banging on the window.

"This way," said Anwar. He grabbed Katherine by the wrist and pulled her behind him as he moved out of the road and up onto the sidewalk.

"The police will come," said Agnes.

"Hey, buddy, you can't leave your fuckin' vehicle here," screamed the driver of the car right behind the truck.

"They will come too late," said Anwar. "This way." He pointed down the sidewalk in the direction of the Lincoln Memorial.

"God willing," said Agnes. She grabbed Aphrodite's wrist with one hand, Lucinda's with the other and followed in Anwar's wake.

"How do you feel, sister?" said Anwar to Agnes over his shoulder.

"The shot you gave me has given me strength, brother," said Agnes.

"Good," said Anwar. He pushed past a family on the walkway and shoved a little girl into the grass as he did so. "It is only moments now, and then you can all rest."

CHAPTER FORTY-EIGHT

"What the hell's going on?" said Yards. He and Bill had crossed the Polo Field and come out on the sidewalk just across the street from the Korean War Memorial. Directly across the street there was a crowd gathered around a pickup truck stopped dead in the roadway.

"No idea," said Bill. He saw that there was a police officer on a horse next to the truck, and, while he watched, the police officer dismounted and appeared to climb in the pickup's cab. Further down Independence Avenue several more mounted cops appeared pushing their horses at a trot through the gridlock.

"Maybe we should find out," said Yards.

"Agreed," said Bill. The two men stepped into the street and wound their way through the mass of stopped cars and trucks to the other side of the street.

As Bill and Yards came up next to the truck, they saw that the windshield was covered with what looked like bloody coffee grounds, and there was a body slumped over in the front seat. The mounted police officer was back on the sidewalk asking the bystanders in the area to take a step back. The other cops were just arriving.

"What's going on?" said Yards. He stepped up in between Bill and the uniformed cop and held up his Maryland State Police badge.

"Not sure," said the officer. "Never seen anything like it. Looks like she vomited blood and died."

"Her stomach filled with blood leaking out of her internal organs," said Bill. He leaned into the cab briefly and then drew back quickly. The stench was overwhelming.

"Who are you guys?" asked the cop. The radio on his hip was crackling. Behind him the other mounted cops drew up and began to dismount.

"We're working the threat," said Yards. "The one Captain Ferrell told you to be on the lookout for."

"Shit," said the officer. He stepped back away from the cab and looked down at his hands as if to search for some invisible contamination. "Don't tell me that that's what killed her."

"Yes," said Bill. He turned, walked over to the cop and leaned in close to his face. "That's exactly what's going on. This woman died of the plague, the same shit that nearly killed everyone in Europe in the 1300's. And she wasn't alone. There were others in this truck with her. Where are they?"

"The truck was empty when I got here," said the cop.

"How long?" said Yards.

"How long what?" said the cop.

"How long from the time she died until you got here?"

"A couple of minutes, I guess," said the officer. "I don't know." He wiped his hands on his trousers. Behind him, the other mounted officers were still trying to push the crowd back and control the scene.

"Who got here ahead of you?" asked Bill. He looked toward the crowd. People were pushing and shoving and taking pictures with their cell phones. In the forefront was a sunburned white man in a t-shirt from an auto parts store.

"Sir, I'm not going to tell you again," said one of the officers. He pushed the sunburned man back a step.

"I need to talk to those guys," said the man.

"That's none of your business," said the cop. He put his hand on the man's chest and then addressed the group as a whole. "Nothing to see folks. Just a medical emergency. Move along."

"Wait," said Bill. He stepped up beside the cop and pushed his hand off the sunburned man's chest.

"Who're you?" said the cop. He squared up like he was getting ready to take a swing at Bill.

"He's with me," yelled Yards. He held his badge up over his head and swung it around so all the other officers could see it as well. "Listen up! We're working a priority national security investigation. This ain't duck pins, people. This is the real deal. Cooperate or get the hell out of the way!" Behind him in the west, the sky was growing dark, and thunderheads were building.

"Did you see something?" asked Bill. He ignored the mounted cop with the mirrored shades and bulging biceps next to him and focused on the man in the auto parts t-shirt.

"She vomited blood," said the man.

"We know that," said the cop.

"Shut up," said Bill. He glared at the cop and then looked back at the man in the t-shirt.

"There were five of them," said the man. "All women, 'cept for one man."

"Which way did they go?" asked Bill. He stepped forward and grabbed the man by both arms. "Which way?"

"That way," said the man. He pointed in the direction of the Lincoln Memorial. "All of them. They got out of the truck and walked away. Like it didn't mean a thing that poor woman just died."

"How long?"

"A minute, maybe two," said the man. "What happened to her?" He pointed toward the truck.

"Was there a blond woman with them?" asked Bill.

"Yes," said the man. "Blond, curly hair. Good looking but with a sad face."

"Thank you," said Bill. He closed his eyes for a brief moment and consciously willed himself to calm down. Aphrodite was alive.

She was alive. She was here. He still had a chance.

"I gave Ferrell a quick shout on that first cop's radio," said Yards. He had appeared beside Bill. "He's bringing in the National Guard and the quarantine boys to take charge of this show.

"Roger," said Bill. He turned and looked down the sidewalk toward the Lincoln Memorial.

"How much of a lead do they have?" said Yards.

"Max two minutes," said Bill.

"No sweat," said Yards. "Easy day."

"Let's end this," said Bill.

"Rock n roll," said Yards.

They began to run.

CHAPTER FORTY-NINE

1401 HOURS, 16 AUGUST 2002.
WASHINGTON, D.C.

Two hundred yards later Bill and Yards found them. There were three of them, all women. One of them was on her knees in the middle of the walkway. The other two had her by the arms and were trying to drag her to her feet. Bystanders were clustered in a ring around the trio.

"Back off!" bellowed Yards as he and Bill approached. He had his badge held high over his head. "Police!" He began to push the crowd away physically. "Give us a ten meter radius!"

"Don't move!" screamed Bill. He had his pistol out and trained on the group of women. The woman who had collapsed was short and looked Lebanese. The woman on the left was black and wearing an American flag ball cap and an "I Love New York" t-shirt. The woman on the right was a light-skinned redhead.

"Our friend needs help," said Sister Agnes, the black woman.

"Game over," said Bill. He walked forward and pressed the barrel of his pistol against Agnes's face. Someone in the crowd started screaming. Sirens began to wail somewhere nearby. "I know who you are. I know why you are here."

"Then kill me," croaked Agnes. She looked like she was about to fall over. Sister Katherine, the woman on the ground, rolled on her side and doubled up in pain.

"God, I would love to," said Bill.

"Send me to Paradise," said Agnes. The redhead beside her, Sister Lucinda, sank down on one knee breathing hard. There was blood running from her nose and a dark, swollen mass on the side of her neck.

"Where is she?" said Bill.

"The blond woman?"

"The blond woman," said Bill. "Where is she? And where is the man who has been traveling with you?"

"You're too late," said Agnes. She tried to smile, but her lips were cracked and bleeding, and she only managed to look more pained.

"Fuck you and your psychotic bullshit," said Bill. He leaned in and pressed the barrel of the pistol tight against the Agnes' forehead. "Where are they?"

"Bill!" yelled Yards. He was standing a foot to one side with his badge in one hand and his gun in the other. A Park Police officer was next to him.

"Tell me!" screamed Bill.

"Bill!" yelled Yards again.

"I'm not coming this close just to lose her," said Bill.

"Nobody's talking about losing anyone," said Yards. "Eleni's infected right?"

"Right."

"So, they can still use her as a weapon right?"

"Right," said Bill.

"So."

"So, this scumbag that has been running this show is going to get her onto the Mall," said Bill with sudden realization. He lowered his weapon and turned toward the Memorial. A hundred meters away was a line of tourists being screened through one of the limited number of entrances in the security fencing.

"That wait is pretty long," said Yards. "We must be right behind them."

"Let's go," said Bill.

"Officer," said Yards to the Park policeman next to him. "Keep these three here and separated by at least ten meters from all bystanders until the command post gets you people to process them."

"Yes, sergeant," said the officer. He had his weapon out and pointed at the cluster of women.

Bill put his pistol back in the concealed holster on his hip and followed Yards to the entrance.

"Police business, investigation in progress," bellowed Yards as they pushed past the people in line and through the narrow gate. He still had his badge over his head. The Park Police officers screening people entering the Mall stepped aside and made no requests for further ID. Bill slid through in Yards' wake.

"Let's split up," said Bill as soon as they were inside. "We can cover more ground that way."

"I don't know what she looks like," said Yards.

"Now you do," said Bill. He pulled a photo of Eleni from his wallet and handed it to Yards. In the picture Aphrodite was smiling and standing on a white sand beach in a pair of shorts and a red halter top.

"You're a lucky man, Boyle," said Yards.

"Just find her," said Bill. He slapped Yards on the back and broke left toward the stage in front of the Memorial. Yards went right and deeper into the crowd.

The noise this close to the stage was deafening. There were huge black speakers on raised stands on either side of the reflecting pool that began almost immediately in front of the Memorial. Right in front of Bill, between him and the closest speaker, was some sort of youth group of teenage girls. They were wearing matching pink t-shirts labeled with the words "Mount Hope Church," and they were dancing and squealing as their favorite country star on stage belted out the words to his latest hit song.

Bill pushed past and through the shrieking girls, around a family of eight eating hot dogs and drinking sweet tea and past a guy in an American Legion hat. A man carrying a boy on his shoulders bumped into him. Several small children playing tag in the crowd banged against his knees. He was only feet from the stage, and he could not see any sign of Aphrodite anywhere.

Bill turned. He froze. Aphrodite was fifty feet away, at the edge of the reflecting pool, looking across the water to the other side.

Bill scanned the crowd. He couldn't see anyone who matched the description of the man they were looking for. Aphrodite turned. She looked right at him.

Bill began to move.

CHAPTER FIFTY

1411 HOURS, 16 AUGUST 2002.
WASHINGTON, D.C.

Aphrodite opened her eyes. At least she thought she did. She could not remember closing them, so she was not sure.

All around Aphrodite were people. It was hot. It was sticky. She could not remember clearly where she was or how she had gotten here. She had a dim recollection of being injected yet again. Her joints ached. Her nose was clogged with congealed blood.

The crowd around her dissolved. It was replaced with darkness. Aphrodite's eyes were open but no longer seeing. The darkness became fear. The fear became horror. Something cold clutched at her heart.

It was death.

◆◆◆

Aphrodite was on a mattress in a cold room. She was naked. There was a man next to her. He was snoring. She did not know his name, and she knew it did not matter.

She was in Athens. She was a junkie.

The mattress smelled of vomit, urine and worse. Aphrodite's body was wracked with pain. Her nose was running. She had goose bumps up and down her legs and arms. The heroin she had shot up the night before was burned off. She was dying for a fix.

Something moved in the room. Loud words were exchanged. A body hit the floor. Someone started screaming.

The man next to Aphrodite came to his feet. There was the sound of a knife going through flesh and cartilage. Another body hit the floor. The screaming continued.

Aphrodite opened her eyes. There was a man standing in front of her. He was square built, like a boxer. He smelled clean, like an American.

The man leaned down. "Are you Eleni?" he asked. She nodded weakly. He held out a hand. "My name is Bill," said the man. He had come for her.

◆ ◆ ◆

Eleni rubbed her eyes. The darkness lifted. The crowd returned. She rubbed her eyes again. The man was standing in front of her. His hair was gray around the temples now. There were dark circles under his eyes. He was still built like a boxer. Behind him the sky was turning black.

It was Bill. He had come for her again. His eyes were glued to her. He began to move in her direction.

Aphrodite looked past Bill. Twenty feet further away, in the direction of the security fence around the Mall, was Anwar. He too was staring right at her. His hand was in his pocket. She knew his thumb was on the switch to the vest strapped to her body.

Aphrodite was wearing a long nylon skirt and a tie-dye t-shirt that the sisters had put on her. She looked down. The hem of the t-shirt was fraying. She grabbed it with both hands and began to tear away a long, narrow strip of cloth.

CHAPTER FIFTY-ONE

1412 HOURS, 16 AUGUST 2002.
WASHINGTON, D.C.

Bill stepped around another father with a young child on his shoulders and momentarily lost sight of Aphrodite. Several hulking young men in University of Maryland football jerseys pushed past and blocked his view again. He moved the other way, walked around a couple of teenagers holding hands and brought Aphrodite back in view.

Aphrodite was maybe thirty-five feet away now. Bill could almost reach out and touch her. He could see the darkness in her face. He could feel her agony.

Bill stopped.

Aphrodite had both hands behind her head. She was holding a piece of some kind of cloth. As Bill watched, she tied her hair up in a ponytail and then turned away.

It was a safety signal, the same one they had always used in Athens. Her hair down meant it was all clear. Her hair up meant danger, stay away.

Bill took a step back. He scanned the crowd again. Nothing. He turned around slowly.

Next to the security fence to the left of the Memorial was a young white man with long blond hair. He had his hand in his pocket. He was staring at Aphrodite.

Bill looked back at Aphrodite. People were swirling around her now. A family with young children had come to stand in front of her and listen to the show. As he watched, she reached down and rubbed her stomach slightly like she was feeling a cramp. Her shirt rode up slightly. Bill could see the bottom of a vest of yellowish plastique.

Bill looked back at the man by the fence. He was still there. Behind him, a storm continued to build over Northern Virginia. A light wind kicked up and blew some dust and trash across the ground.

The math was simple. It was all against Bill. Every second Aphrodite stood in the crowd was another chance for contagion to spread. Any move toward her would mean the vest detonating and dozens of dead. Any move toward the punk by the fence would mean the same.

Checkmate. Bill lost no matter how it played out.

Time to change the game.

The band on stage finished its song and announced they were going to take a quick break. The sound of banjos and steel guitars was replaced by the buzz of thousands of voices. Bill looked at the stage. There were stairs on the left that led from the ground up to where the performers were. He headed for them.

At the bottom of the stairs, a beefy young man in a tight red t-shirt that said "Security" on it met Bill.

"Can I help you, sir?" said the young man.

"National Weather Service," said Bill.

"Excuse me?" said the man.

"Out of my way, son," said Bill. "Severe weather alert."

The young man in the security t-shirt stepped back with a puzzled look on his face. Bill bounded up the stairs and onto the stage.

"Can I help you?" said a man with a ponytail standing next to a panel of controls at the back of the stage.

"National Weather Service," said Bill. "I need to make an announcement."

"I don't understand," said the man. He looked back toward a couple of technicians who were sitting on equipment boxes behind him.

"We have a severe weather alert," said Bill gravely. "I need to make an announcement. I need to reach the whole Mall. I need to do it now."

"I don't think I can let you do that," said the man. "I'll need to call someone."

"Listen," said Bill. He advanced toward the man menacingly. "Any minute now we are going to have a lightning strike in that crowd out there and have a whole bunch of American taxpayers barbecued. Get me on the air. Now." Behind him, he could hear someone coming up the stairs.

"Yes, sir," said the man with the ponytail. He flipped some switches and then handed Bill a microphone connected with a long black cord to the control panel. "Hit the button on the mike, and you'll be talking to a quarter of a million people."

"Thank you," said Bill. He took the microphone in one hand and walked to the front of the stage. Out of the corner of his eye he could see that the young man in the security t-shirt was standing at the top of the stairs. Next to him was an older man in a sports coat. Bill ignored them both.

"Ladies and gentlemen," said Bill into the microphone. His voice boomed out over the mall. Heads swiveled toward him.

"I regret to inform you that we have a severe weather alert in the D.C. area," said Bill.

A collective groan went up from thousands of onlookers.

"Due to the danger of a lightning strike we must suspend the concerts in progress and ask you to immediately leave the Mall area," continued Bill.

The groans grew louder. People began to stand.

"Please take shelter inside or below ground as quickly as possible," added Bill. "That is all."

Bill turned, walked back to the man with the ponytail and handed him the microphone. Then, he headed for the stairs.

"Excuse me," said the man in the sports coat. He was standing at the top of the stairs and blocking Bill's path.

"He said he was a weather guy," said the young man in the t-shirt.

"Can I see some ID?" asked the man in the coat.

"No," said Bill. "Now get out of my way."

"I'm Mr. Lehman. I'm the guy in charge of this concert," said the man in the coat.

"Good for you," said Bill. "Out of my way."

"You're not Weather Service" said Lehman. "What is this some kind of a prank? I'm going to make another announcement and tell people to disregard what you said."

"You do," said Bill, leaning in close to the man's face. "And the deaths of millions of people are going to be on your hands, asshole."

"What are you talking about?" asked Lehman.

"No announcement," said Bill. "Clear the Mall. You have a problem with that, you call Captain Ferrell at the command center and request clarification." He pushed past and down the stairs to the ground.

People were already streaming off the Mall. Bill scanned the crowd for Aphrodite. She wasn't where she had been by the reflecting pool.

Bill walked over toward the gate through which he had entered. People were pushing out in a long queue. Aphrodite wasn't among them.

Bill turned around. On the other side of the reflecting pool on the right hand side of the Memorial the police had opened another exit to accommodate the crowd. People were actually wading across the pool from Bill's side to the other to make it to this new gate. In the middle of the pool, surrounded by dozens of others, was Aphrodite. The man with the blond hair was next to her, pulling her by the elbow.

Bill followed.

CHAPTER FIFTY-TWO

1417 HOURS, 16 AUGUST 2002.
WASHINGTON, D.C.

Bill splashed his way through the reflecting pool and
jumped up onto the grass on the other side. Through the masses of
people in front of him, he saw Aphrodite and the blond man
disappear through the gate and turn left toward the Potomac River.
Bill pushed through behind them.

The man and Aphrodite were less than thirty feet away now.
They skirted across the lawn on the Potomac side of the Lincoln
Memorial and into the circle drive between the Memorial and the
river. The man looked back through the thinning crowd. He
looked right at Bill and then turned and started screaming at
Aphrodite to run faster.

Parked in the drive in front of the Memorial was another of
the D.C. DUKW's used for tours. At the rear of the vehicle, the
folding metal stairs were extended to let people board. The seats
were filled with families and couples.

Anwar shoved Aphrodite ahead of him up the stairs and
stole another look backward at Bill, who was closing fast. At the
top of the stairs, Anwar grabbed the handle to fold up the stairs and

then, with Aphrodite in front of him, hurried down the center aisle of the vehicle toward the driver in the front.

"Hey, buddy, what are you doing?" yelled the driver. He was a tall, ethnic Somali. He stood and turned to face Anwar and Aphrodite down the aisle. The rows of tourists in the pairs of seats on either side of the aisle stopped talking and pointing to focus on the commotion.

"This woman is wearing an explosive vest!" yelled Anwar. He reached around Aphrodite and pulled up her t-shirt, so that the vest was visible. "I have the trigger. Do what I say, when I say it, or we are all going to die right now!"

"Okay, man, chill," said the driver. He stepped back toward his seat. Behind him were the controls for running the DUKW on land and for its propulsion in the water.

"Move, now!" said Anwar.

"Moving," said the driver. He dropped into his seat, started the DUKW and shoved it into gear. The big truck began to roll. "Which way?"

"Into the water," said Anwar. He turned back to the passengers. "Stay in your seats. Keep your mouths shut. You might live through this."

Bill caught up just as the DUKW began to move. He grabbed a hold of part of the mechanism of the folding stairs and desperately tried to pull them down. They were locked. They would not move.

The DUKW began to gather speed. It headed southwest along the circular drive on the river side of the Lincoln Memorial, up over a grassy median strip and then onto a ramp that came off the Memorial Bridge from Arlington and curled toward the Potomac. Bill trotted beside the vehicle searching for a handhold. There were none.

The DUKW went left off the ramp and across an expanse of lawn. It gained more speed. Bill began to fall behind.

At the water's edge, the DUKW went directly across another road, down a short steep slope and plunged into the water. Waves sloshed over the sloping front deck and, momentarily, over the sides. Then the ungainly creation, basically a military cargo truck with rectangular flotation devices on the sides, stabilized and began to pull away from shore. Its propeller kicked up a small wake at its rear.

"Shit," said Bill. The DUKW was moving surprisingly quickly away from shore and down the Potomac. "I need a boat."

"Ask and ye shall receive," said Yards. He seemed to have appeared from nowhere next to Bill. "Priority request," said Yards into the radio in his hand. "Need watercraft for immediate pursuit of terrorist suspect at shoreline south side of Memorial Bridge, east bank. Anyone on this channel, please respond."

"Where the hell did you come from?" asked Bill. He was huffing and puffing between words.

"Saw you hauling ass off the Mall and decided to follow," said Yards. He grinned. "And I gained ground on you the whole way, old man."

"This is Coast Guard patrol Bravo," said a voice on the radio. "I'll be at your location in thirty seconds. We are coming south on east shore from vicinity of Kennedy Center now."

"Roger," said Yards into the radio. He and Bill both swiveled their heads to look north. As they watched, an orange RHIB — a rigid-hull inflatable boat — came flying under the bridge, and spun to a stop right in front of them. There was a light machine-gun mounted at the bow, and two crewmen in tactical gear behind the windshield mounted amidships.

"You rang?" yelled the crewman behind the wheel.

"Priority national security investigation!" bellowed Yards over the sound of the twin 250 HP engines at the boat's rear. "We have a terrorist suspect in a DUKW with hostages trying to flee the scene."

"And one of his hostages is strapped with explosives!" screamed Bill.

"Explosives?" said Yards. He looked at Bill and arched his eyebrows.

"Explosives," said Bill. "Still happy you ran so fast?" He stepped down to the riverbank and jumped aboard the RHIB. Yards followed shaking his head.

"Which way?" yelled the guy at the wheel of the boat.

"There!" yelled Bill. He pointed toward the low, white hull of the DUKW. It was already close to a half mile away in the direction of the Pentagon.

The DUKW moved faster than most people might imagine, close to six miles an hour. The RHIB was in an entirely different class. It was doing close to forty knots in less than thirty seconds. It took less than a minute for it to catch up.

"Come in front of them," yelled Bill to the crewman driving. The other one had gone forward and manned the machinegun. "Make them stop."

"Roger," said the crewman. He was wearing black tactical clothing, a helmet and goggles. Both hands were gripping the steering wheel.

The RIIB curled around the DUKW, turned back toward it and then wallowed to a stop. The engines were chugging in neutral at the rear. The gunner in the bow had his weapon trained on the approaching DUKW.

Anwar stepped forward and said something to the driver of the DUKW. The vehicles' engine cut off. Its speed dropped, and it began to drift.

"Let me talk to them," said Bill.

"Your show, man," said the man at the wheel.

"What are you going to say?" asked Yards.

"No fuckin' idea," said Bill. He stepped around the windshield, walked to the front of the vessel and stood at the bow in front of the machinegun. Less than fifty feet separated the craft now, and the distance was narrowing steadily.

"Back off!" yelled Anwar. "Back off, or everyone dies."

"Smyth!" said Bill. "It's over. "

"Michael P. Smyth died years ago," said Anwar. "My name is Anwar Al-Amriki."

"Okay, Anwar," said Bill. "It's still over. Your plan failed. Time to think about making the best deal you can."

"No deals!" yelled Anwar. He grabbed Aphrodite, who was standing in front of him, by the collar of her shirt and forced her up on the yellow deck at the bow of the DUKW. "This woman is strapped with explosives. You either get out of our way and let us go, or I press the switch in my pocket, and everybody in this thing gets shredded." Behind Anwar the passengers were cowering in terror.

"That woman is my wife," said Bill. The two craft were less than forty feet apart now and still drifting toward each other.

"That must make you Bill," sneered Anwar.

"It does," said Bill grimly. "And it means I'm the guy who's going to blow your head off if you don't let her go."

"She's been saying the same thing since we grabbed her," said Anwar.

"Smart girl," said Bill.

"Dumb bitch," said Anwar.

Bill looked into Aphrodite's eyes. She was staring directly at him. The side of her neck was swollen and turning black. Blood was crusted around her nostrils. Her cheeks were sunken and pale. She was standing at the very bow of the DUKW completely blocking Bill's view of Anwar and the driver.

"Let it go," said Bill. "Enough."

"You lose," said Anwar smugly.

Aphrodite stepped forward off the deck of the DUKW and dropped into the water. Bill drew from the hip and fired twice. Both rounds struck Anwar at the bridge of the nose. He was dead before he hit the deck.

The people on the DUKW began to scream. Anwar's blood pooled on the deck at the driver's feet. Bill dove in.

The water was warm, brown and murky. Bill opened his eyes. He could barely see his hands in front of his face. He spun in a circle a few feet below the surface. Nothing.

Bill surfaced, gasped for air and dove again. Aphrodite was a decent swimmer, but she was wearing a heavy vest and suffering from the effects of the plague. She had gone to the bottom. Bill pulled with his arms and kicked with his legs and swam as fast as he could.

The water grew colder. The light grew dimmer. Bill's lungs began to sting. There was a slight current flowing downstream. He tried to guess how far it might have carried Aphrodite. He kicked harder.

Bill's lungs begged for oxygen. He was past the depth from which he knew he could surface safely. Any deeper and he was likely to drown himself. He kept going.

The sounds of the surface vanished. Everything around Bill was cold and black. He was lost in a void. His arms felt heavy and lifeless. His legs were like lead. He willed himself to keep going.

Bubbles burst from Bill's lips. He was losing the fight to force his lungs to stay closed. Somewhere in the back of his mind the thought was forming that it might not be so bad to just surrender and let the water in. He wondered what that felt like. He wondered absently how deep he was.

Something brushed Bill's leg. He reached back in the blackness to see what it was. He was blind. He couldn't even tell if his eyes were open or close. Something brushed his fingertips. It felt like hair.

Bill swung his arms and kicked his legs. He moved toward whatever it was he had touched. He felt it again. It was hair, long masses of hair.

Groping in the void, Bill felt Aphrodite's head, then her neck, then her shoulders. He grabbed her unto the arms and began to kick with all his might. She moved, but only slightly. He kicked again. They were going up, but far too slowly.

Bill reached up under Aphrodite's shirt. He could feel the vest. He found the duct tape that bound it to her. He fumbled in his pocket, pulled out his knife, opened it in the dark and began to saw at the tape.

The tape was cold and stiff. He couldn't see it. Cutting it away blind, with his lungs screaming, seemed to be taking forever. He kept at it.

Water pushed its way into Bill's nose. He snorted and coughed and almost gasped for air. He kept cutting.

The vest came away and dropped toward the bottom. Bill kicked and pulled. Aphrodite began to move more rapidly. Light began to return around them. The temperature of the water began to rise.

Bill burst to the surface less than twenty feet from the RHIB. Yards dove in instantly, swam to Bill's side and helped him drag Aphrodite to the side of the boat. The crewman pulled Aphrodite up over the side and onto the deck. Then they did the same for Bill and Yards.

Bill rolled over on the deck and came up on his knees. He felt like he was going to pass out. He willed the feeling away and crawled to Aphrodite.

Aphrodite's face was blue. She wasn't breathing. One of the crewmembers began CPR. Blackness closed in on Bill. He lost the fight. He slumped to the deck unconscious.

CHAPTER FIFTY-THREE

1202 HOURS, 31 AUGUST 2002.
SAINT CASIMIR CATHOLIC CHURCH, BALTIMORE MARYLAND.

The organ music started. People began to rise and filter out. The memorial service was over.

Bill remained seated in the dark wooden pew in the front of the church. He was leaning forward, his head in his hands. It didn't get any easier. Somehow he thought it should, but it didn't.

Bill looked to his left. Irene, dressed all in black, was seated next to him. Eddie was on the other side of her. He had cut his hair, shaved his beard and borrowed a jacket from an uncle. He had enrolled in community college the day before. He looked good.

"You okay?" said Irene. She smiled weakly and reached out to Bill. He sat up and put his hand in hers.

"Yes," said Bill. Despite himself he sniffled and wiped away a tear. "But, somehow I think I should be asking you that question."

"I'm okay," said Irene. She squeezed Bill's hand to emphasize her sincerity. "Really. Maybe it sounds strange, but even knowing he's gone, I feel closer to him after this."

"I wish he weren't gone," said Bill. He turned back toward the front of the church and the large picture of Jimmy sitting on an easel in front of the congregation. "Doesn't really seem possible still."

"Come on," said Irene. She stood. "Let's go back to the house. The ladies in the family have been cooking for days. We'll eat and drink and tell stories. That's what he would have wanted."

"Okay," said Bill. He stood up and then turned to his right. "Ready to go?" he asked.

"Yes," said Aphrodite. She looked up and smiled and then, with Bill's help, wobbled to her feet. She had only been out of the hospital a few days. She was still weak.

Bill, Aphrodite, Irene and Eddie made their way down the center aisle of the church to the steps at the front. The priest was shaking hands and thanking everyone for coming. Rogers, Spalding and Yards, who had preceded them out of the church, were standing to one side where the overhang at the front of the church provided some shade from the bright, noonday sun.

"Good to see you up and around, lady," said Spalding. He gave Aphrodite a hug. Yards and Rogers shook her hand.

"She scared me to death," said Bill. "I thought she was gone."

"Good thing those Coasties know their life saving stuff," said Yards.

"That was a gutsy thing to do," said Spalding. He hadn't had a chance to speak to Aphrodite, since Anwar was killed. "What made you jump in?"

"I knew that asshole was holding a transmitter," said Aphrodite. Her voice was clear but thin, like a hoarse whisper. "I knew it could not be that powerful. I figured if I could get the vest, and the receiver on it under water before he could push the button, the device wouldn't function. The signal wouldn't penetrate more than a few inches below the surface."

"When the crime scene boys processed the scene, they found Anwar's thumb on the switch," said Yards.

"I guess your theory was correct then," said Spalding to Aphrodite. "He pressed the switch a fraction of a second too late."

"Yes," said Aphrodite simply.

"What about the part about not drowning?" asked Spalding. "What was the plan for that?"

"Bill was there," said Aphrodite. She looked at Bill briefly and then back at Spalding. "I left it to him."

"Damn," said Yards. "You are one gutsy chick."

"You guys coming to the house for food?" asked Bill.

"We wouldn't miss it," said Yards. "Good eating in Baltimore." He grinned.

"Rogers, I owe you an apology," said Bill. He extended his hand.

"For what?" asked Rogers.

"For biting your head off in the command post that last day," said Bill. "It wasn't your fault we were up against it."

"No apology necessary," said Rogers. He shook Bill's hand. "I think you had more than ample reason to be stressed." He looked at Aphrodite and grinned. He was wearing what appeared to be a brand new cardigan.

"What is the final toll?" asked Aphrodite. She was leaning heavily on Bill's arm. Her face was still pale and there were fading black circles still visible under her eyes. "How many?"

"We got insanely lucky," said Rogers. "The only infected person that ever got into the crowd was you, and you were only there for a short time. CDC is aggressively monitoring emergency rooms and clinics, but so far we're talking only dozens possibly infected, and they are all being aggressively treated. We may save them all."

"The sisters?" asked Aphrodite.

"All three that were captured are still alive," said Rogers. "They will recover. None of them are talking."

"Almost nothing in the press," said Yards.

"Yeah," said Spalding. "The federal government has a way of pushing things under the radar when it wants to. There are a few guys on the web who are talking about an attempted terrorist attack, but nobody's listening."

"How is that possible?" said Aphrodite.

"Some of what people saw is being billed as part of a series of exercises," said Spalding. "Some of it is being linked to gang activity or drug cartels. Some cases of the plague are being blamed on prairie dogs. Some are being characterized as likely Legionnaire's or the like. "

"The boys in Athens were right," said Aphrodite. "It is all lies."

"Sometimes seems that way," said Bill.

"I finally sorted out those Skype names, Addas and Sumaya, as well," said Rogers.

"Hit me," said Bill.

"Our man Smyth, aka Anwar, was using the screen name Addas," said Rogers smiling. He loved knowing things no one else did. "Turns out Addas was a Christian slave during the time of the Prophet Muhammad, who converted to Islam."

"And Sumaya?" asked Bill.

"The white lady whose head you blew off in New Jersey, aka Afiyah, was really Betty McMillan. She used the screen name Sumaya. Sumaya was the first martyr in the history of Islam."

"Fascinating," said Bill. "Seems like I need to read up on my Koranic history a little more. I should have known both of those."

"We presented the Pakistanis with all the evidence we had of ISI complicity," said Spalding. "They denied everything. Blamed it all on some rogue retired officers and said they would put them under house arrest while they investigated."

"Which means they will be doing exactly jack and shit," said Bill.

"Roger that," said Spalding.

"I saw the final write-up on the interviews of the imam at the mosque," said Yards. "Feel sorry for the guy. He thought he was providing a shelter for victims of domestic abuse and ended up being played by some psychopaths."

"Seems so," said Spalding. "Afiyah was sent here sometime back to recruit a team for exactly this kind of op. This thing has been in the works for a while."

"I wonder how many more are in the works," said Aphrodite softly.

"Too many," said Bill.

"Enough doom and gloom," said Irene. She had been standing patiently to one side but sensed this was the time to interject. "We're remembering my father. He would want to hear laughter and see smiling faces."

"That he would," said Bill. "He liked a good time." He smiled at Irene and then at Aphrodite.

"What are your plans, brother?" said Spalding as the group descended the stairs toward their cars parked at the curb.

"Not sure," said Bill. He looked over at Aphrodite briefly.

"Another big adventure, no doubt," said Spalding.

"I don't think so," said Bill.

"No jungles, deserts or volcanoes?" joked Spalding. "No saving the world?"

"I think it's time to tend the home fires for a while," said Bill. He pulled Aphrodite closer to him, and they stepped out into the midday sun together.